THE WOMAN IN BACK ROW

THE
WOMAN
IN
BACK ROW

Herbert Williams

GOMER

First Impression—2000

ISBN 1 85902 871 3

© Herbert Williams

Herbert Williams has asserted his right under the
Copyright, Designs and Patents Act, 1988, to be
identified as Author of this Work.

All rights reserved. No part of this book may be
reproduced, stored in a retrieval system, or
transmitted in any form or by any means, electronic,
electrostatic, magnetic tape, mechanical,
photocopying, recording or otherwise without
permission in writing from the publishers, Gomer
Press, Llandysul, Ceredigion.

This book is published with the support of the
Arts Council of Wales.

Printed in Wales at
Gomer Press, Llandysul, Ceredigion

To my great friends,
the late Reg and Eleanor Kendall,
who showed me such kindness.

AUTHOR'S NOTE

I would like to acknowledge the help of Dr John Hughes of Aberystwyth and Dr Edward Hughes of Camborne, Cornwall, in answering my queries about aspects of medical treatment in the period in which this novel is set. They are in no way responsible for the use to which I have put the information they gave me, nor for any unwitting misinterpretation of the facts on my part. I am also grateful to Mairwen Prys Jones, editor at Gwasg Gomer, for her enthusiastic support of my work. Last but certainly not least, I am indebted beyond words to my wife Dorothy for her patience, wisdom and unfailing encouragement.

Part One

ARROWS

1

From her bedroom window Annette could look right across the valley, and it pleased her to imagine that she could see Steve waving to her from his house on the far side. Of course it was ridiculous, he was too far away and anyway he would never wave, he was too shy for that. But she knew in her heart it was not so much shyness that prevented him doing this as his obstinate refusal to do anything ordinary. She sighed; he was such a peculiar boy.

She stood there in her white cotton nightie, a slim girl with dark chestnut hair and a pale, freckled face. She had a serious look now as she thought about Steve and Ivor, and wondered which of the two she would choose, or whether perhaps there was someone else out there, waiting for her.

A trail of smoke drifted across the valley from the train puffing in from Shrewsbury. As the smoke rose and spread out she stared at it, as if it held the key to the mystery inside her, the mystery of her own identity and of what might become of her.

'Annette! What you doing? It's ar-pas-eight!'

'I'll be down in a minute, Mam.'

'Well, shake yourself for godsake. You're gonna miss that bus.'

'I'll be alright. Don't worry.'

A cough from her parents' bedroom told her that Dad was on the sick again. She frowned out of a mixture of anxiety and disapproval, for she could never be sure of late whether he was really unwell or simply shamming. She had no time to go in and see him now, but still felt a touch of guilt as she ran downstairs after a lick and a promise in the bathroom and a brief session in front of her bedroom mirror, putting on a dab of make-up.

Mam was waiting.

'I'll have to put a bomb under you, my girl. There's no sense, the way you carry on.'

'What's wrong with Dad then?'

'Got a touch of the bronchial again. Why don't you shake yourself in the morning?'

'You getting the doctor?'

'No, he'll be alright. What you having, cornflakes?'

'No time Mam, sorry.'

'You can't go out without nothing!'

'I'll have a cup of coffee in work, don't worry.'

'For godsake, Annette,' and this was another guilt generator, her mother standing there looking harassed and ill as Annette tried hard to avoid the quarrel that would make her feel wretched half the morning.

'I've got to be going, Mam – I'll miss the bus.'

'You should've thought of that sooner. What time you home tonight?'

'Same as usual. Bye Mam. See you later.' And she was out of the back door and flying up the garden path with the old mixture of resentment and worry and guilt in her stomach.

God, but it'd be so easy if she hated her mam and dad! She could go and live on her own then, like Shirley Tucker who'd taken that bed-sitter near the station where she had students round for parties till all hours, if you could believe what people said. And yes, she *could* believe it of Shirley, for she'd always been a flighty one, boasting about what she did with boys even when she was in the juniors and putting on lipstick without her mother knowing.

She practically ran up the slope to the bus stop because she didn't want to be late, not that old Mr Richards minded but it was Mrs Bevan she couldn't stand, with that sharp prying look of hers and the nasty way she had of making ordinary words sound like poison. When she said things like, 'Everything quite well at home then, Annette?' it was like the most evil thing anyone had ever uttered and she wanted to hit her and scratch her till she begged for mercy, the old cow.

The green Crosville bus was just arriving and she sat down at the back with a sudden sense of well-being.

George the conductor ambled down the aisle and clipped a ticket for her in his little silver machine without asking. She smiled her thanks. He gave her the change and went back to the front, standing close enough to the driver to chat with him as they went down Penbryn Hill and under the railway bridge into town.

Annette thought about tonight, and her date with Steve. They were going to a play at the Pier Theatre, something about a cat on a roof, it sounded real barmy. She didn't like plays much, especially when acted by the local amateur dramatics set, because all she could see on stage was a lot of people she knew behaving stupidly. It was different for Steve, he was able to take them seriously, but then he was a much more serious person altogether. She wondered what he saw in her; they didn't really have very much in common. But she still liked him, in fact she liked him a lot, and according to him he was in love with her. Well, she wondered . . . Steve was the kind of boy to be in love with being in love, and she wasn't at all sure if he knew what his true feelings were about her. Maybe she should have stuck with Ivor, he was much less complicated. She smiled at the thought of him. You knew where you were with Ivor, but on the other hand . . . She knew she could never feel deeply about him but with Steve . . . there was something inside her, an excitement, even a premonition . . . She pushed the thought away as she reached the station, and stood up with all the others waiting to step off.

George smiled as she went past.

'How's your Dad? Haven't seen him for a while.'

'Not too good today, George – he's ill in bed.'

'Oh? What's wrong then?'

'Don't know exactly – chest trouble I think.'

Annette saw something in George's eyes that told her he too had his doubts but all he said was, 'Be good then.'

'I'll try.'

She arrived at the office the same time as Mrs Bevan – Big Bertha – who hated her for this because it meant she had nothing to criticise. She clumped about banging things for no reason and Annette was almost sorry for her because her whole life was obviously a misery. What did Mr Bevan do to make her so cross? He was such an inoffensive-looking man. But perhaps, she acknowledged with a worldly-wise humour that brought a smile to her face, it was what he didn't do that was the trouble. And this brought her back to thinking about Steve, and what he wanted her to do next weekend when his parents were away.

She began hitting the keys of her typewriter hard, to stop herself thinking about it and the blush rising to her cheeks. She had told him she felt insulted, but it was not so much insulted she felt now as excited, and mixed in with the excitement was resentment at the way he was forcing this decision on her, and she almost hated him for the trouble he was causing her.

In time she calmed down. Work always soothed her. She loved typing for a start, especially on this machine, for though it was far from new it wasn't difficult like some typewriters. She couldn't get on with the one Rita used over there in the corner, the ribbon was always getting tangled up for no reason at all. She didn't aspire to Big Bertha's machine, *that* was electric, and she didn't really like the look of it – it was too modern and bold-looking, as if it thought a lot of itself. But this machine of hers, it was fine. When she took the dust cover off in the morning it was all she could do not to say 'hello' to it, and 'how are you today?' But if she did, Rita would think she was loopy, and she half-thought that already.

She got into the swing of things, typing out the letters young Mr Allan had dictated yesterday.

> Dear Sir,
> In reply to your communication of the 14th inst, it is my pleasure to inform you . . .

> Dear Madam,
> Further to our letter of the 29th ult, I regret to say that Messrs Drummond and Forbes have rejected our proposal that this matter be resolved in the customary manner . . .

Suddenly she stopped, thinking about her father. Was there *really* something wrong with him? If there was . . .

Impatiently she flicked away a sudden tear. She was too sentimental, she knew it. She would have to grow up. She was twenty-one years old.

2

Hands in pockets, shoulders hunched, Steve Lewis ran up the first flight of lino-covered stairs of the *County Dispatch*, tip-toed up the second and crept past the editor's office at the top. Having safely made the ascent he strolled carelessly into the reporters' room, where Bill Merrick was already clattering out the clichés. Bill was the senior reporter on this weekly paper on the west coast of Wales, a man in whom ambition had long died. His pale mackerel eyes spoke of disappointment and resentment, his thin auburn moustache underlined the impression he conveyed of something inadequately attempted. He nodded briefly at Steve, looked pointedly at the clock and drew on his Player's No. 1, taking the smoke deep into his lungs as he perched the cigarette on the blackened edge of the table. Steve ignored him.

Sitting opposite, the newsroom secretary Brenda Marsden flashed him a bright, unsuccessful smile, then carried on opening the mail. Her tight, cherry-red suit and trendy rimless glasses failed to convince anyone that she would see twenty-nine again. Alone at his corner desk with his back to the flyblown window, old 'Scoop' Matthews, hunched and cobwebby, muttered to himself as he wrote up in pencil his report of the previous day's Rural District Council meeting in Tregaron.

Steve took his notebook from a drawer and frowned down at the poem he had begun a week ago.

> Behold the broken reed, the sterile seed,
> The bare, cropped plain of my desire.
> Arrows of passion . . .

'Something good? Another scoop?' sneered a voice at his shoulders.

Startled, Steve quickly turned the page, with a small-boy-caught-out look that destroyed his carefully cultivated air of sophistication. Ronnie Banks, short, round-faced, slew-eyed behind tortoiseshell glasses, looked down on him derisively.

'Aren't you going to type it out for us all to enjoy?'
'I don't think so, Ronnie. It's not worth it.'
'Pity. Thought it was something worth coming in late for.'
'Sorry about that, Ronnie. The alarm didn't go off.'
'Well, well. Fancy that. We'll have to club round and buy you a new one then, won't we, Bill?'

Bill curled his thin lips into a vulpine smile. Brenda's eyes darkened.

'Anyway, I've got a job for you. If you can spare the time, that is.' Edging away from confrontation, Ronnie waddled back to his cubbyhole office at the far end of the reporters' room. Here, amid a rubble of handouts, old newspapers and unanswered letters, he exercised the twin roles of news editor and sub-editor. His jacket, leather-patched at the elbows, was slung over the back of the chair, for he worked with rolled-up shirtsleeves, Hollywood-style. He had not yet aspired to a green eyeshade but, Steve sardonically imagined, that was only a matter of time.

'Someone called in yesterday,' rasped Ronnie. 'Wants a council house. A Mrs Baker. Says conditions are bad, damp walls, rats in her backyard, usual sort of thing. Might be worth a piece.'

'Where's she live?'

'Back Row.'

'Jesus.'

Ronnie looked sharply up. 'What's that for?'

'Place should be knocked down. It's a slum.'

'What do you know about slums, boy? Living in Dewi Avenue.'

'That's not my fault, is it?'

'Didn't say it was, did I? Anyway go and take a look. Might make a nice human piece. We can do with some, God knows.' He lowered his voice. 'And you're the one to do them,' he flattered, soft-soaping. 'No other bugger here can, that's for sure.'

'What number she live in?' asked Steve, pleased by the compliment but trying not to show it.

Ronnie looked at his scribbled note. 'Four.'

'Know anything about her?'

'Not a thing. Only that she's from away. Been here a year or two, that's all.'

'Does she qualify for a council house then? Won't have enough points yet, will she?'

'I don't bloody know. That's for you to find out, isn't it, lad?'

'I will, don't worry,' Steve said nonchalantly. 'I'll go down there later this morning.'

'Don't push yourself,' said Ronnie sarcastically. 'And buy yourself a new alarm clock!' he called after him.

In unusual good humour, he took his blue pencil to the sheets of handwritten copy from the paper's village correspondents. For all his philistinism and coarseness, Ronnie was the lynchpin of the paper's editorial department, a man surprisingly unembittered by the fact that the rarely-seen editor relied far too heavily on his industry and know-how.

Steve, taking his place at the long table which had been in the *County Dispatch* office since the days of frock coats and quill pens, studiously avoided the enquiring eyes of Brenda Marsden. He knew she fancied him, and was faintly disgusted by the knowledge. She was at least ten years older, with a husband in tow. What the hell did she want him for? Yet he found it hard to resist entirely the allure of those grey-green eyes, and when she came up close, on some thinly-manufactured excuse, he was not above pressing himself against her, deriving a threadbare pleasure from the feel of her full breast against his arm.

Bill Merrick, once-proud ginger thatch now sadly diminished, shot Steve a baleful glance as the young man, without haste, lined up a blank sheet of copy paper on his much-abused typewriter. It maddened him that Steve simply ignored him. Steve, for whom the goading of Bill was a small but significant pleasure, took longer than he needed to begin typing out his report of the previous night's meeting of the town's Chamber of Trade. After a minute or two he stopped, snapped open a silver cigarette case inscribed with his initials (a coming-of-age present), and took out a Senior Service. He tapped this slowly and contemplatively on the back of his hand, then smiled beatifically across the table. 'Could you give me a light, Bill?' he asked. 'I've left my matches at home.'

For a long moment Bill looked as though he might refuse. Then he took a lighter from his pocket and, without a word, flicked a flame into life. Steve leaned across the table. 'Thanks, pal.'

Brenda glanced uneasily from one to the other; she was never quite sure how things were between these two men. Then, with the slightest shake of the head, she resumed the tedious task of entering forthcoming events in the newsroom diary.

It was just after eleven when, his copy safely in Ronnie's In-Tray, Steve clumped back down the stairs and into the streets of the town. It was midsummer in Glanaber and the seasonal visitors were back. There were fewer of them than there had been before the war, for the town was, as everyone acknowledged, 'going down' as a seaside resort. Once it had proudly acknowledged itself to be 'the Brighton of Wales', but now it was not even the Clacton. Its poshest hotel had been taken over by the county council which, according to a malapropist town councillor, was 'like an octopus, spreading its testicles all over the borough.' The expanding university was claiming other seafront properties. Glanaber, quietly dozing its days away in the lotus-eating land of the far west, did well enough from bureaucrats and students without having to exert itself in other ways.

Just the wrong side of twenty-three, Steve had hoped by now to have shaken the dust of the town from his feet. It was too small for him; too Welsh, both in language and habits of thought; too *comfortable*. He felt he was only skimming the surface of life; he wanted to go far deeper.

He was ambitious, but in conflicting ways. One part of him wanted Fleet Street success, but another coveted fame of a different kind. He knew he had poetic gifts, but had still to find his own voice. He was an admirer of

Dylan Thomas, and had attempted poems aping that boozy bard's windy rhetoric. But slowly and very uncertainly, he was edging into a quite different style. He wasn't at all sure that he would ever write 'real' poetry, but took joy enough in words to make the attempt.

Steve was not a handsome young man in the conventional sense, his nose being too large and his red, full-lipped mouth looking oddly out of place, as if it had been stuck on the wrong face. His leanness made him look taller than he actually was, a flurry of wavy brown hair confirming this impression. He wore smart casuals to the office, sports jackets and grey flannels with a red tie plumply shaped into a Windsor knot. He was less confident than he appeared; less experienced sexually than he pretended, having missed National Service – with its ample opportunities for servicing Waafs, Wrens and ATS – because of a heart murmur brought on by rheumatic fever in childhood. Embarrassed by the absence of a common point of reference for young men early in the 1950s, he disguised the fact as well as he could. He was a bit of a loner, avoiding the rough camaraderie of the pubs to take long, contemplative walks during which he juggled words in his brain, spinning and twirling them so that they assumed new, exciting shapes. It was exhilarating, frustrating, daunting, unavoidable.

Back Row was a terrace of old fishermen's cottages overlooking the harbour. Like the harbour itself, it had seen better days. The outside walls, once trimly limewashed, were now smudgy grey. Tired old paint flaked away, lacking the strength to stay longer. Steve knocked and waited.

The door opened suddenly and a small girl with enormous blue eyes looked unblinkingly up.

'Hello. Is your mother in?'

She said nothing but kept staring, so that he wondered if she were deaf, or in some way defective.

'Is Mrs Baker in?' he said, more loudly.

'Who is it, Vi?' came a voice within.

'A man.'

'A man? God help. Ask him in then.'

The small girl scurried inside. A woman appeared, black-haired, brazen-eyed. She smiled.

'Don't just stand there,' she said. 'Come along in.'

She held the door open and glanced up at him, sidelong.

'Well,' she said, following him into a small, dingy room that shut out the sun, 'what can I do for you?'

He stood there, seeing what she was.

'I'm from the *Dispatch*,' he said. 'You went round there yesterday.'

'Oh, that. Yes.' She laughed briefly. 'I thought they'd have sent someone older.'

There was a warm smell coming from her that at once stirred and disgusted him.

'How old are you, then?' she asked.

'Twenty-three.'

'Twenty-three! God help. They'll be having me up for cradle-snatching.'

She did not talk the local way but in the ample, broad-vowelled accent of Montgomeryshire.

'I'm told you've got rats here,' he said brusquely. 'Is that right?'

'Rats! If it's rats you want there's plenty of them on the council. I can tell you a thing or two, that I can. I can give you a few names –'

She stopped abruptly and smiled. 'Come and see for yourself, lad.'

23

She strode through the tiny room to the scullery beyond and unlatched the back door.

'Here. Take a look.'

The backyard was a mess of old cardboard boxes, rusty bits of iron, tin cans and wood shavings. A bicycle wheel with no tyres and bent spokes leaned against a wall. The sun winkled out smells of decay and neglect.

'See?'

She pointed to something at her feet.

'Well?' she said impatiently.

'What is it?'

'What do you think, Scotch mist? It's rat-shit, of course. The place is full of it. It's unfit for human habitation.'

Coming from her, the official phrase sounded stiff and grotesque. Steve said nothing.

'Well, we may as well go back in,' she said irritably. 'No good standing out here. Maybe you'll find your tongue inside.'

The small girl, dressed in a tattered violet frock that strangely echoed her name, stared vacantly from the back doorstep.

'And you can bugger off for an hour,' said her mother forcibly. 'I don't want you hanging round here like a bit of dirty washing. Go down the Gulan, for godsake.'

She shoved the girl aside and Steve followed her into the house, looking apologetically down at Vi as he passed. The girl skipped uncaringly across the backyard.

'Here,' said the woman. 'You see where the damp's coming through? It's ruining everything. We've had the public health here but it's like talking to the wall.

Would you like to live in a place like this? Be honest now, would you?'

'No. I don't suppose I would.'

'Well, that's it then, innit? And I can show you worse. Come and see.'

She grabbed Steve's wrist and led him up the stairs that climbed the dimness opposite the front door. He knew he should shake off her grasp but felt a strange reluctance to do so. He brushed against her. Her hand was hot.

'What's your name anyway?' she said on the landing.

He freed himself. 'Lewis.'

'No, I mean your *first* name. Can't call you Mr Lewis can I, slip of a lad like you?'

'Steve,' he said reluctantly.

'Well, *Steve*, come along in.'

She pushed open a bedroom door and stepped through. There was a double bed that took up most of the room, the pungency of cheap perfume, something else indefinable.

'Well?' she said. 'What do you think?'

'What do I think of what?' he asked awkwardly, acutely aware of his own gaucheness and inadequacy.

'Well – is this the right sort of place for a lady?'

'What's wrong with it?'

'What's wrong with it? What's right with it you mean.' She smiled, showing small and surprisingly white teeth. 'That's what's right with it.' She nodded at the bed. 'That's the only thing that's right with it.'

She looked boldly at him, her fingers playing with the top button of her dress.

'You understand?'

He nodded, his throat tight.

'Well then.' She undid the button. Her skin was brown, her eyes gleamed dark and huge. 'Who's to know then, eh?'

She slipped off her shoes. Her bare feet were shapely, delicate.

A phrase came to Steve: Our reporter made his excuses and left.

He could not move.

Her lips parted as she came to him.

He saw her as if she were already naked.

She closed her eyes and tilted her head back.

He turned and ran down the stairs and out of the door.

Her mocking laughter followed him.

3

She was seeing him that evening: he was doing a theatre review for the paper. She caught the bus home after work, bolted down a skimpy meal and was scolded again by her mother, took the bus back into town. She seemed to spend a lot of her time rushing around, and wondered why people thought everyone lived a quiet life in Glanaber.

She could see from his face, as she stepped off the bus, that he was in one of his moods.

'You're late,' he said, as she came towards him from the bus.

'No I'm not. It's only quarter-past.'

'It starts at half-past. I've got to get a programme and that.'

'We've got plenty of time.'

He began walking briskly across the road behind the parked bus with scarcely a glance to left or right.

'It's alright for you,' he grumbled over his shoulder. 'I'm working, remember. I've got to write about the bloody thing.'

Annette stiffened. She disliked swearing.

She ran a few yards, with difficulty on her high heels, but still didn't catch up.

'Steve,' she said when they reached the pavement opposite. 'Will you please stop still for a minute?'

He turned, scowling.

'I don't know what you're mad about but I know it isn't me. If you want to go on your own I'm not bothered, but I'm not going to be rushed along like a mad thing.'

His face cleared. 'I'm sorry,' he muttered.

'That's alright. Just calm down, that's all.' She smiled and took his hand. 'We'll be there in a few minutes.'

They walked in silence along the street leading to the prom.

'What's this play called, did you say?'

'*Cat on a Hot Tin Roof.*'

'Is it good?'

He smiled thinly. 'It's supposed to be one of the best plays for years, that's all.'

She glanced at him. 'Well, you know how ignorant I am.'

'You're not ignorant. You just don't know.'

'Same thing isn't it?'

'No. You just haven't had a chance.'

Not had a chance to what? she wondered. Go to the county school because she'd failed the scholarship? But it had never bothered her. She hadn't wanted to go particularly. She was always being told at school that she 'could do better' and 'didn't try' but she did as well as she wanted and if she was quite happy what was the point of trying? Anyway she'd learned shorthand and typing at night school and had a good job now with the solicitors, so what would have been the point of going to county and filling her head with a lot of things she didn't understand?

Once more she thought about Ivor. So different from Steve. Far less complicated. She pushed the thought away.

The theatre was part of the Victorian pier that had somehow survived all changes of fashion in Glanaber.

It stretched out from the prom on tall cast-iron legs, like an elderly bather perilously testing the waters. As Steve collected the complimentary tickets from the box office Annette stood uneasily aside, for she could never get used to getting in anywhere for nothing. She felt his disapproval of her awkwardness when he returned with the tickets and a programme; she knew he was still cross about something but couldn't imagine what.

'Cheer up,' she said lightly. 'It's not as bad as all that.'

He gave her a frosty look and she suddenly rebelled.

'Are you sure you want me to come with you, Steve? I can easily go home, you know.'

'No. Please. Don't do that.'

'Well, cheer up for heaven's sake. You look as if you've lost a shilling and found sixpence.'

'I'm alright. It's just something that happened today.'

'What was that then?'

'Oh, nothing.' And his face clouded again.

Secretive, she thought. Always so secretive. Why didn't he open out? Didn't he trust her?

They took their seats in the third row, nearer the front than she would have liked. She felt uncomfortable with what she thought of as the *crachach*, well-to-do people like Wynne Rowlands the coroner, sitting just in front of her, and Mrs Beynon Rees who was on the county council and looked as if she could fall into a cesspit and come up smelling of lavender. She would much prefer to be further back where she belonged, but better still to be at the pictures. Still, she was here now and would make the best of it.

'Like one of these?' Steve asked unexpectedly.

'Oh. Ta.' She picked a pear drop and popped it in her mouth. A phrase of her mother's came uninvited to mind, 'forbidden fruits', and she clutched Steve's hand suddenly, not quite knowing why. Surprised, he gave her a quick, thankful squeeze and they glanced shyly at each other.

At such moments she loved him. But there was too much about him she didn't understand.

He always walked her home, sometimes directly up Penbryn Hill, other times by the path skirting the allotments before climbing the track up to the council estate where she lived. He preferred the longer way because it allowed more chances for snogging but tonight she said: 'Let's go the main road, shall we?'

'Why's that?' he said, disappointed.

'Dad's not well. He didn't go to work today.'

'Oh? What's wrong with him then?'

'His chest is bad.'

He took her hand. His palm was warm, dry, his fingers interlocked easily with hers. She liked his touch; a shiver of pleasure ran through her.

'He's often home ill, isn't he?'

'Not often. Only sometimes,' she said, more sharply than she intended.

'I wasn't criticising,' he said mildly.

'Why should you? He can't help being ill, can he?'

'Course not. Maybe he should see the doctor, that's all I meant.'

'He will do tomorrow,' she found herself saying, though she had no idea whether he would or not.

To their right the sky over the sea was still streaked with the livid colours of a Cardigan Bay sunset. As they crossed the town bridge a fishing boat nosed silently around the wooden jetty into the harbour, watched by a clutch of visitors on the quayside.

They walked in silence for a while. Then he said, as casually as he could: 'Have you thought any more about Saturday?'

'Saturday?'

'You know – about coming over.'

She made no reply.

'You said you would,' he said gently.

'Oh? When did I say that?'

'The other day.'

She felt tense, exposed, as if she were stripped bare.

'It seems too good a chance,' he said.

'Chance to what, Steve?' She stopped. 'What do you think I am? Some kind of – prostitute?' The word was out before she could stop it.

He looked at her, amazed. 'No,' he said. '*No*. I didn't mean that.'

She walked on quickly. He ran to catch her up.

'I didn't *mean* that.' He grabbed her arm. 'Honest, Annette.'

'You're hurting,' she said icily.

He released her. 'God,' he said wildly. 'What did I *say*?'

'You know.'

He thought back. They had been in the room her parents called the parlour, the best room reserved for special occasions. It had a glass-fronted cabinet containing never-used wedding presents – willow-pattern china and dainty cups and saucers, so fragile they looked as if a harsh glance might break them – while a pair of fire-irons and a poker handed down from her grandparents rested in the cold fireplace.

There was a shiny-black settee where Annette and Steve put in some highly restrained snogging, inhibited as they were by her parents' proximity in the next room. The thin dividing wall was not so much a barrier as a warning: through it one could hear clearly the spirit, if not the letter, of normal conversation, and the laughter and applause of studio audiences on the wireless which Ted and Lorna Morris scarcely ever switched off. They listened to it for hour after hour, *Variety Bandbox* and *Ray's a Laugh*, *Family Favourites* and *Up the Pole*, Ted Morris's brays of laughter often subsiding into fits of coughing. Steve despised their tastes but not, he tried to persuade himself – unconvincingly – not the couple themselves.

What *had* he said? He remembered telling her his parents were going away that weekend and he could not help feeling excited at the thought of being alone with her there, absolutely alone. He hoped that he might go much further with her than ever before, not only touch her breasts through her dress or blouse but hold them naked in his hands. He shivered whenever he thought of it, so that he wondered how he could bear to be so near her and do nothing. But what had he *said*?

'I can't remember.'

'Liar.'

Her face was tight as a trap. He felt like a wasp vainly hurling itself against a shut window, furiously buzzing and whirring, the very essence of futility.

'I wish you'd tell me.'

'I wouldn't cheapen myself.'

They walked under the railway bridge and up Penbryn Hill, the main road south out of town. A bus struggled past them in low gear, crammed with picturegoers and pub crawlers. She looked away to where, across the valley, the lights were coming on in the kind of house Steve lived in: roomy, comfortable, with nice carpets and furniture and a bathroom with radiators and towel rails and rugs you could sink your feet into. His parents were different from hers: friendly enough but different. Because they had money.

His words came back to her yet again, the words that at once had confused and excited her, the words she could not get out of her brain: 'We'll be on our own. There'll be nothing to stop us.' What did they mean except *that*? She imagined him in bed with her, felt his body hard against hers, his breath hot on her cheek, his tongue probing her mouth.

Or had he meant that at all?

Suddenly doubtful, she risked a sidelong glance.

He was walking coolly beside her, swinging his arms, looking remote and unapproachable.

He did not return her look.

Sometimes she hated him.

She found her mother sitting on her own, small, dark, resentful. The wireless was off. The room was achingly quiet.

'Where's Dad?' asked Annette.

'What time you call this?'

'It's not late. Not out, is he?'

'Where you been till now, anyway?'

'I told you, the theatre.'

'Theatre!' Lorna threw back contemptuously.

'Well, what's wrong with that? Steve had to go for the paper.'

'Trust him.'

'What you mean?'

33

Lorna Morris's eyes skewed away from her daughter's, as if she already regretted her words.

'Don't you like him then?' said Annette.

'Who said I didn't?'

'You sound like you hated him then.'

'Don't be soft, girl.' Appeasingly she added: 'Why didn't you bring him in tonight anyway?'

'He had to go,' lied Annette, for it was she who had given him the skimpiest of kisses and rushed down the garden path, leaving him standing at the gate feeling wretched.

Lorna Morris smoked fiercely, inexpertly, not inhaling, the tip of the Craven A bright red with every swift intake, her nicotined forefinger tap-tapping the ash nervously into the fag-strewn saucer.

'Where's Dad then?'

'Where'd you think?'

'Not up the Tollbar, is he? He's supposed to be sick!'

'What you mean, *supposed*?'

'Well, he can't be very bad if he's up there, can he?'

'Who says so?'

'It's obvious!'

'Oh, lah-di-dah!' said Lorna, in a mincing little voice. 'Proper little madam these days, aren't you?'

Annette stared at her disbelievingly, then turned and ran upstairs. She *knew* he'd been shamming, she'd known it all along! She flung herself on her bed, fighting back tears. What a night it had been!

After a while, she heard her mother pat-patting upstairs in her slippers. A gentle tap on the door.

'Go away, Mam.'

'Please Annette. Let me in.'

Annette sighed.

'Annette?'

'It's not *locked*, Mam!' cried Annette impatiently.

Lorna edged in. There was something gipsyish about her brown eyes and swarthy complexion, but no boldness in her now. She stood uncomfortably, hands pressed flat behind her against the door.

Annette, still hurt, was not yet ready to forgive.

'I didn't mean it, 'Nette,' said Lorna humbly.

'Didn't you?'

'You know what I'm like. Bull at a gate, me.'

The silence stretched.

'Had a nice time, did you?'

'Please, Mam.'

'I do like him, you know.'

'You don't have to.'

'But I do – he's a nice boy. Bit different to us, but . . .'

'Just leave it Mam, will you?'

'Right. I will.' Lorna paused. 'You're wrong about your dad, you know. He was really poorly today.'

'Why? What's wrong with him then?'

'Bad chest.'

'You get the doctor?'

'No. No need.'

'You should.'

Lorna turned.

'Be nice to him, 'Nette. He's got a lot on his mind.'

The door closed behind her.

4

Jim Lewis hummed a catchy little tune as he thrust a gold cuff-link into place in the big front bedroom of his house in Dewi Avenue. An amiable and generally contented man, he was in an especially good mood that Friday morning. There was the weekend to look forward to, and a very good weekend it promised to be too. After signing the last file of the day at the seafront offices of the Ministry of Pensions, he would be loading up his trusty old Morris Oxford and zoom! off they'd go to the delights of the Vale of Glamorgan.

Or, to be more precise, the delights of a night out with his old pal Charlie Llewellyn, as their wives sat at home gossiping. And where was the harm in that?

It was not that he disliked Glanaber, dump though it was in many ways compared with Cardiff. It was just that he missed Charlie and Bryn and Bob, the three mates he sometimes imagined he'd grown up with, he'd known them so long.

Doing up his fly buttons, he stared out at the magnolia Edna was so proud of, not seeing it at all. If only he'd turned down that promotion, he'd still be living in South Wales. Enjoying a few Friday night jars with Charlie and Bryn and Bob in the old coaching inns of Cowbridge. Going to the Arms Park to see Cardiff take on Newport or Swansea on a Saturday afternoon. Playing a round of golf at Wenvoe on a Sunday. He sighed.

He could never have turned it down, he knew that. Life wouldn't have been worth living, with Edna on the warpath.

But what had he gained? Most of the extra he earned went in tax. Edna, who had been so keen to see him go up in the world, now complained that she missed her old friends. And you could hardly say Steve was a barrel of laughs, the boy was so moody.

What Edna wanted, of course, was a transfer back south on a higher grade still. But he wasn't getting any younger and neither was she, though she'd never admit it. Chances were, they were stuck in Glanaber – though he couldn't see Steve staying there much longer. And why should he? It was no place for a young man. He didn't blame him.

But he had to make one more effort to get him to go with them that weekend, because that's what Edna wanted.

Clad in a lightweight fawn suit, so becoming a middle-ranking civil servant in high summer, Jim ate his breakfast toast and marmalade and waited for his son to put in an appearance. He glanced through the *Western Mail* as he did so, keeping abreast of events in what many people insisted on calling 'the Principality' as well as those in the wider world. He was a smooth-skinned man, not quite baby-faced but looking much younger than his years, thanks chiefly to his pink complexion and pale-blue, innocent eyes, eyes which in his younger days had charmed many a woman and which, even now, were not above a flirtation or two. He sat alone at the table because Edna, his wife, took only black coffee and one slice of dry toast for breakfast. She could be heard now on the phone in the hall, talking to one of her cronies. 'It was absolutely ridiculous, dear. All that effort for nothing! I tell you straight, if it was a daughter of mine – '

But it could not be, because she had no daughters. Only a son.

When Steve slouched ungraciously into the breakfast room Jim looked up eagerly, friendly smile at the ready. Steve inwardly groaned; he knew what was coming. No, Dad, I haven't changed my mind. Sorry, Dad, I'd love to come but I've got work to do. That's what he should say right away, to pre-empt all questions. Instead of which he said nothing, slumping down in a chair and pouring a stream of cornflakes into a bowl.

'I see they're giving us more meat,' Jim said brightly. 'Tuppence a week more on the ration soon. Good, eh?' He slapped the paper approvingly.

'Won't make much difference to me. I don't eat much as it is.'

'Don't have to tell me that, son. Could do with building up a bit.'

'Don't you start, Dad,' Steve chided wearily.

'I won't, don't worry. Just thinking of your welfare, that's all.' He smiled conspiratorially.

Steve did not respond. He stirred the cornflakes uncomfortably, such appetite as he had for them diminishing fast.

'Much on today then, have you?'

'Don't know yet. Nothing in the diary for me. Have to see what turns up.'

'Of course. News waits for no man. That's the nature of the beast, isn't it?'

Seeing Steve's reaction, the glazing of the eye which told him he had missed the mark yet again, Jim pressed on quickly.

'Why not come with us tonight, son? You can do

with a break, I'm sure. They'd be glad to see you, the Llewellyns. They're always asking after you.'

'Sorry, Dad, but I can't. I've got a job on tomorrow.'

'Couldn't someone else do it for you? I'm sure, if you asked . . .'

'I can't, Dad – really. Anyway, why'd you want me there with you? I'm not a kid any more.'

'I know that Steve but – we enjoy your company. Can try a round of golf with us, if you like.' He smiled hopefully.

'You're kidding!'

'Well,' said Jim awkwardly, 'it would please your mother no end.'

'I'm sure.'

The sarcasm turned Jim's face a touch pinker. 'Ah well.' He pushed his chair back, flashed a no-hard-feelings smile. 'If you change your mind just say. You know where to find me.'

'OK Dad. Thanks.'

The phone pinged in the hall as the receiver was replaced. A murmured conversation, and Jim left for the office. Steve pushed his uneaten cornflakes aside and held his head in his hands. Once again he saw the woman in Back Row undo her top button, heard her murmur invitingly, 'Who's to know then, eh?'

What a bloody fool he'd been!

Edna Lewis came in, quiet as a panther.

'Something wrong, son? Got a headache?'

'No – I'm fine.'

'Lost your appetite, have you?'

'I'm not hungry.'

'You can't go to work on an empty stomach. Look, I'll fry you some bacon.'

'No – I don't want it, Mam!'

'Alright then – no need to shout.' She gave him a smile, of lethal understanding. 'I'll get a fresh pot of coffee then – we'll have one together.'

There was no escape for Steve. He took a slice of toast, buttered it, added a blob of Hartley's strawberry jam.

Voices in the kitchen: his mother and the daily, the rat-faced Mrs Teifi Evans. He could not make out the words; did not wish to. He nibbled the toast, wished he'd made his getaway to the office without breakfasting.

Edna, back with the coffee, slid into the chair opposite. At the time of her marriage she had possessed a fragile beauty and had been, for Jim, something of a catch. She had not gone to seed or to fat; was, in fact, slimmer than she had been as a young woman. Her thin lips were lightly made up, her slim body clothed in gauzy materials that gave her a will-o'-the-wisp insubstantiality.

'Did your father have a word with you?' she asked silkily, sliding into the chair opposite. 'About coming away for the weekend?'

'Yes, he did mention it.'

'You will then, will you?'

'I can't, Mam, I'm sorry.'

'*Can't?*'

'I've got too much on. A job's come up. I can't get out of it now.'

'Oh? What job's that then?' She managed a small, stiff smile as she passed him his coffee.

'Oh,' he said vaguely, 'just some meeting. I volunteered for it as I wasn't going anywhere.'

'I see.' She sighed. 'Well, they'll be very disappointed, the Llewellyns. They were so much hoping you'd come with us.'

'I'm sorry,' he murmured.

'They were very good to us, you know – in the war.'

Steve steeled himself.

'And they took such an interest in you . . . when your father was away.'

The Chinese torture, he thought, with words instead of water dripping repeatedly on to one's skull.

'I don't know where I'd have been without them.'

He ate his toast in silence.

'I don't suppose you'll be working – *all* the time?'

'No, I don't expect,' he said calmly, not looking at her.

'You'll be seeing . . . Annette then, will you?' she asked, mouth twisted, as if she had trouble pronouncing the name.

'Yes, I suppose.'

'The reason you're not coming with us, yes?'

'Pardon?'

'Annette. You're staying because of her.'

'No. I told you – I'm working.'

'Ah yes. The meeting.' She smiled thinly. 'But there'll be plenty of time after it, no doubt?'

'Of course. Why?'

'Why nothing, son. But you'll be seeing her over there?' A jerk of the head. 'In Penbryn, yes?'

'I expect so. I usually do, don't I?' A hint of querulousness betrayed him.

'Well. So long as that's clearly understood. We don't want any accidents, do we?'

'Accidents'? he wanted to say. What do you mean, 'accidents'?

Seething inside, his cheeks burning, he sat there in silence, humiliated.

Finishing her coffee, she went upstairs without haste. Mrs Teifi Evans stumped in from the kitchen.

She clattered away the dirty crocks, giving Steve a mean, knowing look.

He knew she'd been listening, the cow.

'She's been back here,' said Ronnie, in his cubbyhole office.

'Who?'

'Who'd you think? The woman in Back Row. Mrs Baker.'

'Oh. Her.'

'Yes. Her. Why, didn't you like her then? Not your cup of tea, I don't suppose. Not middle-class enough.'

Steve flushed. 'There's no need for that.'

Ronnie grinned delightedly. 'Got you on the raw that, did it? Never mind, boy. You can't help living in Dewi Avenue.'

He took a bite of his tomato sandwich, spraying the virgin front page of the latest edition of the *County Dispatch*, hot from the press.

'Sod it,' said Ronnie, not caring much about the mess. The front page was all adverts.

Steve looked down at him distastefully, wondering how long it would be before he left the paper. He had his sights on higher things. Fleet Street beckoned.

'Now look here,' said Ronnie, whisking a handkerchief over the page. 'You can't choose what to write and what not to. There's a good story there. I can smell it.' He squinted up at Steve. 'Let's have it straight from the shoulder. One of your specials, right?'

'But there's nothing in it,' said Steve hotly. 'She's just having us on.'

'Oh yeah? You like to live in Back Row then? I'd give you five minutes. If that.'

'She had nothing to say. All she did was – ' He stopped.

'Yes? What did she do then?'

'Nothing.'

'Oh no? Then why'd you run away like a scalded cat? That's what she says. You run off before you'd been there two minutes.'

Steve's blush deepened.

'Now look here, son,' breathed Ronnie. 'I don't care what she did or what she didn't. I want you back there today and I want a story first thing Monday morning, OK?'

'But there's nothing to say! She's no worse off than plenty of others. Why give her publicity and not them?'

'Because she bloody asked for it, that's why. If the others got off their arses and came round here we might do something for them too.' Ronnie looked up at Steve, playing the hard man. 'Now get going, son. And don't get hoity-toity with me, right? You've got a lot to learn.'

Steve strode out angrily, followed by Bill's gloating eyes. He stumbled into Scoop Matthews in the doorway, muttered an ungracious apology, clattered downstairs. To hell with them all! He'd be doing real stories soon, not garbage like this.

In the Black Ram he moodily ordered a pork pie and a pint, took them unsociably to a corner of the dark bar smelling still of last night's beer. He skimmed through the *News Chronicle* he'd picked up at Smith's first thing that morning: his favourite daily. He might be working for it soon: was it too much to hope for? He turned the page, noticing to his dismay the landlord shuffling over. Joe wasn't a bad sort, but he wasn't in the mood for his company now. Shabby, melancholic and often unshaven, Joe Dobson was the antithesis of the jovial mine host.

'See old Ike's running then,' he hoarsely observed in broad Yorkshire as he swabbed the next table with a damp, grubby cloth.

'Who?'

'Eisenhower. Running for President.'

'God help us.'

'Just what we need.' Joe coughed. 'Bring those North Korean bastards to their senses.'

'What'd he do then, Joe?'

'What? Drop the atom bomb on them of course. Finish buggers off.'

'Might finish us all off.'

'Nah. Them Russkis wouldn't do nothing.'

'No?'

'Not a thing. Should've done it right off and brought the boys home.'

He shuffled back to the bar. Steve, irritated, took a deep swig; the cloudy beer was giving him a headache. But it gave him something else as well: the dutch courage he needed to face Sara Baker again. He remembered her black hair, brazen eyes, the warm smell coming from her. Quickly he drained his glass. There was time for another.

This time she answered the door herself. 'Well, fancy seeing you. Come on in, lad.'

She stood aside to let him pass. He brushed against her, only partly by accident.

'Didn't think you'd be back so soon,' she said, closing the door.

'Didn't you?'

'Not after last time.' She smiled. 'Never seen no-one move so fast in all my life.'

He stood rigidly, hands in the pockets of his fawn gaberdine mackintosh.

'What you think I was going to do then, eh?' she said, coming close. 'Bite you?' She nipped the air with her fine white teeth, then laughed. 'Poor little sod. Frightened you to death, didn't I?'

'Not really.'

'No? You could have kidded me, boy.'

He looked down into her hot brown eyes and his hands itched, either to ravish her or strangle her.

'Anyway,' she said, whirling away. 'Never mind that now. I'm just making a cup of tea. Like one?'

'Please,' he said shortly.

'Right then. Take your coat off. Make yourself at home.' She gave him a seductive, slanting look and went to the scullery, whistling softly through her teeth.

He sat on a wooden chair, his elbow resting on the table. The second lunchtime pint had been a mistake: he'd be wanting a slash soon. Yet he felt better for it, more relaxed. He loosened the belt of his mac then undid the buttons and sat back, legs apart, looking about him. The dark, dingy room, darker and dingier than ever in the gloom of the afternoon, was scantily furnished. It smelt of poverty and neglect and of something else less definable.

'You take sugar?'

'Yes please. One.'

'You can put it in yourself, lad.'

The cup she brought him was chipped. He wrinkled his nose but said nothing. She sat facing him, her cup on the table beside her. Determined not to be caught out again in youthful gaucheness, he tried to ignore the bold, teasing look in her eyes.

'What's brought you back then?'

'You know damn well. You complained about me.'

'No I never.' Her eyes opened wide. 'What makes you say that?'

'Because you did. Ronnie told me.'

'Who's Ronnie?'

'The news editor.'

'What, that squinty little chap with glasses? I never complained. All I said was send you back here, that's all.'

'Why's that then?'

'Well, you buggered off, didn't you? That's no good to me. I want something in the paper.'

'Why?'

'You know why, you're not soft. Want a council house, don't I? Not just for me, for Vi. Don't want her growing up in this rat-hole, do I?'

'Plenty of people want council houses.'

'Daresay they do. I don't give a bugger 'bout them. It's me I'm talking about. Look – what you say your name was now?'

'Steve.'

She grimaced. 'Don't like the name Steve. Knew someone called that once. Proper little pig he was. Look, I'm going to call you Gerry. Any objection?'

He shrugged. 'Please yourself.'

'Well – Gerry – tell me now. Where'd you live?'

'What's that matter?'

'Just tell me, *Gerry*,' she said, half-way between imperiousness and intimacy.

'Well – Dewi Avenue, if you must know.'

'Where's that then?'

He told her.

'Thought as much. Could tell you were a bit posh.' She waved away his objection. 'And your Dad? – clerking or something like that, is he?'

'Something like,' agreed Steve, with an irony she failed to catch.

'Well then. You're doing alright, aren't you? Nice job, nice big house, nice girlfriend too I'll be bound.'

'Look,' he said impatiently, 'where's all this leading?'

'Leading? It's not leading nowhere. But you don't know you're born do you, people like you. You don't know what it's like to live in a stinking hole like this with damp coming through everywhere. Look! There – and there – and there? How'd you like it, eh?'

'I wouldn't.'

'Too right you wouldn't. And your mam wouldn't like it neither, I'll be bound. Not the sort of thing *she's* used to, I bet.' She made an impatient gesture. 'But what's the use. Like talking to a brick wall, people like you. Don't understand, do you? Don't want to, neither.'

Her legs were slightly apart, her brown skirt – unfashionably short – riding up to expose her bare knees. There was a glimpse of white thigh, all the more exciting for its being revealed by accident not design. She crossed her legs and his eyes sheered away. She noticed but did not smile.

'Not easy for you, was it?' she said softly. 'Coming back here today.'

He shrugged, feeling his colour rise.

'Why didn't you refuse then?'

'Couldn't, could I?'

'Couldn't you? What sort of job you got then? Some sort of slave?'

'No – just a job,' he said angrily.

She smiled. 'Sorry lad. Always been a little bugger, me. Never done nothing I didn't want to. That's why I'm like I am, I s'pose.'

'It's not your fault.'

'No?' she said ironically. 'You know what I am, don't you?'

'I can guess.'

'I wonder.' She gave him a long, calculating look. 'Don't know what to make of you, and that's a fact. Sometimes you seem so innocent, and then – '

'What makes you think I'm innocent?'

'Don't be daft, boy.'

'You make me feel a fool,' he said, his cheeks hot.

'No, lad,' she said gently. 'Not a fool. Not by a long chalk . . . How many girls you had then, eh? I mean – properly had?'

'One or two.'

'One or two? God help. You in't even started yet, boy.'

Her skirt rose higher, this time by design. Slowly her leg swung to and fro.

'Bet you haven't had a real woman in your life. Have you?'

'Depends what you mean by that, doesn't it?' he said tightly.

'Someone like me.'

He looked at her.

'No. I don't suppose I have.'

She smiled. 'Well then.'

Ever afterwards he remembered the shabby net curtains, torn at one side, the damp patch in the ceiling, the scrawling cry of the gulls wheeling over the harbour.

He had imagined she might be brusque, mechanical, her practised body judging his inexperience harshly. Instead her hands fluttered lightly over him, as if afraid to settle, her mouth first yielded to his demands and then, with infinite subtlety, initiated deeper pleasures. He held her large, firm breasts exultantly, kissing her nipples too roughly, overcome by haste. He was no sooner inside her than he came, and though he tried to keep going he knew it was over, and he lay on her gasping while she clutched him, sighing.

'Leave it be,' she murmured. 'You lovely boy. Leave it be.'

Then, lying beside her, he took her hand, listening to the gulls and the soft drift of voices from the harbour. Thinking of Annette.

5

It had been a terrible day at Richards and James, Solicitors. Mrs Bevan had been especially obnoxious, finding fault for no reason and bringing Rita to the verge of tears. It was hard to know exactly where they stood with Big Bertha – she wasn't the office manager but she acted like one. Of course she'd been there since Adam and worked mainly for Mr Richards the senior partner, but when it came down to it she was just a secretary like her and Rita. But you try telling *her* that, thought Annette crossly, and then wondered if one day she really *would* tell her.

At last the time came to put the cover over the typewriter, which Annette did with Big Bertha watching her closely. *What d'you think I'm going to do, suffocate it?* The idea made her smile and the older woman gave her a sharp look, as if she were mocking her.

Big Bertha trundled out of the room and the girls looked at each other.

'Bitch,' mouthed Rita.

'Ssh. She'll know what you're saying.'

'I don't care. Anyway how will she?'

'Because she's a witch. She knows everything.'

'Wouldn't be at all surprised. Her bike changes to a broomstick when she gets round the corner, I bet.'

They giggled with the sheer relief of going home.

Rita took her coat from the rack by the window of

their upstairs office, glancing through casually and then standing stock-still, staring.

'You expecting someone, 'Nette?' she asked, in an odd voice.

'No. Why?'

'Well, I think you're in for a shock. There's someone waiting for you.'

Annette gave her a look. Slowly she went to the window.

'Not too close now. He'll see you.'

Cautiously she peeped through.

He was just across the road, outside Morris the Drapers, pretending to be doing nothing special. He glanced up at their office window and Annette drew back sharply.

'What's he want?' she whispered.

'Search me. Better go down and find out, hadn't you?'

'I can't. I'll go out the back way!'

'Don't be soft! Anyway you can't – you know that.'

'Maybe he doesn't want me – he's waiting for *you*.'

'What? That'll be the day!'

Big Bertha stepped back in briskly and gave them a suspicious look.

'What's wrong with you two? Haven't you got homes to go to?'

'We're just going,' said Rita firmly. 'Making sure everything's shipshape and Bristol fashion, that's all.'

'Why shouldn't it be?'

'No reason at all. Can't be too sure though, can you?' She slung her imitation-leather bag over her shoulder. 'Coming, Annette?'

They clattered down the front stairs and paused by the front door.

'Well,' said Rita. 'This is it, kid. But mind Steve doesn't find out – that's all.'

'Don't be so soft!'

Outside, Rita turned right and Annette left, giving each other little fluttering waves of the hand and self-conscious farewells.

Ivor Morgan crossed the road quickly. 'Annette.'

'Oh – hullo.'

'Can you spare me a minute?'

'Suppose so. Why?'

'I'd like a word with you, that's all.'

He stood awkwardly beside her, his long swarthy face anxious and embarrassed. Suddenly she resented him, his unexpected presence there, his working clothes – couldn't he be bothered to *change* before he accosted her?

'Well? What is it?'

'I can't talk here.'

'Why not? There's nothing wrong, is there?'

'No. Least – look, let's go to the Pelican, shall we?'

'Alright, if you must. But I can't stay long, mind. I'm going out tonight – with Connie and them,' she added, then could have kicked herself. She could go out with whoever she liked – what business was it of his?

'I won't keep you long,' he promised.

Briskly they walked side-by-side up Darkgate Street, past shopkeepers putting up the shutters and office workers trailing home. She felt conspicuous beside him and strange too, remembering how, only a year ago, this would have been perfectly natural.

'I'm sorry, Annette. But I never see you these days, do I?'

He spoke calmly, as if, she thought, it was his *right*

to be with her. Yet, for all her resentment and confusion, something in her responded to this direct, almost proprietorial approach. What on earth could he want? Suddenly she wondered if he were getting married and thought she ought to know about it, before word got around. Betty Wilson, she thought bitterly, that plain, podgy thing with the vacant blue eyes, surely not her? Yet she had seen them together a week or two ago, coming out of the pictures, Betty gazing up at him with a gooey look in her eyes. She thrust away the memory, surprised by the fierceness of her jealousy. And felt still more cross and uncomfortable.

They turned into Pier Road and crossed the road to the Pelican. Let's hope Steve isn't in here, she thought grimly. This'll take some explaining.

It was between-times in the cafe, the daytime bustle over, the more leisurely evening trade not yet begun. She deliberately chose a table on the far side, away from the front windows. He took his time at the counter, chatting with Mario, the breezy Italian who ran the place with his father. Standing there, tall and slim, Ivor had a natural dignity which impressed itself on Annette. His working clothes no longer mattered; she had a sense of his fitness in the scheme of things in this town. She knew, in the depths of her soul, that whatever happened to her, he was Glanaber through and through. He would remain here, part of the mosaic of life, perhaps an important part in time to come. And suddenly she was afraid.

'Well,' she said lightly, 'what's bothering you?'

Slowly he licked the froth from his spoon and her stomach lurched, as if his tongue were again in her mouth.

'How's your dad these days?'

'Dad? He's OK. Why?'

He sipped his coffee, every movement slow, ponderous.

'He said anything about his work?'

'No. Nothing special. What's this, Ivor? What're you getting at?'

'So you haven't heard,' he said, giving her a straight look.

'Heard what? For heaven's sake, Ivor, out with it!'

'He's been suspended.'

'Suspended? What d'you mean, 'suspended'?'

'What I say. Suspended from work.'

'What on earth are you talking about?'

Ivor sighed and began stirring his coffee again, holding the spoon still now and then, playing with the froth in a way that maddened her.

'You're out of your mind,' she said wildly. 'What do you mean by bringing me here and – '

'Listen,' he said sharply. 'I want you to know before someone else tells you. Knowing your mother – '

'What's wrong with my mother?'

'Nothing's *wrong*. But she won't tell you, will she? She'll try to protect you. And then you'll find out from someone else and that'll be awful.'

'Find out what?'

'He's been stealing, Annette. Stealing letters.'

'*Stealing*?' She glared at him, outraged. 'How dare you say that? How *dare* you?' Her hand went to her cup, to throw coffee over him, and his eyes followed the movement, suddenly wary. 'How *could* you say that. You of all people. How *could* you.'

'I'm sorry. It may not be true – '

'Of course it's not true. It's a lie. You're telling lies!'

A woman sitting alone near the door turned and stared.

'I had to tell you,' he said miserably. 'It's what people are saying.'

'Let them say,' hissed Annette. 'Let them say what they like!'

Trembling, she put her hands to her mouth, biting her fingers, not noticing the hurt.

'I don't want to believe it. You know how I like him,' said Ivor.

'Like him. A good way of liking him I must say!'

Furiously she opened her handbag, dabbed her eyes, blew her nose. She had a weird sense that this wasn't really happening, that any moment she'd find herself stepping out of the office and going straight for the bus. She wanted all those horrible words cancelled out, never spoken. And then, through her tears, she saw Ivor's face and went suddenly cold.

She put her hankie back in her bag and clasped it shut.

'Well,' she said calmly. 'Thank you for telling me.'

She stood up, her coffee untouched, and slowly, like an actress playing a part, walked out of the cafe.

They were eating fish and chips and listening to a repeat of *Ray's a Laugh* on the wireless. They looked up guiltily, almost furtively, as if they already knew what she had found out.

'Alright love?' wheedled her mother. 'Cup of tea?'

'No thank you,' she said shortly, sweeping through the room like an avenging angel. She ran upstairs, flung her dress on her bed and went into the bathroom in her slip, locking the door hard, savagely, as if to keep out the world. She washed herself thoroughly, to remove the stain that was in her, then went back to her bedroom and locked that door too. She put on a different frock, an old one she'd bought at a sale in London House two years ago, and sat on the bed thinking. Wondering what was to become of them.

Dad would lose his job, if he hadn't lost it already. He might go to jail. They'd have no money, except what she was earning. Oh the shame of it, the shame of it!

He'd be up in court. He'd have his name in the paper. *Steve* might put it there. She stared hard at the wall opposite, willing all this to go away.

She had no doubt he was guilty. It was in the way he'd been behaving lately, how he looked at her, as if something had gone out of his soul.

She'd *known* something was wrong. But why hadn't they told her? And why had he done it? They weren't rich, but they had enough money to live on!

She thought of the way Ivor had told her. The miserable look in his eyes. He had almost touched her, his hand extending then drawing back.

A murmur of voices downstairs. Talking about her, she knew it. No wireless now. Just the voices, distant, the words indistinguishable.

The living-room door opened and she froze. She wouldn't talk to them, she couldn't! Then it closed again and she imagined her father creeping out of the house, hiding his shame.

A sense of utter desolation possessed her. She felt as if she did not know her father, had never known him. When had they last talked to each other, really talked? They were like strangers within the same walls, drifting steadily apart. She could cry but she would not: she felt cold, hard, pitiless.

The silence below reached out a long, stony arm and touched her. Steeling herself, she went down to face her mother.

The living-room was empty. She was alone in the house.

Steve sat at his desk in his bedroom in Dewi Avenue, saying the words of his poem aloud.

> Behold the broken reed, the stunted seed,
> The bare, cropped plain of my desire.
> Arrows of passion . . .

What arrows? What passion?

The passion he had felt for the woman in Back Row?

That had spent itself in the hot spurt of semen into her body.

Staring down at the page, crazily patterned with crossings-out and doodles, he saw only her, gipsyish and inviting, the slow smile that told him anything was permissible, the breasts he enfolded with hot, wanting hands.

He could still smell her and feel her on his skin.

The words before him meant nothing.

He put them aside, to think about her all the more deeply.

Annette waited up for them.

They came lurching in just after eleven, the raucous camaraderie of the tavern still on their tongues, and stared at her sitting there, trying to focus on the fact of her presence.

'What you doing here then? Thought you were going out,' said Lorna Morris.

Annette ignored her. She looked at her father, his eyes wide open yet vague, then blinking rapidly in the way that had become habitual of late, a moth-like, nervous flurry.

'Lost your tongue, have you? Well, there's a thing now. Least she could do is be civil after all we've done for her, Ted, innit?'

He made an almost imploring gesture, begging the world to ignore him, then with a quick, diving motion tried to escape.

'What's this I hear then, Dad?' asked Annette, her clear voice cutting across his path, barring his way.

'What?' he mouthed feebly.

'About you stealing.'

'Stealing?' cried Lorna. 'What you mean, stealing? You watch what you're saying my girl, or I'll give you what for – '

'Shut up! I'm talking to *him*.' Annette shot to her feet, the sudden, incisive movement causing her parents to step back instinctively, as if struck by the wave of her anger.

'Why d'you do it, Dad? I want to know.'

He flapped his hands feebly. 'I didn't do nothing. It's all rubbish. I'll fight them all the way. I'll – '

'Course he didn't!' said Lorna. 'You ought to be ashamed. Call yourself a daughter – '

'Keep out of it! I'm asking *him*.'

'Of all the – ' But she gave way, leaving her husband exposed.

'Why, Dad? Why? Tell me. You must.'

He turned to face her out but failed, flopping into a chair, hands to his head, a picture of weakness and despair.

'I want to know, Dad. Tell me!'

Annette loomed over him, at once pleading and threatening. And all he did was shake his head, moth-like and beaten.

She stared at him, unbelieving.

'Leave him alone,' cried Lorna, rising again to battle. 'See what you've done – wicked girl.'

It was as if she had not spoken.

'Dad,' said Annette. 'Please.' She touched his shoulder.

He sat there, unresponding.

'So it's true,' said Annette softly.

Almost imperceptibly, he nodded.

'Why, Dad? Tell me. Why?'

After a long moment, he shrugged.

'It was for you!' Lorna burst out. 'He did it for you! You're always out there spending!'

'Don't be so stupid,' said Annette coldly.

Exhausted, Lorna sank to a chair. Ted sat silent, unmoving, his head in his hands.

Annette looked from one to the other. Then, without haste, she quietly left the room and went to bed.

6

He woke up that Saturday morning with a hard on. His fingers itched to touch himself but, resisting, he turned over hotly. There had been strange, lurid dreams of which he remembered only the atmosphere, not the detail. They had been drenched with sexuality, a sense of wild excesses. Now he remembered her and groaned. He smelt that warm animal smell coming from her body, felt her tongue stick to his as they sucked at each other's mouths, saw her crimson nipple harden.

He would have to see her again.

Oh no, he would not.

He was seeing Annette that afternoon. Oh, Christ.

If he'd gone to South Wales with his parents . . .

He stretched out an arm for his watch. Half-past eight. Jesus. He was due at work at half-nine.

He lunged into the bathroom.

She woke up with the knowledge inside her.

She thought about the night before, the day ahead.

She didn't want to see Steve now. She didn't want to see anyone.

She just wanted to go back to sleep.

She dragged herself out of bed to the bathroom. In her parents' bedroom, her father coughed.

She gave herself a good wash, patted back to her room and got dressed. She didn't care what she put on because she'd resolved not to see Steve after all.

Downstairs her mother greeted her with a smile.

'Hullo love. Got a lovely bit of bacon for you.'
'Ugh! No thank you.'
'But you always do on a Saturday!'
'I can't. Not today. It'd make me sick.'
'Aw, come on, 'Nette. I've got some tomatoes to go with it, look – '
'I said no thanks, Mam! I'll just have some toast. I'll make it.'

Her mother barred the way to the kitchen.

'Excuse me, Mam, I want to get past.'
'You don't care do you, you little slut.'
'What?'
'You heard me. You just don't care.'
'What's that you called me?'
'He only did it for you, to get us some money – '
'What you *talking* about?'
'You try doing things on his money. We haven't had a holiday for years – '
'He shouldn't have done it, Mam, you know that as well as I do!'
'Running upstairs like Lady Muck. You're always doing that! Who'd you think you are?'
'For God's sake let me get *past*, Mam!'
'Think you're too good for us, don't you? Is that it? Just because you're going out with *him*.'
'Please, Mam!'

She tried to thrust past but Lorna pushed her, so hard she staggered back against the living-room table. She grabbed a chair to save herself falling.

'Slut! Slut! You little slut!'
'I'm not,' cried Annette wildly. 'I'm not I'm not. Why do you call me that?'
'Because you are. You've slept with him haven't you? I know your sort. You little slut.'

'What's wrong with you, Mam?'

'I was pure when I married your father. He's the only man I've ever had in my life. What about you then, eh? First Ivor then *Stephen*.' She spat it out like a curse. 'What was wrong with Ivor then, eh? I'll tell you this, he's a better man than the one you've got now. That rubbish from South Wales. They're all the same down there. Have your knickers off as soon as look at you.'

'Mam – don't – ' gasped Annette.

'How many times he done you then, eh? Ten times, twenty? Little slut! I can see it in your eyes, don't you worry.'

'Stop Mam, stop.'

'It changes you, you know that? It changes the look of you. Oh yes, I can see it. You can't hide it from me. That's right, cry. Cry, you baby. But all your weeping won't wash it away. You stinking little slut.'

Annette sank to her knees.

Lorna stared at her, as at a stranger, then went from the room and clumped heavily upstairs.

He stood on the steps of the King's Hall, waiting for her. It was twenty-past-two and he was ten minutes early. A brisk wind from the bay flattened his trouser legs against his thighs.

God, this town. I'll have to get out of here quick.

On the nearby bandstand the Everard Orchestra was scraping out songs from the shows. *Oklahoma*, *Annie Get Your Gun* and the latest Ivor Novello. The small audience hunched in their deckchairs, squeezing out a sliver of pleasure from the grey afternoon.

Fleet Street. That's where I'll be soon. *The Daily Express* perhaps, not the *Chronicle*. Working under

Arthur Christiansen, a whizz-bang of an editor. Or the *Mirror*, with Hugh Cudlipp. More my scene. The *Express* was a Tory rag.

He pictured bright, humming newsrooms with people pounding out stories. *Real* stories, as he kept telling himself, not pathetic little pars about sales of work and spring fayres. And he would be there, keeping up with the best of them. Making a name for himself: Steve Lewis, rising star of the Street!

So what was he doing, waiting there for Annette?

She could be trouble. Huge trouble. If she got pregnant . . .

Would she want to go with him, anyway? To London? Every time he spoke of his ambitions she changed the subject, she just couldn't face facts! What good was that?

He ought to ditch her, he should be free; there were plenty more fish in the sea.

Like Sara Baker. No, no! He must not think of her, he must *not*. Because she had been an Experience, simply an Experience, and Experience of all kinds was what he wanted.

And because she aroused in him a mixture of disgust and excitement.

Annette was not only late but sulky, uncommunicative.

'What's up?' he asked.

'Nothing.'

They walked briskly along the prom, the dull grey sea pounding miserably on the gritty sand.

'If you don't tell me . . .'

'There's nothing to tell.'

'Oh alright then, be like that.'

It wasn't as if he needed her. He could get along very well. She was holding him back! He wouldn't stay in this dump for her, no, not in a million years. He'd end up like Ronnie and Bill and Sam, pathetic creatures, every one of them. Or old Scoop Matthews. Christ, what a fate.

Suddenly it struck him. She'd started her period, that's what. Today of all days, with the house empty! Bloody hell.

'Why are you wearing dark glasses?'

She stopped. 'Why are you speaking to me like that, Steve?'

'Like what?'

'You're a bully. Do you know that?'

'Me? A bully?'

The thought amazed him. 'I'm not a bully,' he said, catching up with her. 'What makes you think that?'

'Because you are. You're always so – aggressive.'

'No I'm not,' he said, half-laughing. He couldn't believe she meant it, because it was so unlike his own image of himself. 'I'm not at all.'

Beside him, she was a tight ball of anger.

'I wish you'd tell me,' he said, a little later.

She slowed down. 'It's Dad,' she said. 'He's been stealing.'

They sat in the Pelican, only two tables away from where she'd been sitting the day before with Ivor.

'I can't keep it out of the paper, Annette. But I won't cover it. Someone else can.'

'I know that. I don't expect you to.'

She'd taken the glasses off. Her eyes were sore from weeping.

'Maybe he didn't do it. We can't tell,' said Steve.

'Yes he did. I know he did. He told me.'

'But why?'

'I told you. I don't *know*.'

He felt sorry for her, desperately sorry. But a part of him said it might be easier to get her into bed now.

She had slipped off her red mac to reveal a white sweater. Her pointy breasts thrust out, her thin white wrists tormented him.

'I'm moving out,' she said.

'What do you mean?'

'What I say. I'm getting my own place.'

'But why?'

'There was a row.' She bit her lip.

'Who with?'

'Mam. It was horrible. She called me – '

'Yes? What'd she call you?'

'I can't tell you.'

'Yes you can. Come on, I want to know.'

'A slut,' she said, her voice breaking.

'What?'

'Don't *talk* about it, Stephen!'

She thrust back her chair. He followed her out, wonderingly.

They caught a bus to the stop nearest his house. He was on edge, afraid that for some reason his parents might have come home again. He dare not look, for fear of seeing his father's Morris Oxford in the drive. When he knew for certain they'd left he felt dizzy, light-headed.

As he groped for the Yale key in his pocket she stood beside him like a martyr, eyes lowered. He felt afraid of what he might discover about her, something unexpected, unreal.

He unlocked the door and gestured her inside. She

shook her head and he stepped in before her, closing the door behind them.

'Annette,' he said thickly. And took a step towards her.

'No!' she cried, flinching. 'Not here. Please.'

'In here then.'

He opened a door and she followed. She had never been in this room before. It was patently 'the best', with paintings on the walls and the kind of furniture she'd only seen before in the pictures. The carpet was inches deep, the sort you could sink your feet into. A tall harp stood by the deep bay windows with their heavy velvet curtains.

She hesitated.

'Come on,' he said, smiling. 'Make yourself at home.'

At home! As if she ever could be, in a place like this! She felt sorry she'd come. What did they have in common? He was a rich kid, she was council house trash. A slut!

'I'd best be going home,' she said unhappily.

'No! Why'd you say that?'

'I don't belong here.'

'Yes you do. You're with me.' He smiled, drew near. 'Where are they then – your folks?'

'I told you. They've gone to South Wales.'

'They might come back.'

'No they won't.' He put his arms round her, made to kiss her.

'Please, Steve!' She turned her face aside, yet still clung to him. He stroked her back, then the nape of her neck.

She began to cry.

'Annette,' he breathed. 'I love you. Darling.'

She tried to shake her head but found herself kissing him. His hand moved to her breast. His hardness dug into her.

She loved the musk smell of his maleness, the thick rod of black hair running down his chest to his navel.

She was whiter than anything he'd imagined. Her nipples small, precise, outsticking. Her bush of hair a copper flame.

He made to put the johnny on but she cried 'No! Don't. Just.'

She gasped, and dug her nails into him.

He thought of a pierced hymen, blood on the carpet. There was none.

Part Two

SHADOWS

7

Ivor Morgan had begun the day by feeding the chickens. They were a dead nuisance sometimes. He could kill the little buggers.

They cluttered around him, clucking and squawking, climbing on each other's backs, stupid creatures. He scattered the feed and they scrabbled for it, tiny beaks darting.

Sometimes he could wring their necks. He smiled. Because come Christmas, he would have to.

There weren't many of them but they made a good sideline, and Mam could do with the money. Still with two mouths to feed, and Sally to visit in the sanatorium. Of course he gave her his keep and a bit more, but when all was said and done it didn't go far. Maybe Prosser would give him a rise soon. Maybe pigs might fly.

Ivor unlatched the chicken coop and stepped out into the greyness of the morning. At least he didn't have to work every Saturday, that was something. Three in every four, that's all. This was the fourth.

He trudged along the concrete path back to the house, trying to ignore all that needed doing in the back garden. The once-neat vegetable patches were a jungle of couch-grass and briars, the flower beds choked with weeds, the roses rambling back to a state of nature. Dad would break his heart if he saw them. He'd be ashamed of them, ashamed.

He kicked the mud from his boots and went into the small whitewashed cottage, where his mother was having an up-and-downer with his younger brother.

'You eat that bacon, my boy, I cooked it for you special.'

'I can't, Mam, I'm full up!'

'Not so full you can't find room for it. Go on, eat it!'

'Oh, Mam!'

'Do what your mother says,' said Ivor sternly. 'And none of your lip.'

Lennie pulled a face, then golloped the bacon down, jaws chomping furiously. Freckle-faced, twelve years old, he looked nothing like his big brother. Ivor's dark, saturnine features resembled those of the man in the photographs on the mantelpiece, the father sanctified by death. Lennie had his mother's pert look, his snub nose not merely a physical feature but the embodiment of an attitude to life. Facing him at the table the youngest of the family, Megan, dreamily nibbled her toast, her faraway look a contrast with her brothers' emphatic masculinity. Occasionally she moved her head from side to side, or her body, catching the rhythm of the music that was forever in her brain. This was the morning of her dancing class: she had to be there in half an hour. She took after Ivor and her father in appearance, whereas Lennie had the fair skin and strawberry blonde hair of the mother; her quickness of temper, too, that strain of Irish excitability.

'You going to see Sally today?' Ivor asked his mother, when the breakfast was at last cleared away.

'Of course,' said Eileen Morgan, washing up. 'You're not coming then, are you?'

'No, I can't. I've got a match.'

'In July?'

'I told you. It's this special cup competition. For charity.'

'Oh. That makes it alright, I suppose.'

'Makes what alright, Mam?' he said irritably.

'The football, of course,' she replied calmly. 'What else?' She gave him a look.

'I don't know. I don't know what you mean half the time.'

'Well now. Fancy that.'

She swilled out the chipped enamel bowl under the tap. He noticed the thinness of her shoulders, the grey streaks in her hair.

'It's not that I don't want to see her.'

'Who suggested such a thing?'

'I go there when I can.'

'Of course you do, son.'

Delicately she wiped her hands on the roller towel hung on the back door.

He began drying the dishes, looking fretful and unhappy.

'I saw Annette yesterday.'

'Did you now? And what did young madam have to say for herself?'

He let the sarcasm pass.

'I told her about her father. The rumours and all that.'

'What on earth for?'

'I thought she ought to know. You know what her mother's like.'

'You shouldn't interfere, Ivor. It's none of your business. What did she say anyway?'

'Nothing much. She just got upset and walked out.'

'Serves you right for interfering.'

'I had to do it,' he said stubbornly.

Eileen Morgan, temper rising, snatched the tea towel from him. 'Give that here! You're too slow to catch a cold.'

Furiously she dried the remaining dishes as if to rub the pattern off.

'Bet that took her down a peg or two.'

'Don't talk like that, Mam!'

'And why not? Didn't she treat you like dirt? Going out with that reporter feller when you were practically engaged to her?'

'It wasn't like that, Mam.'

'It was and you know it.'

She clattered the dishes away, slammed the cupboard door.

'Anyway I'm not sorry,' said Ivor. 'Somebody had to tell her.'

'Well, I hope she's grateful. That's all I can say.'

She swept from the scullery. 'Haven't you gone yet?' she bawled at Megan. 'You'll miss your bus!'

Megan, piping up in self-justification, was cut short.

'Don't answer me back! Begone with you.'

Ivor sighed. It was going to be one of those days.

The journey from Glanaber to Highland Sanatorium took nearly three hours by bus. It involved changing at Llangurig, which in stage coach days had been a wild outpost on the fringe of the Plynlimon mountain range. It was still an outpost, though less dauntingly so with its cheerful inn and garage-cum-general stores.

Eileen found the journey wearisome and would arrive home exhausted late in the evening. But she would not miss it for anything. She did not go every week; she could not afford it. And there was the bother of getting someone to look after Lennie and Megan, for they were too young to be left by themselves and as for Ivor . . . well, Ivor was Ivor, a law unto himself. Her friend Louisa came round to look after them when she could; only if pushed would she ask her neighbour Mrs Todd, who generally contrived to make Eileen feel she was being done a very big favour.

Eileen put up with all this for the sake of seeing her daughter Sally for a couple of hours; she would have put up with a good deal more, for she loved her and was afraid for her.

Sally had been in the TB 'San', as the patients invariably called it, for just over eight months, and was still on permanent bed rest. When she first went in, old Dr Cullen, the family doctor, had told her she would be there for six months, but Eileen had not believed him, and neither – if the truth be known – had Sally, though she pretended to, for the sake of her mother. Eileen had heard of people being incarcerated in Highland for two years or more, confined to bed most of the time before being allowed up for a series of graded exercises designed – so the theory went – to make them fit enough to be discharged. To her mind these 'grades', as they were called, were nonsense. If someone was fit enough to walk a mile or two a day, clean windows, weed flower beds and cut the grass, then they were fit enough to go home, in her opinion. It was simply cheap labour; and, she had decided, her daughter would have none of it. When Sally was allowed to stay up all day, she would demand her release, whatever the doctors said. There were one or two sadists among them, she reckoned; and the orderlies were even worse, great hulking women who looked like prison warders.

But she would forgive the San everything if Sally was cured.

There were five or six regulars on the bus, like her, visiting relatives. They nodded and smiled at each other, exchanging greetings and small talk about the weather. But they tended to sit separately, as if too close a friendship might imply a degree of permanence in this shuttling to and fro.

Eileen liked sitting alone, staring out of the window and enjoying her thoughts. She did not normally have much time for thinking, what with bringing up the children and working part-time in the post office. She was a counter clerk, so knew all about Ted Morris's thieving long before the news leaked out. She thought him a fool but still felt a bit sorry for him. There was no real harm in him; he was just a weak, vague man with a stupid wife and a stuck-up daughter who needed her bottom slapped.

She was glad Ivor wasn't in danger of marrying Annette, but still felt furious with the girl for throwing her son over.

She had with her a few things for Sally, some apples and bananas, a bar of Bournville plain chocolate, an assortment of magazines and the local rag, the *County Dispatch*. Unlike some of the other visitors she did not take cigarettes because Sally didn't smoke, though there was no absolute ban on them. Eileen thought it mad, people being allowed to turn their bad lungs into kippers by puffing smoke in and out.

Slowly the bus ground its way up the steady ascent towards Eisteddfa Gurig, the highest point of the journey. In winter, the road was often impassable. Today, on a July afternoon when a fitful sun sported with high, fluffy clouds, the bare mountain slopes seemed like giants half-asleep. Eileen could never be entirely at ease among them; even in their softest moments they seemed threatening. Her Irish imagination, fed on the folk tales told by her grandfather in County Clare, peopled them with ghosts. Up at Highland, amid hills almost as daunting as these, the cards seemed stacked against Sally. But when Eileen had wavered about sending her there, the consultant had been brutally honest.

'You know what TB is, don't you, Mrs Morgan? They used to call it consumption. The White Plague. It eats away the lungs and the flesh. If you keep her at home, she'll be dead in a year.'

What answer was there to this? So Eileen had consented, while wishing Eddie were still alive so that the decision need not be hers alone. She still felt angry with him for dying, leaving her to cope all alone.

The dead had it easy, she complained in the depths of her soul; but fervently she prayed, that Sally might remain in the land of the living.

'Here. Ivor! Oh, for Chrissake!'

The Brynpadarn skipper, Tony Webb, held his head in despair as Ivor sliced the ball into touch.

Pansy, thought Ivor brutally; show-off. He did sod-all himself anyway, apart from sticking on airs and graces and trying fancy dribbles that never came off.

'Mark your man, Ivor. Mark your man.'

That's what I'm doing you daft bugger, Ivor silently retorted, crunching into a tackle. He won the ball but the referee's piercing whistle cancelled out his triumph. The ref, small, bullet-headed, rancidly assertive, charged across. 'What the hell you playing at?' he snarled. 'Any more like that and you're off the field.'

'Nothing wrong with that, ref,' Ivor protested.

'You arguing, son?' The ref reached for his notebook.

Ivor said nothing, backing off for the free-kick. It was taken quickly, a swift pass to an unmarked man who steadied himself and shot, bringing a fine pass from the Brynpadarn goalie.

Tony Webb glared at Ivor before haring upfield.

I'm going to pack it in, Ivor vowed. What was the point?

But he knew he wouldn't because he loved everything about football: putting on his boots, tying up the laces, trotting on to the pitch with the others, the little thrill when the ref's whistle started the match. The first touch of the ball – nothing quite like that – the long punt upfield, the clip of the short pass, slithering through mud for a sliding tackle. He loved heading the ball! And the quick run upfield from the right-back position, taking their opponents by surprise, even feinting and dribbling when the mood took him. And the shower afterwards (when you were lucky), the water too hot or too cold but lovely, lovely!

No, he wouldn't miss it for anything.

He had quite a good game after his early lapses and Tony said grudgingly, 'Did alright in the end, Ivor. That header off the line saved us.' For they had come out 2-1 winners.

'See you tonight, Ivor?' Dai Sam called out as he left.

'Aye, I 'spect.'

'You better. You owe me a pint!'

Yes, he'd be there. With Dai Sam and Horny Bowen and Bill Browning and Terry Mason. Swilling down pints in the Black Nag as one of the boys. But in his heart he wanted to be somewhere quite different. With

Annette. Lovely Annette. Kissing her, cupping his hand round her breasts.

And now she was with that arsehole reporter.

She was with him at that moment, that very moment. He knew it in the depths of his being. He knew it with an inner rage that turned his pleasure to ashes. He knew it in his head, his heart, his balls.

Suddenly he kicked out at a tussock of grass and crunched along the ash path leading from the council playing fields to the main road.

As she passed through the sanatorium gates and began her long walk up the drive to the huts and wards where the patients were incarcerated, Eileen felt the familiar dread that always accompanied her on these visits. She hated this place, the institutionalised horror of it, and wanted to snatch Sally away. But all the doctors said she'd be cured here, that at home she would die however loving the care. And Sally believed them, she had faith in the treatment. But if it was nothing more than fresh air and rest, reasoned Eileen, couldn't she get that at home? And better food into the bargain? Mind, there were other things they did, such as collapsing the lung by fancy methods to rest it, but whether this did any good at all she took leave to doubt. In her heart of hearts Eileen believed it to be all a big fraud, designed to give jobs to doctors and nurses and to soak up the money left by that rich man Lord Davies to finance the whole caboodle. And all he'd been doing was salving his conscience for the way he'd treated the miners in his stinking horrible pits, that's how she saw it. Conscience money.

Bitterly she made her way to Newtown Block; even the places of incarceration were named after the towns and villages of his lordship's county.

The sanatorium resembled a prisoner-of-war camp, with its long rows of huts strung out in parallel lines on a hilltop fringed by woodland. The patients were mainly in individual wooden cubicles known, curiously, as 'chalets', as if this were a posh place for consumptive toffs high up in the Alps. Set apart from the rest was the sombre grey slab of Powys Block, a place of shivering night sweats and racking coughs and hollowed-out cheeks and hope abandoned.

Sally, at twenty, was two years younger than Ivor. She was fair of hair and skin like her mother, though more akin to her late father in her steady temperament. She shared a ward with three other patients, Tessa, Carol and Veronica. Tessa was huge, her rolls of fat libelling the tubercle bacilli's reputation for reducing human flesh; Carol smooth, self-contained, socially superior; Veronica a cheerful older woman who of the four was the most obviously consumptive. She had a high colour, coughed daintily into her handkerchief and spat or, as the authorities put it, 'expectorated' into a metal container like a small cup with a lid, kept in a special compartment near the top of her locker.

Eileen was convinced that Veronica, who liked to be called Vee, was not long for this world, and it took no special gift of second sight to see this.

Sally sat up in bed as straight as she could against the fluffed-up pillows, and smiled brightly at her mother.

'How's it going then, alright?'

'OK Mam, thanks.'

It was the unvarying greeting and response, followed by a kiss and the predictable sinking of the heart that Eileen always felt when she set foot in Newtown Block.

'I've brought you a few things.'

'That's nice of you, Mam.'

'It's not much, don't get too excited.'

Sally glanced sympathetically at her mother, as if she were the visitor and Eileen the patient. She knew the strain her mother felt, caught the false note in her voice, realised the impossibility of her ever behaving naturally in this place. She was aware, too, of her mother's distrust of the San, her want of belief in the system. And she felt sorry, that Eileen could not share her faith in it. For she was convinced it would make her better, however long it might take.

'What's your temp like these days?' asked Eileen, knowing the importance of the twice-daily thermometer reading in the theology of the sanatorium.

'Oh, not too bad. Up a bit last week. I was put back on R1 a couple of days.'

'R1.' Eileen frowned. 'Bad that, isn't it?'

'Could be worse, Mam. I could be on Powys Block,' said Sally, with mock gaiety.

'Powys Block!' cried Eileen in anguish. 'Don't say that.'

'Alright, Mam. Don't worry. Only joking.'

'Call that a joke?'

Inside Eileen's head, the terminology of sickness whirled around. R (for Rest) 1, total bedrest, with the indignity of bedpans; R2, consent to walk to the toilet block for calls of nature. Oh, how she hated everything about this place! How she longed to wrap Sally up and take her home with her!

'How's everyone at home then?' asked Sally brightly.

'Same as ever. Megan's in a world of her own and Lennie's a little heller.'

'In trouble again, is he?'

'When isn't he? I wish his father was alive. He'd deal with him better than I do.'

'You do alright, Mam. And Ivor helps, doesn't he?'

'Ivor!' It was almost an expletive. 'Don't talk to me about Ivor.'

'Why – what's wrong?'

'What do you think? That girl.'

'Annette, you mean?'

'Who else? Flighty little bitch.'

'Mam!' Sally glanced around the ward; she knew, from the rigid way Carol held herself, that she had overheard.

'Well, she is, isn't she?'

'Annette's alright.'

'Oh, is she now. And what do you know about it?'

'Why, what's she done then, Mam?'

'You know what very well. Thrown your brother over for that reporter feller.'

Sally frowned. 'But that was ages ago – before Christmas, wasn't it?'

'What difference does that make? Still a rotten trick, wasn't it?'

'But if it wasn't working out, Mam . . .' said Sally patiently.

'Working out . . . I'd give her working out, and no mistake.'

'Not still brooding over her, is he?'

'What do you expect? Not made of stone, is he?'

'No, but all the same . . .'

'And you know what's happened now, don't you? Her father's been caught thieving.'

'What? Annette's father?'

'Caught red-handed. Stealing the mail. Stupid man.'

'Oh, that's awful . . . Does Annette know?'

'She does now if she didn't before. Ivor told her yesterday.'

'What he go and do that for?'

'Don't ask me. That's what I'd like to know.'

Sally looked thoughtful.

'He'll be up in court, of course,' Eileen prattled on. 'Go to jail, I shouldn't wonder.'

'No! Not as bad as that, is it?'

'It's a serious offence, stealing. Always has been, always will be.'

'Poor Annette.'

'Poor nothing. It'll do the little madam good. Teach her a thing or two.'

When she had gone, after the two-hour visiting, Sally put on her dressing-gown and slippers and joined the procession of women down the corridor. There was a sense almost of relief when the visitors left; they were creatures from another planet, lacking meaning in the context of the San. They reminded the inmates of the world beyond the Sanatorium gates, where people got dressed every morning and went about their business, the world of work and dances and going to the flicks, of dating boyfriends and seeing kids off to school and simply being alive.

For this wasn't life; this was something apart. A punishment for past sins or sins not yet committed; a thing to be endured.

Sally lingered as long as she dared in the toilet block, spinning out the evening wash they were allowed before settling down for the last few hours of another day.

Back in her ward, she stretched out in her bed again.

The atmosphere was strangely subdued; no-one felt much like talking. Tessa was listening to the radio through her headphones – the Light Programme, invariably; Carol, reading a Graham Greene novel from the hospital library, looked curiously compact, as if the bed and the lifestyle were made to measure; Vee, whose bed had been surrounded by far more than the two visitors officially tolerated, had slumped into an exhausted sleep.

The french windows were flung wide, as they were even when wintry winds knifed into the ward. Beyond were the hills of Radnorshire, but Sally was blind to them. She was thinking of home, with a poignancy made sharper by the news she had just been given. All this was happening, and she had no part in it! She felt sorry for her brother, but sorry too for Annette, whom she could not bring herself to dislike. How would Ivor react to her family trouble? She wouldn't be surprised if he tried to muscle in again, but she didn't think Steve would stand for that. Steve . . . she knew hardly anything about him, but had seen him around town, with his devil-may-care manner and air of sophistication. A thought suddenly struck her: would she, one day, know him a good deal better? The strangeness of it made her shiver and she turned on her side, trying to make sense of a notion she found peculiarly disturbing.

8

Annette went straight up to her room when she arrived home that Saturday evening. Her parents, eating a supper of baked beans on toast, glanced at her, then at themselves.

'Lost your tongue?' Lorna called after her, only to be ignored. 'Needs her bottom smacked, that girl,' she said across the table to Ted. She sliced her toast ferociously, needled by her daughter's behaviour, her husband's indifferent response. Upstairs, Annette sat on her bed, in total confusion. Why had she let him do it? She hadn't intended to. She had led him on, going home with him like that! But she had enjoyed it, oh, how she had enjoyed it! Her mouth twisted as she relived her abandon.

And what now? She did not know if she loved him. Sometimes she thought she did, but then something happened and they would seem light years apart. Yet, that afternoon, she would have given up everything for him, the world's gold if she'd possessed it, the planets and the stars. For he'd been so *good*, so kind and understanding.

She did not regret it. No! She'd do it again if he wanted.

Her hands clenched and unclenched as she thought about his nakedness.

You're a slut, Annette Morris. Just like your mother said.

'I don't care,' she told that taunting inner voice. 'I don't care one little bit.'

She had it out with her mother next day, when her father was taking his Sunday afternoon nap. They were together in the living-room, Lorna knitting a jumper for her sister Hilda's latest. She stared at Annette disbelievingly.

'Shirley Tucker? What you mean, you're gonna live with Shirley Tucker?'

'What I say.'

'You can't do that, girl.'

'Why not?'

'She's a vampire, that's why.'

'Vampire?' Annette laughed. 'You're talking rubbish, Mam. You don't know what a vampire is.'

'Yes I do. She sucks up men, that's what she does. Sucks 'em up and spits 'em out again.'

'No she doesn't, don't be so soft. Where'd you get that from?'

'Everyone knows it, you can ask anyone. She's got a reputation, that girl. I don't want my daughter getting one an' all.'

'Huh! That's good. I've got one already, 'cording to you!'

'What you mean?'

'The things you called me yesterday. You've forgotten that already?'

'I lost my temper, girl. Take no notice.'

'Take no notice! How can I when you call me – '

'Look! I didn't mean it.'

'Then why'd you say it?'

'Don't you say things you don't mean?'

'Not things like that.'

'Oh, get away with you.'

'Slut! That's what you called me. Slut!'

'I said I'm sorry, didn't I?'

'You said I'd been sleeping with boys. Ivor, Steve . . .'

'Sorry sorry sorry! How many times must I say it?'

'That's what you think of me though, isn't it? You think I'm that sort.'

'No I don't!'

'You must do!'

'No! It's because – don't you see?'

'What?'

'The way you are!'

'How am I then?'

'Well -' Lorna made a vague, hopeless gesture, her hands flopping down to her sides.

'Tell me, Mam.'

'You're so lah-di-dah!'

'What?'

'Lah-di-dah! You know you are!'

'*Me*?'

'Yes – ever since you took that job.'

'Don't be so stupid!'

'You think you're better than us! And now this – with your father – '

She began to cry.

'Don't, Mam,' said Annette, appalled.

'I can't stand it, girl. Don't you see? It's going to be the death of me!'

She dabbed her eyes with her apron.

'Oh, Mam,' said Annette.

Helplessly she looked at her. She wanted to put her arms around her, but could not.

They arrived back late on the Sunday evening, as Steve was just finishing typing out the story the paper needed first thing next morning.

'Steve? You in?' Edna called.

'Yes, Mam. I'm working up here.'

She pat-patted upstairs, formally tapped his bedroom door, poked her head through.

'Oh, sorry. Busy, are you?'

'Yes. I had a story to write up.'

'Oh yes. Of course. You said you had something on, didn't you? Can I come in for a minute?'

'Course.' He took the paper from his typewriter, put it face down on the desk. 'How were they then – all OK?'

'Oh, we had a lovely time *bach*, pity you couldn't come.' She bent and kissed his brown curly hair, wafting over him the Sunday-best smell of lily-of-the-valley and mintoes. 'They wanted to know all about you, what you were doing. They're such *nice* people, the Llewellyns, I've met no-one like them up here. It brought it all back, the good times we used to have.'

Steve smiled wryly. All he could remember was his mother's constant complaints of how cold the house was, how awful the people were, how much she missed living in Hendon.

'And what do you think! Doris is working in a bank – in Leeds! What do you think of that?'

Steve, who thought nothing of it, found it hard to frame an answer.

'Nice girl, Doris. So clever. I always knew she was going places.'

Yes, thought Steve. Leeds.

'Well, and what have you been doing with yourself? Haven't had your nose to the grindstone all weekend, I'm sure. You saw Annette, I take it?'

88

'Yes, we went for a walk. On the prom.'

'That's nice. Raining, was it?'

'No, it wasn't. Why'd you say that?'

'Because it always rains up here, doesn't it? Never known such a place for rain. Anyway, how is she, alright?'

'Of course. What's this, Mam, an inquisition?'

He pushed his chair back, fussed with the papers on his desk, hoping this small fluster of activity might be assumed to account for his slowly reddening cheeks.

'Inquisition, what sort of word is that? I'm only asking. No harm in asking is there?'

'No, none at all, but you're always so – '

'Yes? Always so what, Steve?'

Icy now, she stared him down.

'Oh, nothing.'

'Good.' Her heavy breathing filled the silence. 'Only got your interests at heart, son. That's all.'

When she had gone, he sat miserably on his bed. She hadn't asked the question he'd dreaded – had he brought her back *here*? – but he knew she had no need to do so. She read him like a book.

Slyly, deviously, she would winkle it out of him. How he'd invited her back – but, he would insist, only because he felt sorry for her, after the quarrel with her parents – how her father was up for stealing, how Annette was moving out.

She'd find out the truth about anything, he thought bitterly.

But she'd never know for certain what had happened between them. Unless –

But that was something he could not bear thinking about.

'Good,' said Ronnie. 'Bloody good.' He slapped his hand on the typewritten pages theatrically. 'Best thing you've ever done for us, boy. It's got heart. That's what we want on this paper. Heart.'

'Thanks,' said Steve awkwardly. When Ronnie praised him, he didn't know how to respond.

'What's she like then, eh – this Mrs Baker?' He leered up at Steve. 'Bit of alright, is she?'

'She's OK. Quite friendly.'

'Friendly!' Ronnie cackled. 'That's what I mean, son – how friendly?' He held out an open packet of Capstan Full Strength. Steve took one. 'Sit down a minute, have a chat.' He lit their cigarettes. 'They say she does a bit – that right?'

'I wouldn't know,' said Steve, poising himself carefully on a rickety-looking chair.

'No?' A leering Ronnie, Steve decided, was even worse than a sarcastic Ronnie or a bollocking Ronnie. 'You sure?'

'Positive.'

'Didn't try to – *bribe* you then, did she?'

'I thought we weren't supposed to take bribes.'

'We aren't, but – there are bribes and bribes now, aren't there? A bit of the old collateral, you know?'

'I don't know what you mean, Ronnie.'

'Don't you, son? Ah well. Maybe you're too young.' He took a drag, flicked ash on the lino-covered floor. 'Got a girlfriend, haven't you? Ted Morris's girl.'

'Yes.'

'Mm. Nice girl.'

Steve said nothing.

'Nice parents too. Known them all my life. You get on alright with them?'

'Of course. Why?'

'Nothing, son, nothing. Only Ted's a bit – ' He looked carefully at Steve. 'You know the word *didoreth*?'

'No.'

'You wouldn't, would you? From South Wales. Can't help that, I know.' A smile as feeble as his jest passed lightly over him. 'It means careless. Slap-happy. You know? Not quite as you should be. Wonder they gave him a job as postman in the first place.'

Ronnie dragged on his fag again.

'You been hearing any rumours about him?' he ventured.

'What sort of rumours?'

'About his job.' Ronnie held his cigarette at arm's length, dreamily tapped it, not looking at Steve. 'You know he's been suspended, don't you?'

'I did hear something, yes. Don't know if it's true though.'

'Oh, it's true alright. True as I'm sitting here. He's been nicking the mail. Silly bugger.'

For the first time Steve felt the weight and shock of it, felt its reality for Ted Morris, not simply its bearing on his relationship with Annette.

'He'll go down for it,' said Ronnie. 'You know that, don't you? He'll be down in Swansea Jail before you can say Jack Robinson.'

'It'll be smashing. But – do you really mean it?'

Shirley Tucker, eyes burning, looked at Annette, who turned aside to stare through the front window of the flat they were viewing. It was on the first floor of a four-storey house on the southern and less popular end of Glanaber's promenade, part of a terrace built in late

Victorian times for local people of substance. It had long declined in the social scale, most of the houses now being turned over to bed-and-breakfast places or flats. Annette lifted the lace curtain to see, all the more clearly, the slow drift of passers-by.

'Yes,' she said quietly. 'Of course I mean it.'

'You don't sound it! Cor, we'll have some great times here, mun!'

Normally Shirley's over-enthusiasm would have grated on Annette, but now she accepted it calmly. Everything seemed to have an inevitability these days, her moving out from home, the sharing of a flat with Shirley, her brief moment of passion with Steve.

She turned, with an effort. 'Of course we will,' she said simply.

For a moment she feared Shirley was going to throw her arms about her. But she only said, 'Right. That's settled then.'

Shirley picked up the bright blue plastic mac she'd thrown on the back of the faded, melancholy-looking settee. 'How soon can you make it, did you say?'

'Any time. Soon as you like.'

'OK. We'll tell him then, shall we?'

Annette nodded. At the door, Shirley gave the room a last, lingering look. 'I can't believe it. We won't know ourselves. All this room to ourselves!'

The man from the agency was waiting downstairs in the hall. He listened impassively.

'Well, you know the terms. A month's rent in advance, three months' notice to quit, no pets of any kind. You can move in as soon as you like once you've signed.'

'I'll be round there tomorrow!' cried Shirley. 'Or will you want us both?'

He made a small, impatient movement, a mere twitch.

'As I explained to you earlier . . .'

He was a pale, exhausted-looking man in middle age. Annette had often seen him around town, harassed and distracted. He did not look at them as he spoke, wanting only to get this settled.

'Now, do you have any questions, either of you?'

Shirley glanced briefly at Annette, then shrugged.

'Right. Well . . .'

He gestured and they went through the front door and on to the prom. The evening spat rain and the waves tumbled in the brisk breeze from the west.

'That's it then. I'll expect you tomorrow.' He nodded and sloped off in his dark, hooded way.

The girls stood, unmoving.

'Well,' said Shirley solemnly. 'We've done it now.'

'Suppose we have.'

'Not changing your mind? Sure about it?'

'Absolutely.'

'But why?' asked Shirley impulsively. 'I mean, I thought you were such a home bird.'

'I am. That's the point.' Wildly Annette stepped into the road, not looking, to cross to the seaward side of the prom. 'That's why I have to get away!'

Shirley followed, laughing uncertainly. 'You're a funny one and no mistake.' She drew level with Annette, clutched her arm. 'But I know we'll have some fun – I know it!'

Fun. Is that what it was going to be?

The word seemed meaningless. What *was* fun?

Lying with him on the carpet – had that been fun?

Something grasped her stomach as she thought of it – grasped it and twisted it.

No. It hadn't been fun. It had been much more than that.

She was seeing him tonight. For the first time since.

She yearned for it, yet dreaded it.

She was afraid of what sort of a person she was.

'What I thought we could do tonight,' said Betty Wilson, munching a Crunchie Bar in the Cormorant Cafe, 'is go to the Forum. It's got that flick with Jane Russell in. *The Outlaw.*'

'I've seen that before,' said Ivor irritably, hating the way she spoke of 'the flicks' instead of 'the pictures.'

'So've I. But I don't care. I like it. It's – sensual.' She gave him a look that aimed at provocation but veered into absurdity. 'Anyway, you like Jane Russell, don't you? Her – you know . . .' She thrust out a bosom that was itself fairly ample, though suffering from its proximity to a generous waistline.

'I'm not all that bothered.'

'Not bothered?' Betty giggled. 'That's a funny thing to say.'

'What do you want to do then?' she added poutily, when Ivor failed to respond.

'I don't know. Nothing much. Stay here maybe.'

'Stay here? We've been here ages. We'll be looking like the place soon. Anyway we can't. They'll be closing in a minute.'

As if in confirmation, a woman began clearing the remaining crocks from the tables with a clatter and several meaningful looks at Betty and Ivor, the sole customers left.

'Let's go then,' said Ivor suddenly, thrusting his chair back.

'Hey, hang on!' Betty hooked her handbag over her

shoulder and stumped after him. 'Not much of a gentleman, are you? You should let me go first,' she complained outside.

'I'm not a gentleman, I don't pretend to be. I'm a carpenter, remember? I work with my hands. Gentlemen don't do that.'

'What's got into you then, cross-patch?' Her plump legs tried in vain to keep up with his long stride. 'Oh, wait a minute,' she said, slowing down. 'I know.'

He stopped. 'Know what?'

'Why you're like this. It's because of him, isn't it?'

'Who?'

'Thingummy's father.'

He took a step closer. 'Who the hell's thingummy?'

'You know who I mean. And don't swear at me, Ivor Morgan. And don't look like that, neither. Who do you think you are?'

The arch, knowing look had given way to one of distinct nervousness.

'If you mean Annette,' he said coldly, 'say so. And don't jump to conclusions, right?'

'Oh,' said Betty weakly, 'sorry I spoke.'

She trotted by Ivor's side as he set off again at a less headstrong pace. His face was hard, shut-off, sullen. After a while she took his arm. He made no objection.

'Where we going then, Ivor?'

'The Forum.'

She sighed happily. 'I know you'll enjoy it, dar . . .' She let the half-endearment hang limply in the air, and gave his arm a squeeze. 'We always do, don't we?' she said, with an attempt at Hollywood huskiness.

His face became harder, his heart harder still. He didn't know why he was with this stupid cow-eyed girl. He'd been on the rebound from Annette, thinking she might at least provide a quick shag, but there was none of that, only kissing and fumbling in the back row of the pictures. Still, he would have to watch himself. For if he put her up the spout he'd had it. And some day – some night – she'd let him do it. He was as certain of that as of anything.

A short distance away, Annette and Steve sat on a knoll overlooking the sea. Behind them were the grey, scarred ruins of Glanaber Castle, before them the unruffled waters of Cardigan Bay. It was a place for calm reflection, but they were neither calm nor reflective. Their nerves were stretched taut, their emotions confused.

'So you're moving out then – after all,' he said, after a strained silence.

'After all what?' she asked in a high, brittle voice.

'I didn't think you would.'

'You don't know me then, do you?'

'Don't I?' He gave her a slanting, sideways glance she found mean and sly, like the leer of a peeping tom.

He flushed, as if reading her thoughts. 'You may be sorry. You might find you don't get on with Shirley Tucker,' he said brutally.

'I might and I might not. I don't know till I try it, do I?'

'She's got a bad reputation. You know that, don't you?'

Annette stared at him, amazed. 'You sound just like my mother. How dare you say that about Shirley!'

'It's not just me,' he said defensively, but wishing he'd never started this. 'Everyone says it.'

'Just because she's got friends. Just because she likes a bit of fun. Not like most of the people round here.'

He was silent, thinking what a fool he was. Once Annette was with Shirley, there'd be far more opportunities . . .

'Well,' he said, his tone altering. 'It may work out OK. Hope it does, anyway.' He gave her hand a squeeze, to which she did not respond.

She looked at him suspiciously. 'Soon changed your tune, haven't you? Why's that, I wonder?'

He said nothing, not knowing how he stood with her. His thoughts turned to Sara Baker, and a shiver of pride stirred him. To have had two women, within a few days of each other! He was making up for things now, making up with a vengeance!

A pleasure boat chugged back to the harbour. Gulls cackled and snarled in its wake, fuming up in a grey-white cloud. The setting sun flung a glittering pathway to the shore.

Annette saw none of these things. Her eyes were directed inward, as she tried to make sense of what had happened. She felt now that they were strangers, though she resisted this feeling. He *was* something to her, she *had* wanted him. Suddenly she felt she must have him again soon, or all would be meaningless. She put her right hand near him, hoping he'd take it. He did not.

'You're not moving out – because of me?' he asked.

'Why you?' She snatched her hand away, not wanting to touch him now.

'Well – because of Saturday.'

'No,' she said eventually. 'Don't be silly.'

'That's good.'

The warmth in his voice made her glance at him gratefully. He took her hand, fondled it. She felt he could do anything to her.

'It was great – wasn't it?' he said.

'Mm.'

He nuzzled into her. They kissed. She caught her breath. She held his hand tightly, so that it would not do things she wanted.

'Let's go somewhere,' he breathed.

'No . . . no . . . not tonight Steve . . . please.'

If only he insisted, she would!

'Alright then,' he said at last.

They drew apart. She felt empty, and shivered.

He walked her to the bus. She had to take a seat on the far side, so as it pulled away he could no longer see her.

He stood at the bus stop awhile, as the dusk thickened. He felt lonely now without her. Yet deep inside him was the dread he could not escape, that even yet he might be dragged down to a life of inconsequence on the *County Dispatch*.

9

The local rag was out again. People bought it automatically, grumbled, scoffed, scanned some of its pages eagerly and others indifferently, claimed they never believed a word (for no-one admitted to taking it seriously), but all read it. Devouring the *County Dispatch* was the one thing the people of Glanaber had in common. It was a kind of social glue binding academics to business people, small-town society to council tenants. Now, the big rotary press silent, the printers tapped the keys of their hot-metal type-setting machines more slowly, the run-up to the next publication day still comfortably distant; and in the newsroom the hacks took a broader view of the world, touching on issues of the day as judiciously (and possibly as effectively) as the leader writers of *The Times* and the *Manchester Guardian*.

Scoop Matthews, in whom Great War shell-shock had precipitated a latter-day childishness, was excited by the latest news from the Far East.

'Five hundred bomber raid, mister. That's the stuff to give 'em.' His eyes glittered. 'The Yalu River power stations, mister. Target for tonight.' He cackled, wheezed, clapped his hands.

'You don't approve of that, do you?' said Steve, appalled.

'Approve? Approve? Settle 'em once and for all. Bring the boys home from Korea.'

'Quite so, Mr Matthews,' said Bill Merrick. 'Quite so.' He dragged on his fag. 'That's the only thing they understand, these Commies.'

'Commies!' exploded Steve. 'That just about sums it up, doesn't it?'

'How so, my friend?'

'Well . . . that stupid word. *Commie*!'

'But that's what they are, isn't it? Correct me if I'm wrong,' sneered Bill.

'They're Communists. Not *Commies*. And they're just people too. You ever think of the workers in those power plants they're bombing?'

'War is war,' said Bill casually.

'Total war!' exclaimed Scoop. 'That's it, mister. Total war!'

'You're mad,' cried Steve. 'All of you.'

He pushed back his chair, stormed out to the lavatory.

'What's wrong with him?' asked Ronnie, emerging from his burrow.

'Upset by the latest news from Korea. The Yanks' 500-bomber raid,' said Bill.

'Oh, that. Bit of a red isn't he, our Stephen?'

'*Bit*?'

'I don't think he is,' said Brenda, 'not really.' She blushed as Ronnie and Bill stared at her, then glanced knowingly at each other.

'Well,' said Bill softly, 'you should know, Brenda.'

She flashed him a hateful look but said nothing. If only she *did* know.

Steve, suspicious of the silence, glanced self-consciously around as he came back. He failed to notice the heightened colour in Brenda's cheeks, as he failed to notice anything about her at all. She was just the office secretary, the willing dogsbody who opened the mail, sorted out handouts from letters, took dictation from Ronnie and the rarely-seen editor who was winding down to retirement, answered the phone, made the coffee and tea and put up with a thousand tiny humiliations: just Brenda, not at all dowdy or unattractive but simply ten years too old.

An hour later, she handed him the phone over the desk with a look that failed to register.

'Mrs Baker. Of Back Row.'

'Oh.' She turned away from the gleam in his eye, the pretended indifference.

'Hullo? Steve Lewis speaking.'

'Gerry, is it? Where've you been, love? When you coming to see me?'

'Oh.' He thought quickly. 'So it was alright then, was it – the piece I wrote? Heard anything from the council yet?'

'Of course it was alright. Very much alright. I like a young man's. You know what I mean?'

'That's good,' he said jauntily. 'Well, I hope it'll do you some good. Maybe I can do a follow-up some time – keep the pot boiling.'

'You can do that any time, darling. You boil my pot alright. Boils right over, it does. Know that, don't you?'

'I'm glad to hear it, Mrs Baker.' Heart pounding, Steve half-turned in his chair to avoid the looks Brenda was giving him.

'So when you coming then, eh? Quick now – can't stay in this kiosk all day. There's somebody waiting.'

'I'm not sure about that.'

'This afternoon – come this afternoon! Two o'clock – before Vi gets home!'

'Well . . . possibly.'

'Good lad!'

The phone went dead. With a feigned look of surprise, he carefully put it back in its cradle.

He could not be unaware of Brenda now.

'What did she want?'

'What? Oh, nothing much. Just thanked me for the write-up, that's all.'

'It's the second time she's rung. She rang yesterday, when you were out.'

'Did she? You didn't tell me.'

'I didn't think you'd want to know.'

Bill Merrick gleefully banged his typewriter.

By the flyblown window, Scoop Matthews chuckled and whinnied.

"Five hundred bombers, mister,' he cooed, clapping his hands. 'Five hundred Yankee bombers. That'll show 'em mister. That'll show 'em!'

On warm summer afternoons like this, Annette and Rita took their lunchtime sandwiches to the prom and watched the world go by as they ate them.

'Wish I had the guts to leave home,' said Rita. 'But I haven't got the nerve. Mam would explode.'

What could Annette say? She knew it was perfectly true. Rita would never step out of line.

'Can I come and see you there?' asked Rita. 'I mean, when you're properly settled in?'

'Course. Come for a coffee one night. Bring Gwyn along.'

'Ooh, I'd like that. Hey, you'll have a smashing time there. Looking out to sea and everything.'

'Ye-e-e-s.' Strangely, the view meant nothing to Annette. She wasn't one for views; what mattered to her was people.

'What does Steve think of it then? All for it, I bet.' Rita chanced a sly, prurient glance. 'Be able to have a nice little cuddle, won't you? I mean – times Shirley's out.'

'Oh, I don't know about that, Rita,' said Annette levelly.

'What? Who're you trying to kid?'

Her nose slightly out of joint from the put-down, Rita added, 'Course, I suppose Ivor may have something to say about that.'

'Ivor? What's it got to do with Ivor?'

'Well – ' Rita shrugged, feeling the ice crack under her feet.

'I've got nothing to do with Ivor, Rita, and you know jolly well I haven't!' cried Annette hotly, aware of the snooty tone her voice took on when she was angry, as if she'd been to some posh private school.

'OK, keep your hair on. Sorry I spoke.' And Rita too could be proud, in her down-to-earth way, wondering where Annette found the cut-glass voice that made you think her dad was Lord Muck instead of a common little thief.

The girls sat in silence, unhappily munching their sandwiches.

'Don't take no notice of me, 'Nette. I'm just a jealous little twit.'

'No you're not.' Annette looked fondly at her friend, squeezed her hand. 'You'll be the first to come and see us, Rita. I promise you that!'

The afternoon was a clamp of heat on Steve's skull, defining the fury inside it. He knew he was a fool to go but could not help it. He made his way along Shipwrights Road, now dozily belying its long-redundant name, and stood a moment at the top of the broad flight of stone steps going down to Back Row. Should he or shouldn't he? Even now it was not too late to draw back. Up here he was still the respectable young reporter, down there he would be just another of Mrs Baker's seedy clients. No! – not client! He did not pay. Did she charge anyone? All was supposition and rumour. All he knew is that she gave herself freely to him, had given herself once and now would do so again.

To be lingering here invited comment. He thought he saw a lace curtain twitch and plunged down the steps, two at a time. Without further thought, fired only by the need for excitement and adventure, he rapped the door of number four. He was about to knock again when it opened.

'Oh? So it's you. Didn't think you'd come. Come in, lad.'

Knowing his mistake now, he wanted to flee but could not. She stood before him in the short brown skirt she had worn the last time he had seen her. Now she had a red blouse on, not white. A thin stain of grease ran parallel with the top buttons. The bulge of her breasts made him clench and unclench his fists unthinkingly.

'Well, what's wrong? Lost the use of your tongue?' She wetted her lips, goading him. He stepped forward, exulting in the warm smell of sex that came from her. As he embraced her she unexpectedly lowered her head, pressing her face into his chest. He kissed the top of her dark head, noticing for the first time the odd strands of grey. He squeezed her, rocking her gently.

'Best go, lad. Now. Before it's too late.'

He pressed his fingers into her buttocks.

'Did you hear me? Go away. I shouldn't have rung you. It was wrong.'

'No. It was right. Right.' He tried to kiss her but she turned her head aside.

'Look. I'm twice your age. I'm a bad woman. Leave me be.'

'I can't, Sara. I can't.'

Never had he used her name before. It hung in the air like a statement.

'Why did you come? I didn't think you would. I was just trying it on like. A bit of devilment.'

'Kiss me, Sara. Please.'

'No!' She thrust him away, suddenly strong, and looked at him pleadingly. 'I can't be the same with you like I can with the others. Don't you see?' She sat heavily on a chair, and her plump bare knees excited him to a pity mingled headily with passion.

He did not move. 'For God's sake,' she said wearily.

He stood over her. Very gently he put a hand to her breast. Then the other.

He bent and kissed her. She moaned.

His fingers moved over her breasts, her nipples.

Her fingers came slowly alive.

She took his hardness into her mouth.

He gasped, trembling above her.

'She'll be back,' said Lorna Morris. 'Don't you worry. She'll be back.'

Her false teeth squelched into the pear. A thin dribble of juice ran down her chin and she wiped it off with her apron.

'Even if she goes that is. She might change her mind yet. Wouldn't be at all surprised.'

Ted shook his head. 'No she won't. She's made her mind up.'

Lorna's eyes darkened. 'Don't know when she's well off, that girl. Done all we can for her, and now look.'

Ted pressed a hand wearily over his eyes. 'It's all my fault. If it wasn't for me . . .'

'Now don't start that again! She'd have gone anyway. You know what she's like. Ever since going to work for them *solicitors*.'

She took a last bite, threw the stump venomously into a small round bin at her side.

'That Shirley Tucker! I could kill her, and that's the honest truth.'

Ted stared vacantly at the frayed edge of the mat by the Rayburn cooker, next to which he was squatting on a chopped-down chair resembling a stool. The Rayburn, which gave off a fierce heat in winter, was cold now, cold as the house would be when their daughter moved out.

They sat in a heavy, brooding silence.

'Don't know how she can afford it. Cost a small fortune, them places on the prom. Make a hole in her pocket, that's for sure,' said Lorna.

'God,' she cried a moment later, 'say *something*! Don't just sit there like I dunno what.'

Ted, thin, exhausted, his moustache a sign of something attempted but not sustained, looked at her.

'What you want me to say?' he said.

Lorna raised both her hands and flopped them down again hopelessly.

The afternoon wore on, grinding them down into failure.

He lay panting with the woman straddled across him, trying to squeeze it into herself yet again. Sweat ran shamelessly down her face, her eyes burned with the heat of a thousand summers. He willed his cock to rise again but it was limp, yet still she tried to push it where it would not go.

'I'm sorry, Sara,' he breathed. 'I'm sorry.'

'No need,' she said. 'This is good. Bloody good.'

She stroked it, slid down the bed and sucked it. And it began to fill again with blood, the miracle happened. She jogged up and down on it, feeling it grow stiff inside her, jogged harder and harder as if testing it to see if it might break.

His hands cupped her breasts, the silky softness of them. He thought – how could he not – of Annette's more angular breasts, the youthful pertness of them. Sara's were full, mature, the nipples deep brown, several shades darker than Annette's. Intoxicated by his new-found strength he kept pace with her rhythm, felt the semen boil up again, held it back then let go with a cry. She banged the bed with her fists, mouth twisted in triumph, then threw herself prone on him, digging her nails into his shoulders. He was filled with immense and ungovernable pride. He was a *man*, proving himself over and over. No longer a boy, he thought, no longer a boy, the words singing in his brain. Their sweat and their stickiness bonded them together, and over the harbour the gulls cackled and mewled.

Slowly they calmed, their heartbeats drumming less brutally. Their breaths mingled, their sweat cooled.

'Wonderful,' he murmured. 'Wonderful.'

She spoke with her hands, stroking him gently. He ran his fingers down her spine and then up again, resting them finally on the nape of her neck. She sighed.

There was nothing he wanted more in the world than this.

She raised herself on her elbows. 'You shouldn't have,' she said seriously. 'You silly boy. You shouldn't have.'

He smiled, tracing the outline of her nose and mouth with his finger.

'You shouldn't have let me,' she said, looking down at him. 'By Christ.'

She kissed him softly, rolled on to her side. 'Go on, boy. Get moving. Vi will be home soon.'

She watched him dress.

'What will you say to your girlfriend?' she asked.

'Nothing.'

'You won't tell her?'

'Course not.'

'Have you done it with her?'

'Once.'

'Jesus.'

Lacing up his shoes, he asked: 'Is it true what they say about you?'

She looked at him steadily. 'Depends what they say, doesn't it?'

'You know.'

'That I'm a whore?'

He flinched.

'Only sometimes,' she said.

He stood up, tightening his belt another notch.

'Shouldn't have asked, should you?'

'I wanted to know.'

'Won't come again now, will you?'

'You want me to?'

She shook her head.

'Why not?'

'It's not good.'

'Oh,' he said. 'Wasn't it?'

'Not that.' She smiled. 'Come here, Gerry.'

He paused, then sat on the bed again.

'Closer.'

'That's better.' She took his hand in both of hers. 'Listen, lad. I'm thinking of you. You're a boy. I'm just a slut. No – don't go now – ' for the word had reminded him of Annette – 'it's true, that's what I am. I don't want to hurt you. I like you.'

'Like?'

'Yes. You don't want me to say I'm in love with you, do you?'

He looked away.

'Go back to Annette now. Quick. Before I smack your bum.' She gave him a nudge.

He did not move.

'Gerry now. Play fair. Please.'

'What's fair?' he said. And bent his head and kissed her.

'God help me.' She put her arms around him. 'God help me.'

It came in the night. The blood, crackling first in her chest then boiling up to her throat, choking her. She coughed, gasped, spat it out, sitting upright in bed, shaking.

'Jesus,' cried Tessa, waking hugely, 'whass wrong with you?'

Vee was at her side, switching on the light, arm around her shoulders, soothingly, 'You're alright, love. Don't worry. All over now. Don't worry. Ring the bell.' This to Tessa. 'Go on. Ring the bloody bell. She's mopping.'

'Jesus Christ.'

Carol pulled the bedclothes over her head, refusing to have any part of it.

Sally coughed, spattering flecks of blood on to the counterpane, beside the bright red stain of the haemorrhage.

'Take it easy now. You're OK. Just breathe gentle. That's all.'

Vee put her free hand to Sally's brow, like a mother soothing her sick child.

Footsteps running down the corridor. Night sister, small, freckled, briskly taking control. Pillows propped behind Sally, mouth wiped clean, Vee dispatched back to bed, Tessa aghast, crying, Carol not wanting to know.

Then the doctor, male, quickly assessing. And Sally weak, trembling, but no more blood, only wretchedness.

Long hours of fitful sleep, lurid dreams. And in the morning the death sentence: a transfer to Powys Block.

Ivor woke with a start, knowing something was wrong. He tried to clutch hold of his rapidly-dissolving dreams but could not. He felt something more than menace but less than dread, something that affected somebody close to him. He turned over, knowing who it was. His sister, Sally.

The thought of her brought a hot, crawling sensation to his scalp. He tried to beat back the memories but they took shape with ghastly cunning. They were in the loft once again, dustmotes dancing in the sunlight shafting down through the skylight. A huddle of rags on the floor, an old blanket, scattered toys and boxes.

She was in a thin cotton dress and white socks and looking at her he felt strange. She wasn't just Sally but something else but he wasn't sure what. He felt the hardness he'd felt before but didn't know what was happening. Her thin legs drew his eyes to them over and over as they played. What was different about them now? And why did he want to see what could not be seen, and why this spit in his throat that made him gulp?

'Let's play a different game,' he said suddenly.

'Alright then. What?'

She was sprawled on the floor, white legs flung about anyhow, dress high above her knees.

'I don't know,' he replied.

'Well. You can't tell anyone then, can you?'

With a sudden, twisting movement she turned her back on him. Propping her head on her right elbow, she began drawing invisible patterns on the floor with the forefinger of her left hand.

He could neither move nor speak.

She half-looked over her shoulder.

'I don't mind,' she said casually.

There was no sound outside. They were the last people on earth.

'Lie down,' he said thickly.

She went on doodling for a few seconds, then stopped. She edged over to the rags, tidied them, stretched the blanket over them. Then lay down on the blanket, legs stretched out straight, eyes closed.

Her dress was all rumpled and she did not put it straight.

Slowly he walked over, stood above her, then knelt. A knot in the plank floor dug into his knee. He did not move but let it hurt him so that he would always remember.

His right hand reached out and touched her knee. Then lifted the hem of her skirt.

He touched her where he shouldn't, then pressed his fingers down hard. She gasped.

He recoiled as if burnt and stared at her, aghast.

'What's wrong?' she said fearfully, looking at him.

Filled with shame, he sprang to his feet.

'Ivor! Don't!' she cried, sitting up.

'Please! Ivor!'

He scrambled down the loft ladder.

'It's only a game!' she called after him. 'It doesn't matter!'

They never went up the loft again. She was never afraid to look at him, but for days he would not look directly at her.

Now, in the half-light, he felt the shame and the curse of it. If only he hadn't touched her, defiled her. The sickness was his. It had entered her body through his evil, questing fingers. For years it had lain dormant. Then something had roused it to unspeakable life. And he could not face seeing her, confronting the sickness of his own making.

But what had happened to her now?

He got out of bed and stood at the window, naked.

Part Three

DOUBTS

10

Every day Annette faced her mother's reproachful eyes, her father's pained silence, her own sense of guilt. She thought several times of staying put after all, but resolutely set her face against it. If she didn't move out now, she never would.

'You'll give me a hand tomorrow, won't you?' she asked Steve at the Pelican.

'If you like.' He gave his coffee another stir, unnecessarily.

'You don't have to if you don't want to,' said Annette, bridling.

'Course I do.' He looked up, smiling. 'Wouldn't let you down, would I?'

She gave him a long look, so ambiguous that he wondered for a moment if she had found out about Sara Baker. He turned pink and said, a little too loudly, 'Got much stuff to take, have you?'

'No, not much. My clothes, mainly. They'll go in a couple of cases. Shirley's lending me one. You can help me with my books, if you like.'

Steve sipped his coffee, considering. 'You've got quite a lot of them, haven't you?'

'Not all that many.'

'Couple of boxfuls, I'd say.'

She kept them in her bedroom. He'd been in there once, when her parents were out for the day. They were in a bookcase her father had bought for her, proud of her 'learning.' They'd snogged on the bed, she'd let him take her blouse off and feel her breasts through her bra, nothing more. He never thought he'd get where he had with her a week ago, not without marrying her. Yet, so suddenly had things happened, he was already comparing her with Sara.

'Maybe Dad will come and move them in his car, if I ask him nicely.'

'No thank you.' She smiled, to take away the edge of her refusal. 'I wouldn't like to bother him, Steve.'

'It's no bother. He wouldn't mind.'

She shook her head gently.

A group of students barged into the Pelican, talking loudly. Mario bantered with them as he served them, the coffee machine hissing and spluttering. Steve looked at them distastefully, absolved for the moment from any further persuasion. Then he said: 'I think you've got the wrong idea. About Dad.'

Annette looked at him questioningly.

'He's not against you.'

She smiled faintly. 'Not like your mother?'

He shrugged, infinitesimally.

'No, that's alright, Steve. I'll manage.'

He was silent a moment. The students subsided to their table.

'We'll take them down in the bus then,' he said. 'Couple of journeys should do it.'

Outside, she took his arm. By unspoken assent they walked the short distance from the Pelican Cafe to the prom. It was one of those beautiful evenings that come to Glanaber in summer, the declining sun sending a glittering pathway along the sea from horizon to shore. The sky was a wash of pink, deepening to orange. Her grip on his arm tightened.

'Oh, Steve. Isn't it gorgeous? Why does anyone want to leave this place, I wonder?'

He stiffened. 'Lots of reasons.'

She bit her lip. She had spoken impulsively, and he had taken it personally. Unhappily she glanced at him.

'I didn't mean you, Steve.' She gave his arm a squeeze. 'I know you want to get away. What do you want to do . . . exactly?'

'I don't know. See some life, I suppose. I can't bury myself here, can I?'

The words 'life' and 'bury' repeated themselves in Annette's head. What did they mean? What was life, what was burying? Weren't they alive now? Were they buried? She felt a sudden emptiness, the gulf between them. She had given herself to him . . . for what? They had scarcely mentioned it since and he seemed more distant, as if he were regretting it. But how could she talk about it, and what precisely did she want to talk about? Suddenly she wanted him again, wanted him inside her, not just his body but himself, wanted him entirely a part of her. She could not bear this cool, aloof Steve who seemed a perfect stranger.

'Fancy a walk?' she asked abruptly.

'Where?' he said, surprised at the change in her tone of voice.

'I don't know. Anywhere. Let's go down the flats.'

'When do you have to be in by?'

'I haven't *got* to be in any time,' she said impatiently. 'What d'you think I am, a schoolgirl? Anyway I'm moving out tomorrow, remember?'

'I know that. Thought you might want an early night, that's all.'

'There'll be plenty of early nights when I'm dead.'

He looked at her wonderingly. There seemed

something desperate about her. What had changed her? That shag on the carpet, her father's thieving? Or maybe both? Uneasily he wondered what this might mean for him. Would she become more demanding, insist that he marry her? If she became pregnant . . . oh hell, why hadn't he put a johnny on? But it had been wonderful without, the sheer sensation of it . . . just like it was with Sara.

Suddenly he felt huge, masterful. An older woman and a young one; both hot for him! He could fill them both, fill them till they screamed for mercy. He was Steve, super Steve, Steve the shagger, Steve the fucking poet!

'What're you grinning for? You're like a Cheshire cat.'

'Just thinking, that's all.'

'Well, why don't you share 'em? I can do with a laugh.' She tugged his arm. 'Well? Coming?'

The flats were beyond the allotments they passed on the longer way back to her house. They were a plain, ambiguous area just outside the town, neither wholly urban nor wholly rural, a series of scrubby-looking fields where cattle from a nearby farm were often put to graze. Here, dispirited men tended to wander at dusk, finding comfort in the anonymity and desultoriness of the setting, and here too lovers would lie kissing and fumbling in the coarse grass. Annette and Steve had always skirted this region till now, keeping to the path around the allotments before crossing the river and climbing the hill to the Penbryn council estate. But tonight Steve sensed a strange mood in Annette. He glanced at her uneasily, trying to work it out. She stopped. 'Well?' she said, with an odd little laugh. 'Shall we?'

'Shall we what?'

'Don't have to spell it out, do I?' She nodded towards the adjacent field.

'Oh.' He smiled slowly. 'OK then.'

He took her hand, led her stumbling down the short, steep slope from the path to the field. She bumped into him at the bottom and he kissed her suddenly, roughly, so that she protested. He kissed her again, slowly, gently. 'That's better,' she said softly. 'Much better.'

The worry that had fretted away obscurely all evening in a corner of his mind was dispelled by desire. He wanted her, wanted her! As they kissed again his hand touched her breast and she shivered.

'Mmm,' she mouthed with a shake of her head, and taking his hand she led him farther away from the path. Their feet softly brushed the grass, thistles stinging her ankles and clinging to his trousers. It was hard to see where they were going now and, unromantically, he feared they might any moment find themselves ankle-deep in cowshit. Suddenly she stopped, her hand gripping his so tightly that he winced. 'What's that?' she breathed, as a shape loomed out of the gloom.

'It's only a cow,' he said a moment later in relief, and allowed himself a brief laugh.

'Oh God. Let's go back.'

'Don't be silly,' said Steve, bolder now that he sensed an indefinable danger retreating. 'It won't hurt you.' He tried to kiss her but she wriggled away.

'I'm sorry. I hate cows. They're so big,' confessed Annette.

'Don't worry. It's gone now.'

'I don't care. I want to go home, Steve. I'm sorry.'

His desire too had died. Irritated with each other without quite knowing why, they scratchily made their way back to the path. Above them, a new moon leaned back on a cloud. He hardly noticed it, but for her it was so impossibly romantic that, thinking about it later in bed, she had to brush away a tear.

Eileen, white-faced, confronted Dr McKee across his bare, austere desk in the sanatorium. He was a slender, finicky Scot with thinning, auburn hair and a freckled forehead. She sat on the edge of her chair, obscurely feeling that she should have remained standing, to give herself some moral advantage.

'How ill is she?' she asked. 'Is she going to die?'

Dr McKee wrinkled his nose. 'We don't talk in those terms,' he said. 'She's being well looked after.'

'That's no answer. No answer at all.'

The doctor looked down at his desk, hardly bothering to hide his distaste.

'I want to see the medical superintendent,' said Eileen. 'Where is he? I want to see him now!' She stood up, startling him with the abruptness of her movement.

'My dear Mrs Morgan – '

'I'm not your dear – don't call me that! Where's Dr Campbell? I insist on seeing him, I tell you!'

'He's not here, madam,' said McKee coldly. 'He simply isn't here to see anyone.'

'Why not? Where is he then?'

'He's at a conference in Copenhagen.'

She knew he was inwardly laughing at her, this thin-lipped, sardonic man.

'Do sit down, Mrs Morgan.' He waved a cool hand.

She shook her head. 'A pretty kettle of fish. My daughter's dying and he goes off on a jaunt somewhere.'

'It's not a jaunt, Mrs Morgan. And your daughter isn't dying. She's had a setback, that's all. I'm sure she'll respond to treatment.'

'Oh yes, I'm sure. I wish *I* was sure. A full-scale lung haemorrhage. That's what she's had, isn't it?'

McKee inclined his head. 'It's not all that uncommon, Mrs Morgan. We know how to cope with these things.'

'She's on Powys Block, isn't she? That's a death sentence!'

McKee sighed. 'I don't know where you get these ideas from, but I assure you – '

'They're not my ideas, they're hers. They're everyone's here – you know it!

'They certainly aren't my ideas, Mrs Morgan. And they shouldn't be hers either – she has no right to think them.'

'No right, no right. Nobody has any right here – only the doctors.'

'If you think that – '

'I do. I certainly do.'

McKee fiddled with Sally's chart, the record of her treatment. He was fortyish, his abating hairline emphasising the peculiar roundness of his head, his cheeks spotty and puckered, as if he were enduring delayed teenage acne.

'I'm thinking of taking her from here,' said Eileen, breaking the silence.

McKee, startled, met her eyes. 'You mustn't,' he said, with unexpected warmth. 'You really mustn't.'

'Why not? You aren't doing her any good. She's getting worse.'

'You really think you can do better than us?'

'I can have a damn good try.'

'If you did that, Mrs Morgan,' said McKee clearly, 'she'd be dead within a month.'

'Ah! So she *is* critical. You admit it.'

McKee gave her a long, careful look. He seemed to have shed a mask. 'Come here,' he said. 'I'll show you something.'

He went to an inner room and she followed. He flicked through a filing cabinet, removed something.

'This was her condition when she came in here,' said McKee, as they looked at the illuminated X-ray. 'You see this?' He pointed to the apex of the right lung. 'That's what we call a spot on the lung – the earliest sign of TB. But there was also this.' He indicated the lower lobe of the left lung. 'You see that small hole? That's a cavity in the lung, caused by the infection.'

'Both lungs,' said Eileen. 'They never told me that.'

'I daresay. The prognosis wasn't good, I'm afraid. But she's been doing quite well, in fact. Look.'

He put another X-ray beside the original. 'This was after six months. You see? The spot's disappeared from the right. It's here the problem is. No progress to speak of.'

'So that's what gave her the haemorrhage.'

McKee nodded. 'She's still got a long way to go, Mrs Morgan.'

'It's not a long way to the grave,' said Eileen bitterly.

'Don't say that, please. It doesn't help.'

'What does help then? What are you going to do?

'There are various options. We'll probably collapse the lung, to give it maximum rest and a chance to heal properly.'

'You mean that big operation – where they cut away the ribs?'

'Not at this stage, Mrs Morgan. In fact, not at any, I hope. What I have in mind is something much simpler.'

He explained the technique of pumping air into the pleural cavity to partially collapse the lung; in the sanatorium jargon this was an AP, short for artificial pneumothorax. Eileen was familiar with the term. But, she wondered, why was everyone so secretive here? Why keep people in the dark until you made a big fuss?

'Well! Here we are! Great, isn't it?'

Surrounded by still unemptied boxes and bulging suitcases, Shirley flung her arms wide as if to embrace everything in the flat, the faded blue carpet trodden by many tenants' feet, the scratched but solid furniture, the anaemic paintings of wilting landscapes, the gas fire stuck in the middle of the tiled Victorian fireplace.

Shirley swept some stray strands of her smoky blonde hair from her eyes.

'Well, say something girl, even if it's only sod off!'

It was the gas fire that fixed Annette's attention. It looked cold, forlorn, a summary of the emptiness of the lives of all the people who had drifted into this flat and then drifted out again, meaninglessly, irrevocably.

'It's fine,' said Annette, blinking back the tears.

'What's wrong with you then? Why the water-works? Sorry now, are you? I knew you would be.'

Shirley, dashed, lifted a heavy trunk and humped it into the bedroom.

Annette pressed her hands to her eyes miserably, thinking of her father slumped on the little chair by the Rayburn, her mother turning her back on Steve as he carried out the biggest of her boxes.

Her heart thumped so loud that she felt everyone passing on the prom must hear it. Then she blew into her hankie, straightened and went through to Shirley, who had commandeered the bed in the middle of the room rather than the one which, pushed against a wall, had a modest and apologetic look, as if it had no right to be there.

Shirley, hanging clothes in the big wardrobe with inevitably cracked mirror, self-consciously kept her eyes turned away as Annette tentatively entered.

'Nice, isn't it?' said Annette feebly.

Shirley made no reply, her strong arms busy, her broad back a reproach to any weakness or indecision.

Annette sat on the bed by the wall, her legs suddenly weak.

'Look,' said Shirley, turning. 'You don't have to stay if you don't want to. I'll get someone else to share. You can just take your things back home and pretend it didn't happen.'

Annette shook her head. She seemed dazed by Shirley's energy, the fierce sense of commitment she carried around with her like a banner.

'I knew you didn't want to really. It was just an impulse because of what happened at home. You wanted to get away and – and – now you don't. Do you?'

She faced Annette boldly, challenging.

'Yes I do,' said Annette.

'No you don't! Don't give me that! You were crying your eyes out a minute ago.'

'No I wasn't.'

'Well.' Shirley softened. 'We all cry a bit sometimes, I suppose.'

She looked at her friend, sitting forlornly but bravely on the edge of her bed.

'Tell you what. Let's have a snifter.'

Annette looked queryingly at her.

'Don't you know what a snifter is? You haven't lived, mun!'

She produced, as if by magic, a half bottle of whisky. Annette stared, as if at some secret potion.

'Ever had any of this? It's the best. Haig's Scotch Whisky, matured in the wood. Here – let me get a couple of glasses.'

She thrust one into Annette's hand.

'Don't stare at me like that. You look as if you're going to be shot!'

Shirley giggled as the amber liquid splashed into Annette's glass.

'Not too much! That's enough!' cried Annette.

Shirley laughed robustly, holding the bottle before her with both hands.

'Go on! Try it!'

'But – don't you need something in it?'

'Try it as it is!'

Obediently Annette put the glass to her lips. The fumes from the drink almost made her faint. Tentatively she sipped, coughed, held the glass away.

'Ugh! I can't drink that – it's horrible!'

'Yes you can. Wait a minute.'

Shirley flurried away, produced a small bottle, took the top off expertly with an opener.

'What's that?'

'Dry ginger of course. Look, where've you been living all this time – in a convent?'

She poured the ginger generously into Annette's glass. 'There now. Try that. Go on! It'll be different, I promise you.'

'I hope so.'

Annette took the tiniest of sips, considered, took another. She looked up at Shirley. 'It's nice.'

'Nice! I should say it's nice! It's the best. I tell you.'

She poured herself a drink, with half the measure of dry ginger she'd given Annette, and raised her glass.

'To us,' she said solemnly.

The girls clinked their glasses and drank.

11

'Give it me!' yelled Megan.

'No! It's mine!'

'Give it *me* I say!'

The children fought over the comic as only brother and sister could. Teeth clenched, they struggled until the inevitable happened and it tore apart.

'Look what you've done now!' cried Lennie.

'It's your fault.'

'No it's not.'

'Yes it is, it is, it *is*!' And Megan stamped her foot, the very picture of girlish outrage.

Eileen whirled in, catching Lennie by the scruff of the neck and throwing him into a chair, hauling Megan to the foot of the stairs and commanding: 'Upstairs now! Directly! And don't you dare come down here till I say!'

Megan charged upstairs, fearful of her mother, crying but pausing on the landing to shout down: 'It's not fair! You're not sending *him* to bed!'

'I'll say what's fair and what isn't, young madam. In your room before I give you a leathering.'

Megan's wails increased in volume until modified considerably by the closing of her door. Grimly Eileen returned to the living-room.

'Don't think I'm letting you off because I'm not,' she told the boy, who sullenly avoided her eye. 'I want you out here right away.'

'Where?'

'In the garden, where d'you think? Come along.'

A moment's pause, to salvage the merest sliver of pride, then Lennie followed. Like his sister, he feared his mother's temper.

'Now,' she said, 'you can weed these for a start.'

'*Weed* them?'

'Yes. Haven't you heard of the word?'

She pushed a trowel in his hand.

'Go on. They won't bite.'

'Do I have to?' he said miserably.

'Yes, you do. So the sooner you start the sooner you'll finish. Here's some papers to kneel on so you won't dirty your precious knees.'

Defeated, he knelt and began prodding the earth ineffectually around the peonies and sweet williams. Eileen knew he would achieve little but it would keep him out of his little sister's way till they both calmed down a bit.

Wearily she pegged the washing to the line. It was hard bringing up these two on her own. She dreaded the adolescent years ahead, the painful scrabbling towards manhood and womanhood of these lively, squabbling children. If only Sally were here, if only Ivor would help out more, if only Eddie were still alive. He'd been gone three years now, gone before his time, cut down by that stupid heart attack. The pain of his absence struck her now and she stood motionless with one of Ivor's shirts in her hand, seeing Eddie smiling at her from across the garden, those jolly laughing-sailor eyes beneath the beetle brow and frizzy black hair. It was as if she'd just lost him, the tears came, and she blindly pegged up the shirt before wiping them away.

Ivor looked out from the back door, doing the cuffs of his shirt up.

'What's wrong with Meg, Mam? She's crying her eyes out.'

'She knows what. They've been fighting.'

'Fighting? Over what?' He stepped out, saw Lennie. 'Good God, what are you up to then? Gardening? Turned over a new leaf, have you?'

Lennie, still sulking, ignored him.

'What they been scrapping about then?' Ivor asked his mother good-humouredly.

'Nothing. A stupid comic.'

She knew he wouldn't notice she'd been crying, wouldn't notice anything.

'A comic. Fighting over a *comic*, is it?' He picked Lennie up, the boy struggling and shouting, 'Lay off, will you? Put me *down.*'

'I'll tan your arse for you in a minute, you see if I don't.' He held his brother up high then put him down, ruffling his hair. He stood there placidly, the picture of contentment.

Eileen felt a dark fury boil up inside her, a rage with his indifference to herself and Sally, his obsession with the girl who'd thrown him over, a rage against the young manhood he epitomised, standing there like a god while she trembled with loss and frustration.

'Aren't you going to work?' she said sharply. 'Or have you got another Saturday doing nothing?'

'I'm going now, Mam,' he said quietly, looking at her in surprise. 'I don't have to be there till ten.'

'Oh, don't you now. Cushy little number you've got, haven't you?'

Ivor took a step nearer. 'What's wrong, Mam?'

'Nothing's wrong. Why should there be anything

wrong?' She took a petticoat from the wicker basket on the thin garden path and pegged it up.

'You sound put out about something. Kids, is it?'

'Everything.'

Ivor looked down. 'She'll get better, Mam. Don't worry.'

Eileen gave him a glance. 'Who's talking about Sally?'

The boy, bent unhappily at his weeding, stiffened. Both brother and mother were painfully aware of him.

'I'll go to see her next week, Mam – I promise. I can't today.'

'Of course not. First things first,' she said sarcastically.

'It's the semi-final. I can't let them down.'

'Naturally.'

Fiercely Lennie dug the trowel in, pushing it down and down, his hand white with the effort, till it would go no further.

'Well, I'll be going now. See you later.' Ivor strode back into the house. 'And see you get all those weeds up,' he threw at his brother.

Lennie said nothing. His mother dourly went on with her task. The chickens clucked morosely in their coop at the end of the garden.

'Right boys. I know it's only a charity cup but I want us to win it.'

Solemnly, Tony Webb addressed his assembled team. Looks just like Errol Flynn winning the fucking war against the Japs, thought Ivor.

'Now, let's go over the plan again.'

Plan, plan, what a load of balls. All it was was a game of football. Kick the ball, kick the other lot if

130

you can get away with it, put the ball in the net and sod off for a pint with the lads. That's what the game was all about, wasn't it? He could stuff his plan up his nancy-boy arse.

'You listening, Ivor?' Tony's eyes grew steely, a trick learned in drama school. He'd been there for a year and come back to Glanaber, to take a job as a teacher and to act spare-time with the local dramatic society, yet another wannabe without the guts to see the thing through.

Ivor nodded. Some of the lads grinned. He was known as a prickly character, a rebel, and saw it as a compliment, acknowledgement that he hated the shit that Tony Webb put about.

'So that's it. Let's go out there and win. And when we've got the cup in our hands, first round's on me!'

Cheers, some more shaded with mockery than others, and an arse-licking voice. 'What, all of us, Tony?' piped up Cy Reynolds.

'All of you. No exceptions.'

Smart, brittle, authoritative, Tony pushed his shoulders back, the essence of silver-screen leadership.

'OK boys?' The ref looked in, small, moustached, blinking disconcertingly as if short-sighted. 'Off we go then.'

The teams trotted on to the pitch. The match was being played on Town Field, home of Glanaber FC, winners of the Welsh Senior Cup in the long-ago days when footballers' jerseys reached down to their knees and the great Billy Meredith chewed a toothpick as he swayed down the right wing for Manchester City.

Ivor felt gutted. He knew he should have pulled out, gone with his mother to see Sally. What kind of a brother was he?

In the kick-about before the game began, the ball rolled towards him. Viciously he kicked it anywhere, seeing it slew into the small knot of spectators behind the goal. Tony gave him a hard look. Ivor looked down at the ground then stooped, pretending to do something with his laces.

Calm down, he thought. Calm down. Now you're here don't make a prick of yourself.

He stayed crouching for a moment, as if frozen. Then bounded up, doing a swift run-on-the-spot that won a small, approving smile from Tony.

And then he saw Steve. Up in the grandstand. With his stupid notebook in his hands.

And it all came back, the way Annette had two-timed him, the way this arsehole of a reporter had taken her off him, God knows how, the way he was stuck now with fat Betty who didn't even have a brain in her bum.

And he felt a hatred that burnt his guts to cinders.

He tried to control himself but could not. All he felt was a blind rage with everything. It focussed into a rage with death, which had taken his dad away and now might take Sally. He remembered his dad's face in the coffin, the waxy unreality of it, like some shopwindow dummy.

And he went into a tackle with both feet so that the poor bastard went flying.

'Off,' snarled the ref.

'What?'

'Off the field. I'm not having any of that nonsense round here.'

'Christ, ref, what for?'

'Jumping at an opponent. Dangerous play. You know the score. Off. But give me your name first.'

132

'Stanley Matthews.'

'Joker, eh?' A snarling smile lifted the ref's small, ginger moustache. 'I'll get you for something else if you're not careful. Now out with it.'

'Ivor Morgan. You know that anyway, don't you?'

'Got to ask you, son.' The ref wrote the name in his notebook. 'Now go on, there's a good lad.'

The man he'd fouled was writhing on the grass, moaning. The trainer, magic sponge active, manipulated his left leg to and fro.

'You could have broken his leg you daft cunt,' said the trainer.

'Well I didn't, did I? He's only shamming anyway.'

Tony Webb was alongside him. 'Bad show, Ivor. What the hell got into you?'

'Oh, piss off.'

'Hey, hang on. You can't talk to me like that.'

'I'll talk to you as I bloody like.'

Tony stopped. 'This is the last match you play for us while I'm captain,' he said clearly.

Ivor turned, looked him full in the face and gave him the V-sign, both hands.

The men on the touchline laughed and cheered.

The desk in Steve's bedroom deliberately faced a blank wall. He wanted no distractions.

He frowned over the line he'd just written.

In the winter of my youth I sing

There was something wrong with it, the echo of a half-remembered line. Then it came to him; Shakespeare's 'winter of our discontent.'

He crossed out 'winter' and substituted another word.

> In the December of my youth I sing

Better. Much better.
A smile played over his full lips; he was filled with the sense of fulfilment that came only when his writing took wing and began to mean something.

His fountain pen moved rapidly over the page.

> A song of awakening seed

His seed. Awakened by Annette. And Sara.
His heart thumped and his prick stirred at the mere thought of them both.

Two women. *His* women. Both of them. Jesus!

> ... awakening seed, and blood
> burning like desert sand

Christ, no!
He tore the page out of the writing pad and called up images of heat, staring at the blank wall, oblivious of time. Then he wrote again.

> In the December of my youth I sing
> A song of spring-awakened seed and blood
> Scorching my jungle veins

The veins *were* a jungle, weren't they?
He paused, read it through.

> Mad with desire and ...

No! Another cliche.
Drunk with desire, he murmured.
That was better..

> ... and pounding passion

No, not *pounding*.
He turned the line around in his head.
Desire-drunk, he wrote, and passion-proud.
He started a clean page.

> In the December of my youth I sing
> A song of spring-awakened seed and blood
> Scorching my jungle veins,
> Desire-drunk, passion-proud.

He read it aloud softly. Not bad. Not bad at all.
But would anyone publish it?

That Sunday afternoon Sally lay still, very still, in her white bed in Powys Block. She could not get used to the quiet. There had always been something happening in Newtown Block, Tessa and Vee chatting, the girls on exercise passing along the verandah as they took their regulation walks, even the tiny diversion of the slamming of a dustbin lid outside the nearby kitchens. But there was silence here, apart from the occasional cough in one of the other cubicles, or the grating ugliness of phlegm being dragged up and spat into one of the small metallic pots which every patient kept at her bedside.

The silence of the grave. Sally tried to force the phrase away, but it clung to her, as her nightdress clung to her in the small hours when she awoke drenched in the night sweat that was a symptom of consumption.

The bug had got her alright and she was going to die.

No. No. No.

She thought of Steve, the mischievous smile never far from his lips, Steve the family enemy, Steve who had snatched Annette away from Ivor.

But she could not see him as an enemy.
He was her secret.

A tap on the bedroom door.
'Yes?'
'It's gone five. Aren't you coming down for tea?'
The voice of his mother, sharpness edging in despite her efforts.
'Alright. In a minute,' said Steve. He too made an effort; to subdue his impatience.
He screwed the top back on his fountain pen, put the pad in a drawer.
Poetry came second to Sunday afternoon tea in Glanaber.

12

'So that's it then, yes?' said Shirley eagerly. 'A flat-warming.'

'If you like.'

'Well, who'll we invite?'

They had been in their flat for nearly a fortnight, and things were falling into place. Annette's initial doubts were already history.

'Well . . . there's Steve,' ventured Annette.

'Of course.'

'And Roy.'

'Roy? I've finished with him.'

'Since when?'

'Oh, a long time.'

Shirley lifted a hand and let it drop, as if an eternity had passed since last seeing him.

'You went out with him last week – I remember,' said Annette spiritedly.

'Well, what of it? I'm not going out with him again.'

'You said a long time.'

'So what? Seems a long time to me. I hate him.'

'Why, what's he done to you then?'

'Nothing. I'd like to see him try.'

'There must be *something*.'

'He's a creep, that's all.'

'What way?'

'Everything. Oh, I don't want to talk about him 'Nette.'

'OK then. We won't.'

The girls lapsed into a brief, contented silence. Outside, a low-flung Sunday sky was turning to drizzle. Annette felt warm, relaxed, as if her real life were only just beginning. Her parents were still there in her mind, edgy and distracting, but for the moment she felt in control, determined to make the most of her freedom.

'How many shall we invite then?' asked Shirley.

'I don't know. I've never been to a flat-warming before.'

'Yes you have. You came to mine.'

'No I didn't.'

'Why not?'

'You didn't invite me.'

'That's not true! I'm sure I did.'

'I'd have come if you'd asked. But I didn't know you so well then.'

Shirley looked thoughtfully across the room at her. She was on a pouffe by the fireplace, Annette in the easy chair placed in the bay window overlooking the prom.

'Funny that,' said Shirley. 'I feel I've known you for years.'

Annette gave her a friendly smile, but there was something in Shirley's expression that made her feel awkward.

'What's he like then?' asked Shirley.

'Who?'

'Steve of course, who'd you think?'

'He's nice.'

'*Nice*,' Shirley mocked.

Annette looked at her queryingly.

'Is that all?' said Shirley.

'What do you want me to say?'

'What's he kiss like? Does he – you know – ' She jabbed her tongue through her lips.

Annette blushed.

'Thought so. They're all like that from South Wales.'

Annette gazed out at the passers-by on the prom, raincoated and umbrella'd against the fine rain teasing in from the sea.

'Does other things too, I bet,' ventured Shirley. 'If you let him.'

Annette's blush deepened.

'Don't say you have,' Shirley said disbelievingly. 'Have you?'

'Leave it, Shirl.'

'Jesus.'

'I haven't said anything, have I?'

'You don't have to, kid. I can see it in your face. My God.'

Annette felt a tight knot of pride; one in the eye for Shirl, who thought she knew it all.

'Hope you take precautions,' said Shirley, businesslike. 'Don't want to get landed.'

'I'm alright, thanks.'

'Proper dark horse, aren't you? Thought you were a little innocent, I did.'

'Thought wrong then, didn't you?'

'Looks like it.' She threw Annette a complex look, made to say something, changed her mind. She smiled. 'Another snifter, yes?'

'What, again?

'No law against it, is there?'

'OK then,' conceded Annette. 'Just a small one.'

'Right!' Shirley slapped her thigh, got up. 'But remember, 'Nette – what's sauce for the goose is sauce for the gander.'

Annette stared at her, puzzled. Briskly, Shirley strode to the kitchen.

Next day, the Monday morning post plopped through the letterbox of the Morrises' council house in Penbryn. A postcard from Butlins at Clacton-on-Sea (their friends Florrie and Mike having a great time and wishing they were there), a circular from a mail order firm and an official-looking envelope that made Lorna's heart sink to the soles of her frayed carpet slippers.

She held it in her hand, wishing it would disappear, then took it upstairs.

Ted was in cheerful mood, smoking a Woodbine in bed as he drank his morning cuppa, till he saw her face. Without a word, she gave him the letter.

Carefully he stubbed out his fag in the saucer before tearing it open.

His lips silently moved as he read the contents. Then he handed it back.

'September the sixteenth,' she said, scanning it bitterly. 'Not much time, is it?'

'Long enough.' He plucked a thread of strong tobacco from his lips, his fingers trembling. 'Want to get the thing over.'

'Swines,' said Lorna. 'Hope they all rot in hell.'

She continued to gaze blankly at the letter.

Gently he took it from her, scanning it again.

'Magistrates,' he said. 'That's a laugh. People like Bertie Ross. He'd do his own mother in as soon as look at her.'

'Bertie Ross. Is his name down there? Why, whass he doing with you?' She held her hand out. 'Give it here, Ted, let's have a look.'

'No, there's nothing to see mun. He's on the bench though, in' he? That's all I said. People like him'll be deciding it.'

'What, Bertie Ross? He in't a judge, is he? All he is is a grocer. Made a mint outa the black market in the war too, biggest crook around. Mean to say *he'll* have summat to do with this?'

'He may do, he may not. All depends who's on that day, I suppose. But he could do – he's been on the bench for years.'

'Whass this bench you're talking about, Ted? I dunno what you mean, mun.'

'It's just a word,' said Ted impatiently. 'There'll be two or three on 'em, I 'spect – I dunno, I've never been there before.'

'Oh, Ted.' She touched his knee through the bedclothes. 'It's gonna be orright, innit? I mean – they aren't gonna put you in – ' She began sniffing.

'Course it'll be orright,' said Ted bravely. 'We've got a good man, haven't we? This young solicitor chap – he knows a thing or two.'

'Oh, I dunno 'bout him,' said Lorna doubtfully. 'He's so young, in' he? Straight from college, by the look of him.'

'Well, he's got to start some time, hasn't he? Seems a good little chap to me. Knows what he's saying.'

'I hope so,' sighed Lorna. 'Oh, I hope so.'

'Ah well . . . what's it matter. All be over soon, anyway. Out of my way, gel – I'm getting dressed.'

'Have some more tea, Ted – I'll get you another cup.'

'No – I'm getting up. Want to take a walk up the Dinas. Clear my head.'

He swung his legs out and stood up, a thin figure in faded pyjamas.

She looked up at him. 'You want me to say anything, love? I mean – to them judges?'

Ted smiled. 'No, love. No need for that.'

'You're a good man. Better than all them put together.'

She bent her head, brushing away a tear.

'Do you really want to say this?'

Sam Evans, sports editor of the *County Dispatch*, stood over Steve, pudgy finger stabbing his just-typed report of the charity cup match.

'Yes,' said Steve coolly. 'Why?'

'Bit strong, in't it?'

Steve shrugged. 'It's fair comment.'

'He'll have your guts for garters, boy. I would anyhow.'

Bill Merrick looked keenly across, sensing blood. Brenda Marsden stared at Steve.

'Well, there it is,' said Steve dismissively.

'No,' said Sam. 'No. There it bloody isn't.' Slowly he tore up the copy, put it on Steve's desk, walked slowly away.

Bill smirked, dragged on his fag, hummed softly as he resumed typing. Brenda, worried, entered something in the editorial diary. Steve blushed deeply.

He sat quite still for a moment, then picked up the torn-apart sheets and took them over to Sam.

'Here's my copy, Sam,' he said levelly.

'I don't want it. You know what you can do with that.'

Sam, fortyish, blond hair clinging to his scalp as though stuck on with glue, avoided Steve's eye. His chest heaved, as though he were having trouble breathing.

'My copy, Sam,' repeated Steve. 'Stick it together and sub it.'

He plonked it down on Sam's cluttered desk, and went back to his own. Bill gleefully glanced from one to the other.

Sam was as one cast in stone for a moment. Then he deliberately put Steve's report on the spike which was the receptacle of all unwanted material.

Ronnie emerged from his lair. 'What's all this then?' he said uneasily.

'Ask Sam,' said Steve.

'Sam?' said Ronnie, half jocularly. 'What's going on then, eh?'

Sam glared. 'He's given me some unusable copy, that's all. I've spiked it.'

'Unusable? Why?'

'It's libellous.'

'Libellous? What the hell you been writing, Steve-o?'

The 'Steve-o' was a signal that Ronnie wished all this to pass off lightly, so that reference need not be made to the editor so rarely seen, who left practically everything to Ronnie.

'I don't know what all the fuss is about,' said Steve. 'It's just a report of Saturday's cup match, that's all.'

'Well, what have you said then? Slagged the ref off, have you?'

'No.'

Brenda, increasingly uncomfortable, shot questioning glances at Steve, who was entirely oblivious to them. Bill found it hard to contain his excitement.

'Who then?'

'One of the players,' said Sam.

'Let's have a look.' Ronnie, conscious now of his status as arbiter in the crisis, ambled over. Sam wrested the copy back off the spike and gave it to Ronnie without a word.

'Christ, what a mess. Bloody jigsaw puzzle this,' grumbled Ronnie, playing for time.

Deliberately he took it to a table long relegated to a dusty corner of the office and perched uncomfortably on the edge of it. He pushed the bridge of his glasses to the top of his nose, then jiggled with the pieces of paper.

'Where is it then? Don't have to read all of it, do I?'

'Near the top. You can't miss it,' said Sam brusquely. He seemed calmer now, the challenge made, the matter taken out of his control.

Ronnie was silent, reading.

'Christ,' he said.

Steve stared unseeingly at his notebook, theoretically writing a report of last Friday's Chamber of Trade meeting.

Ronnie slid off the desk, went to Sam, put the copy on his desk.

'That's OK,' he said. 'Stick it together and sub it.'

Sam stared at his retreating back.

'OK? It's bloody libellous!'

Ronnie turned to face him.

'Trouble with you, Sam,' he said slowly, 'you're scared of your own shit.'

He slid into his cubbyhole office. Brenda shivered, she knew not why. Steve, transfixed, dared not look at anyone. Bill's face was a mask of disappointment.

She lay at an angle, the foot of her bed raised up by the blocks of wood placed under it. She had been told why, but could not remember. All she knew was that she had to be as still as possible, to allow rest to work its miracle. Rest, rest; the need for it permeated her tired body, the idea of it soaked itself in the sweats that drenched her nightly.

She was on Absolute; the ultimate treatment. Absolute Rest, one step from the death it imitated. She must not move more than necessary, for movement required energy, and energy must be reserved for the fight against the enemy. It was a war within her, the brave red corpuscles battling against the evil invader, the tubercle bacilli which had taken one citadel after another in her lungs. The haemorrhage had been a famous victory, signalling a fierce advance, her body's army in full retreat. But now she pictured it regrouping, the tattered remnnants rallying and finding new courage. Churchillian tones echoed inside her: 'We shall fight on the beaches ... we shall never surrender.' And no, she would not. She might at last die, but she would fight to the last drop of her blood. So she lay still, still, while her imagination took flight. There was no subduing that. It was as lively as her body was comatose, and through it she lived a secret life that no disease could touch.

She thought of home, the home that now seemed so distant. Her mother busy about the house, Lennie frowning over his homework, Megan practising her dance movements in a trance. And Ivor, her big brother, so strong and purposeful. Ivor especially; she loved him with a special love, different from any other. She loved the idea of him, had always done so, the maleness that encompassed him from head to ankles. And she thought of her father, whose touch had been so warm and comforting when she was little. If she had remained so, cradled in his arms, nothing evil could have touched her. It was his death that had made her vulnerable to disease, the unspeakable invader that had battened on to her grief and forced its way in with such cruel ferocity.

Then she thought of a man she scarcely knew, the reporter Steve Lewis, in his mystery and otherness. He was assuming a strange importance in her life; she did not know why. Her mother had made him a part of her mental circle by speaking of him with such loathing, on the day when she had told her about Annette's family problems. Now, having little else to think about except her own body's corruption, she dwelt on the idea of him with curious satisfaction. The Steve Lewis she conjured up in her mind's eye was a creature of her own making; she knew it. But what harm could come of these secret imaginings?

Thus she justified herself, not knowing the power that dreams have to reach out and touch those who inhabit them.

13

Steve walked briskly along Shipwrights Road. It was two in the afternoon, he was obviously on a job, his mac buttoned-up against the drizzle wafted in from the bay by the warm sou'westerly. Only a psychic could have detected in his manner any of the nervousness he felt at drawing nearer to Annette's flat on the prom, although he did not intend going that far. He was seeing her that evening, when they would meet in the cafe that was their second home, where Mario held court behind the hissing coffee machine. Briefly he wondered if he would miss Mario when he left Glanaber, miss the bonhomie of the coffee shop that was the town's entrée into the new world taking shape around them, a world without rationing in which new talents were coming out on 78rpm all the time, Billy Eckstine and George Shearing and Alma Cogan and Dickie Valentine. No, there would be smarter coffee shops in London, and bigger record stores, and Mario was expendable, and so was everything else about this one-horse town on the edge of the world where the waves crashed endlessly on the gritty shore and where everything was dying.

Even Sara was expendable. But he must make the most of her while it lasted.

Officially he was making some of the regular calls that might yield a paragraph or two in the paper or might not. They could wait, not least because he still felt sore with Sam Evans for creating that scene over his football report a few hours earlier. Christ! If Ronnie hadn't backed him up he'd have handed his notice in right away, and to hell with everything. It was typical, just typical. He frowned as he thought of it, then stepped suddenly aside to avoid someone coming the other way, a cadaverous figure with staring eyes who looked reproachfully down from a great height as Steve mumbled an apology.

'Mr Stephen Lewis,' it pronounced. 'In a great hurry, and for what, I wonder?'

'Doing the calls,' said Steve impatiently, seeing no need to offer explanation for anything to Goronwy Pritchard, resident bard of Glanaber and minor functionary with the town council.

'The calls,' the gloomy voice repeated. 'And what calls might they be, may I ask? The calls to repentance, possibly?'

'I'm sorry, Mr Pritchard, but I can't stay.'

'Can't stay?' A skeletal hand gripped him suddenly by the lapel. 'Never say can't, boy. It's not a word in my dictionary. Now tell me, *where are you going*?'

Pritchard's near-black, manic eyes bore into him. 'To see Fred Barclay, if you must know. Now would you please let me *go*, please?'

The double apology struck a chord of amusement in Pritchard.

'A likely story,' he said, a rare smile contorting his death-mask features. 'Fred Barclay indeed!' He gave vent to a short, explosive sound that was his nearest approach to laughter.

'For God's sake, Mr Pritchard.' Steve wriggled free and hurried on.

'Take care!' Pritchard called out after him. 'The Lord is listening!'

Mentally Steve gave him the V-sign.

'Take not his name in vain!' Pritchard warned. And then, just as Steve turned the corner that would take him out of sight, he called again. 'Beware . . .' His next words, carried away by the wind, were unclear but sounded like 'whore of Babylon.'

Shocked and dismayed, Steve almost stopped. Had he really said that? Did he know about Sara? How could he?

A voice inside him said, 'Everyone knows everything here,' but he did not wish to hear it, did not want to have done with Sara yet. For what was this, after all, but the windy rhetoric of a religious maniac?

Down the flight of stone steps he rushed, to rap the door of 4 Back Row. Vi answered and, without a word, stepped back to let him in.

Sara was flopped in a low, shabby chair by the fireplace, the only chair in the room with any pretensions to comfort.

She looked at him with surprise, even alarm. 'What you doing here, this time of day? You shouldn't be here, lad.'

'Why, what's wrong?'

'I'm ill, boy. Can't you see?' Her round face looked slippery, the sweat a sheen against her flushed cheeks.

'What's the matter?'

'Christ knows. I feel half-dead. If I didn't have Vi here . . .'

The child looked dispassionately up at Steve, like an elderly dwarf.

'Have you seen the doctor?'

'Doctor, what would I want with doctors? Don't believe in 'em, never have. I make my own medicine.'

Steve felt suddenly out of his depth. A witch

woman, part-time whore faced him from the depths of a tattered settee in a Glanaber slum. What was he doing here? What was happening to him?

'What brings you here now? I thought you'd be working.'

'I am,' he said defiantly.

'Are you, be devil. Funny sort of work. Sort I'd like, eh Vi? Nice work if you can get it, that's what I say.'

'I thought you'd be glad to see me,' said Steve resentfully. 'You always have been before.'

'I know I have, more's the pity. But I told you to stay away, didn't I? Look after your girlfriend, that's what I said.' She stiffened in the chair, moaning softly. 'Make the man a cup of tea, love,' she told Vi. 'Put the kettle on, there's a good girl.'

'I don't want one, thank you. Don't bother.'

'Don't bother now, is it? That's a fine thing. Here, take your coat off and sit down. You're making the place look untidy.'

Steve hesitated then sat down, still with his coat on.

'I've just had a visitor. If you can call him that.'

Steve looked at her inquiringly.

'Man from the council. Bit touched in the head, if you ask me.'

'Why do you say that?'

'Because he was, that's why. Screwy as they come. Looked like a madman, talked like a preacher.'

'What was his name?' asked Steve, knowing the answer.

'How should I know? Who cares anyway? He's only been gone a few minutes. Must have seen him, didn't you?'

'I think so. Goronwy Pritchard, was it?'

'That's the one. Cheeky bugger. Wanted to know all

my ins and outs. I'd have told him to go to hell if I'd felt better.'

'What did he want then?'

'What didn't he! What my name was, where I come from, not much he didn't want to know, real nosey parker he was.'

'But what was he *doing*?'

'Doing? Doing? Just told you, haven't I?'

'The house, Mam,' said Vi, appearing in the scullery doorway. 'He said it was all about the house.'

'The man knows that, I told him so! Didn't I?'

'No, you didn't,' said Steve. He turned to Vi. 'You mean he talked about getting you a council house?'

Vi nodded. 'Don't ask her, ask me!' exploded Sara. 'I'm not stupid, you know. What the devil d'you mean, asking her? The kettle's boiling, go and make the tea!' she told her daughter. 'God, the things I put up with.'

'So you've got the chance of a house – that's great!'

'I'll believe it when I see it. And if the rent's too high I won't take it. It's bad enough here, living in this pit of a place. I won't go if it's too far out either, them new houses up Penbryn cost a fortune in bus fares.'

'But aren't you pleased?' asked Steve, astonished.

'Pleased, why should I be pleased? They've kept me waiting long enough. There's some only been here five minutes and they get a house. It's who you know, the old story.'

Vi appeared again. 'Want some sugar?' she asked Steve.

'Bring the bowl in!' commanded Sara, before he could answer. 'Let the man put it in for himself.' She closed her eyes, exhausted.

Steve, head bowed, felt resentment and, more insidiously, self-disgust. He had given himself to this stupid, shallow woman, a part-time whore who felt no gratitude towards him whatsoever. She was the kind who took everything for granted, lacking the imagination to appreciate what was being done for her. And here he was, putting everything at risk for her, his relationship with Annette, his very career . . .

Vi stood at his side, carefully holding a cup and saucer. She looked at him solemnly.

'Thanks, Vi,' he said. 'That's very kind of you.'

He took a spoonful of sugar from the bowl she offered and smiled his thanks.

Sara slipped into a doze.

Vi went upstairs.

Steve sipped his tea in the uncanny quiet. When it was only half-drunk, he tip-toed out.

Lennie was being as good as he knew how. He knew he was a nuisance because everyone told him so, but the word had ceased to mean anything because he rarely meant to be bad but only did what came naturally.

No-one could possibly accuse him of being mischievous now. He was reading the *Dandy*, his favourite comic, and as he enjoyed the latest adventures of Desperate Dan and Keyhole Kate he felt safe and comfortable, here with his Mam without his big brother teasing him or his little sister pestering him.

The faintest of sounds, not much more than an exhalation of breath, made him look up. His mother was gripping the paper they called the local rag, and suddenly she slammed it down on the table. 'The cheek of it! The brazen cheek!' she exclaimed.

Eileen had a quick temper but Lennie feared more her quiet rages, the cooped-up tension that showed in her smouldering eyes and clipped sentences.

'What's wrong, Mam?' he ventured.

She did not answer but simply strode out to the kitchen, where she banged things about.

All his pleasure in the *Dandy* left Lennie. Cautiously he went to where she'd been sitting and looked at the paper.

It was open at the sports page, unusual reading for his mother. Then he saw the headline, 'Player Sent Off in Tough Cup-Tie.' He read the report underneath and went quietly back to his chair, so that when she bustled in a few moments later his eyes were still apparently riveted to the comic.

'You seen it?' she said.

'What, Mam?' he asked innocently.

'You seen what they said about your brother in the paper?'

'No.'

'Read it. But for God's sake don't tell Ivor. He'll find out soon enough.'

She thrust the paper into Lennie's hands. He pretended to read it for the first time. Under the headline were the words: 'by Steve Lewis.'

Brynpadarn 0, Glanaber Rangers 3

> It sometimes happens that a football match is ruined before it properly gets under way, so that the result is entirely predictable.
>
> So it was at the Town Field last Saturday, when these two old rivals played their eagerly-awaited semi-final tie in the Lloyd-Taylor Charity Cup competition.
>
> Within a few minutes of kick-off, Brynpadarn full-back Ivor Morgan hurled himself into a two-footed tackle on Rangers defender Mike Potts, and was rightly sent packing by referee Hubert Evans.

'It was a reckless foul that could have had the direst consequences for the defender concerned,' said Mr Evans after the match. 'We don't need that sort of thing in this locality, especially in charity competitions of this kind. It's entirely against the spirit of the game.'

Sadly, Morgan – known as one of the most uncompromising of players – compounded his crime by making an obscene gesture to the spectators, and I understand that his conduct will be discussed at the next meeting of the Glanaber and District League Executive Committee, under whose aegis the competition is organised.

Not surprisingly, this unfortunate incident decided the course of the game, the entire pattern of Brynpadarn's play being disrupted and Rangers running out easy winners.

Their first goal was the result of . . .

Lennie looked up, his main feeling one of embarrassment that Ivor should be mentioned at all in the paper.

'Isn't it diabolical?'

Lennie shrugged. 'Don't know what all the words mean.'

'You know enough. That's slander, that's what it is. I've got a good mind to take them to court.'

Lennie didn't quite follow. 'But he *was* sent off, Mam.'

'Who said he wasn't? But all *this*.' Her hand struck the page. 'The referee *saying* things – it's outrageous! And you see who's written it, don't you? You see who's behind it?'

Lennie looked up blankly.

'Oh, never mind! You don't know a thing, do you? Just as well I suppose. Here, give it here.' And she snatched the paper from him.

He put his head in his hands, all the joy gone from the day. Why *was* it like this? Sally in hospital, Mam shouting, Ivor in a bad mood more often than not.

When Dad was alive . . .

But that was so long ago it didn't seem real any more.

He picked up the *Dandy* and turned the pages miserably.

'I've read it,' said Ivor that evening, as they sat on a green bench near the tall castellated tower that had once been the pride of an English king.

'Well,' said Betty, 'what you gonna do? You can't let them reporters say things like that about you. It's not fair.'

She crossed her plump legs, letting her skirt ride up an inch or two.

'I dunno yet. I'll think about it.'

Betty sighed and put the newspaper clipping back in her handbag. He didn't tell her anything, that was the trouble.

She hitched her skirt up another inch, without him noticing.

'What we gonna do tonight then?'

'Haven't got a clue.'

'Can't stay here all night, can we?' she said, giving him a sly look.

'No,' he agreed, not rising to the bait.

She sighed again. Why didn't he say yes, let's stay here all night? It'd be cold up here on the castle grounds, with the wind whipping in from the sea like it always did, but if they cuddled close they'd be warm. She'd put her hand inside his jacket, and he'd wind his arms round her and give her kiss after kiss, and she'd moan like she always did when he got going, and after a while they'd . . .

And why not?

He was being a right old slowcoach. Not at all what she'd been led to expect of Ivor Morgan, who had a bit of a reputation.

Was she to blame? Was there something bad even her best friend wouldn't tell her, like they said in those adverts in the paper?

'Ivor,' she said in a small voice.

'Mm?'

'Is there something about me?'

He was staring out to sea, not listening.

'Ivor,' he said impatiently, 'I'm talking to you.'

'What is it?'

'I said is there something about me?'

'What?' he said blankly.

'You know. Something you can't tell me.'

'What you mean?'

'Oh, you're hopeless!' She pushed her skirt down furiously. Why did she bother?

'What're you talking about, Betty? I don't understand you.'

'No, that's the trouble. You don't understand me one bit.'

'Why, what have I done now?'

'Oh, nothing!' She dabbed her eyes.

'There must be something. What is it?'

'I just asked you a question, that's all.'

'What?'

'If there's something about me – bad breath or something.' There! It was out now.

'Bad breath? What you talking about?'

'Well, what is it then? Why you so –'

Behind the tears, her eyes sparkled. He looked at her strangely.

'What, Betty? Why am I so what?'

'Oh, I don't know. It doesn't matter. Come on, let's go.'

'No.' He put his hand out to stop her. 'I want to know. Please.'

She shrugged.

'What's wrong, Betty?'

She looked at him.

'You don't like me, do you?' she said. 'Not really.'

'Don't be so soft.'

'It's true and you know it.'

'I wouldn't be here, would I? If I didn't.'

'I don't know, I'm sure.'

He started to say something else but stopped.

'Come on, Ivor,' she said wearily. 'It's getting cold. Take me home.'

She stood up.

He sat there a long moment.

'Coming?' she asked.

Slowly they walked down the flight of stone steps from the castle ruins to the prom. His hands were deep in his pockets. When they reached the bottom they paused a moment, looking at one another. Then they resumed their walk, more jerkily this time because, quite casually, he had put his arm around her shoulders.

14

'Will this be enough, d'you reckon?' said Shirley, suddenly anxious.

She looked at the stout, almost opaque flagons of beer and cider lined up on the kitchen table, like a doomed army awaiting the call to action.

'It'll have to be,' said Annette. 'It's too late now.'

'Oh God, I hope so.'

'What're you so worried about? There's enough here to sink the fleet!'

'Do you think so? You don't know them like I do. I think Dennis Rees would get through that lot on his own.'

'Well, if they don't like it they can lump it,' said Annette impatiently. 'Anyway they'll be bringing bottles themselves, won't they?'

'I hope so. That's what we've asked them, isn't it?'

Annette nodded. She wasn't sure now if this flat-warming was a good idea or not. She was feeling a bit guilty about having such a good time, with her father's case coming up soon. She even felt guilty about moving out. And there was something else bothering her, something she dare not talk about with anyone.

'Who'll be first, d'you think – Steve?' asked Shirley provocatively.

'I don't think so for a minute,' retorted Annette, cross with her friend for suggesting it. She knew very well he wouldn't be, so why say it? But then, Shirley was getting very funny about Steve. Every time she mentioned him, there was a strange look in her eye. As if Shirley knew something she didn't. Once or twice, she'd been on the point of saying 'Out with it!' but something stopped her. Next time she'd have it out with her, but not now. Not just before the party.

'Well,' said Shirley bravely. 'In for a penny, in for a pound.' Annette gave her a sharp look but let it pass. It was one of those meaningless remarks she was prone to making.

Ernie Ball was the first to arrive, ringing the doorbell a minute after eight when Shirley wasn't even ready.

'Go and let him in girl, whoever it is,' she panted, squeezing into a new frock which Annette reckoned was a size too small for her. 'Silly bugger, coming so early.'

'We did say eight o'clock start,' said Annette, with a last look in the cracked wardrobe mirror.

'Yes, but everyone knows that means half-past at the earliest. God, this'll kill me! I can hardly breathe!'

Ernie was just raising his hand to ring again when Annette opened the door.

'Hullo Annette,' he boomed. 'Hope I'm not too early.'

'Course not. Come in, Ernie.'

'Ta.' He lumbered in, bulky with goodwill, and stood in the hallway, beaming.

'Here,' he said, handing her a bottle of British sherry like a ticket of admission. 'Thought I'd give you a special treat.'

'Thanks, Ernie,' said Annette, touched by his generosity. She only drank sherry at Christmas but thought she might try a drop of this. 'That's very nice of you.'

'Don't mention it.' His broad, pink face radiated pleasure. 'Well, where do we go then? Lead on.'

'It's up here.' She climbed the stairs, Ernie following.

'Many here yet?'

'No. Actually you're the first.'

'Am I? Well, all the more for me then!' He laughed, filling the stairway with his bonhomie.

In the bedroom, Shirley grimaced. Why the hell had they invited him? But then, Ernie was the sort of person you couldn't leave out. Broad and bluff, known to everyone in the town, he was like a big benevolent family pet.

'How'd you like it here then? Suit you OK?' asked Ernie, taking a glass of Roberts Original Brown Ale from Annette. 'Ta.'

'Yes, fine.'

'Surprised to hear you'd moved out, mind. Thought you'd be too comfy at home.'

'Yes ... well ...' Annette temporised, feeling a stab. 'Got to be independent some time, haven't you? Can't depend on your parents all your life.'

'I dunno. I'm quite happy myself, living at home.' He hesitated, then plunged on. 'Hey, sorry to hear about your Dad, Annette. Hope everything will be OK, you know?'

'Thanks, Ernie.' She felt at once embarrassed and relieved. Trust Ernie to mention the unmentionable! But she was glad in a way because everyone else skated round the subject, as if her father were himself a fatal disease, too dangerous to talk about.

'Can you open this for me, please?' she appealed, holding out the sherry bottle. 'I'm not sure I can manage it.'

160

'Aye, of course!' He leapt up, eager to please.

By the time Shirley showed her face, two others had arrived, Paul and Sandra, recently married and still self-conscious about it. Sandra kept twiddling with her wedding ring as if it might vanish any minute, while Paul had a nervous attentiveness towards her, as if on probation as a husband.

Shirley, her nerve about to crack, shot desperate glances at Annette and drank two glasses of cider very quickly.

Relief came in the shape of Dai Flat, a student who flung his arms around Shirley in the front doorway and kissed her neck with Dracula abandon.

'Stop it, Dai, for God's sake!' she squealed ecstatically. 'Where'd you think you are?'

'I know where I'd like to be,' he replied, 'and that's not in the kitchen.'

'Go on, you.' She punched his arm playfully. 'We're all upstairs.'

'Great! My luck's in!'

'It's where we live, Dai.'

'Oh, is it? Pity.'

He hadn't brought a bottle, but then he never did. Dai traded on student poverty as he traded on the mischievous charm that allowed him to say things others daren't.

Dennis Rees more than made up for Dai's lapse by bringing a flagon of mild and a bottle of Blue Nun. 'Bloody lovely, if you'll excuse my French. You tried it?'

'No, don't think I have,' said Shirley. 'I haven't drunk much wine, to tell you the truth.'

'Don't know what you're missing, girl.' Dark-eyed, swarthy, he was in his late twenties, older than most of her friends and all the more attractive for that. Not short of a bob or two either; he worked in the Midland Bank.

He poured out two glassfuls and they faced each other, drinking them, Shirley soon melting into what Annette thought of as her Mata Hari mould, the mysterious and enigmatic woman who would in time be transformed into the giggling and shrieking drunk.

It was well past nine now; where was Steve?

Sara sighed. 'That's better. Thanks, Gerry.'

She handed the cup back to Steve.

'I was parched. Dry as the bloody Sahara.'

'Want some more?'

She shook her head. Sweat freckled her brow. Propped up on pillows, eyes closed, she lay still, her arms resting on the faded counterpane. Her breast rose and fell gently, the only obvious movement in her body. Watching it, all desire for her washed away by her illness, Steve felt a tenderness for her he would not have thought possible.

The air in the bedroom was impure, tainted not simply with her sickness but with all that had happened there. He had been part of it, a small part, along with many others. How many? He neither knew nor cared, for he was not in love with this woman. Yet she mattered to him, in a way he could not have described. He had felt a compulsion to come and see her, on his way to the flat-warming, and had found her like this. Vi had let him in before sidling out, saying she was going to her friend's, and Sara had been too weak to argue, even if she had been so inclined.

He had filled a cup with water from the scullery tap and taken it to her, the only offering he could make.

'You ought to see a doctor,' he said.

It seemed she had not heard him, until: 'Whassat?' she breathed stickily.

'I said get a doctor. You need one.'

'I don't need no doctor, lad,' she retorted, eyes feverish-red. 'Only time I want a doctor, when I'm dead and gone. Don't trust the buggers. Have me up the Union soon as look at me.' The old name for the workhouse still persisted, though it had long been converted into Glanaber General Hospital.

'But you're ill.'

'So's my fanny. Doesn't mean to say I need some clever dick squinting at it.'

Did she mean it, or was it just a figure of speech? Startled, he had visions of VD clinics, rotting noses and ears, madhouses, shame.

'Only joking.' She smiled wanly. 'Clean as a whistle, me. Only let gentlemen do it. Not any old ratbag.'

He found himself taking her hand, in relief and contentment. He liked being with her, for there were things in her to which his soul reached out. She settled again into a shallow sleep and, not wanting to disturb her, he resisted the temptation to turn his wrist around to look at his watch.

He would have to be leaving soon. But not yet.

The front door opened, a voice called, 'Sara?'

'Up here, Beryl,' she croaked, instantly awake.

'Who you got up there, your fancy man?'

'No, just a friend. Best be going,' she said softly, releasing his hand. 'Go on.'

He stood up, feeling helpless. A peroxide blonde breezed in, looking Steve sharply up and down.

'Hello, who's this then? One of your regulars?'

'Bugger off Beryl, he's young enough to be my boy.'

'You can say that again. Just out of nappies by the look of him. What you doing here then son, bit young for her aren't you?'

'I told you, Beryl – '

'I just came to see how she is,' said Steve. 'I heard she wasn't well.'

'How'd you hear that then son, read it in the paper, did you? Hey, wait a minute. Seen you somewhere before, haven't I? Yeah, you're that reporter bloke who come to Stan's funeral, aren't you? What you doing here then, eh? What's she to you?'

'Leave him alone. I told you, he's just a friend.'

'Friend? That's what you call it now, is it? Think me green?' The red slash of her mouth curved in mockery. 'Bet you got lost inside her, didn't you, son? Started yelling for your mam, thinking you was in a tunnel!'

'That's enough of that, Beryl. For Chrissake go, Gerry. You can see what she's like.'

'Yeah, I can see what he's like too. Filthy devil.'

'I'll be seeing you then,' said Steve, trying to ignore her.

'Yeah, don't worry 'bout me. I'll be OK,' said Sara.

'Dirty swine. Go back home to your mother!'

Beryl's invective followed him downstairs and out of the front door. On the pavement opposite, a small group of neighbours stared at him as he hurried away. Raucous laughter taunted him as he climbed the stone steps to Shipwrights Road. Never had he felt so ashamed, never so vulnerable.

'Steve-o!' cried Shirley. 'Where've you been, boy? Annette's been looking for you. Under the table, everywhere.'

'I had a job on. Kept me late.'

'Well, go on up. Follow the din, you'll find out soon enough.'

A slab of noise hit Steve as he reached the landing. Shrieks of laughter, loud voices, Billy Eckstine booming 'Taking A Chance on Love' full-blast. There was only one thing to do, arriving cold sober like this. Elbow your way through to the drinks, grab a glass, fill it with anything going, get smashed as fast as you could.

He pretended not to see Annette, staring coldly at him across the maelstrom.

He ignored Ernie Ball, silly fool, ducked away from Penny Gibson, boring bitch, joined Dennis Rees and Mal Hughes, who were at least tolerable. Why the hell had he come here? He just wasn't in the mood.

Damn. He was stuck here now, good and proper.

'And this stupid idiot said – you know what he said? Oops, sorry.' Dennis, theatrically gesturing, caught someone's elbow, a spillage of Babycham cascading on to the soiled carpet.

Mal, glazed of eye, not noticing, waited for the punchline.

'He said – hey, watch it!'

A bull of a man, stepping suddenly backwards, barged into Dennis, his glass of Roberts Bitter emptying on to his shirtfront.

'For Christ's sake!' cried Dennis, pushing the bull away. 'Look what you've done, you stupid sod.'

'I'm not stupid, who're you calling stupid?' Vernon Pott, huge, menacing, stared down at Dennis.

'Well, can't you be more careful?' Dennis, mopping up with white handkerchief, struck a marginally more emollient note.

'I'll be as careful as I like, mate. And I won't ask your permission neither, right?' He grabbed Dennis by the lapels, heaving him on to his toes. 'And just one thing, arsehole. Don't call me a sod unless you want your face out the back of your head. Understand?' Glaring, he let Dennis go, then elbowed him aside.

'Big show-off. Take no notice.' Ena Parry, small breasts fetchingly outlined by revealing silver bodice, sidled up to Dennis. 'He always gets like this,' she consolingly offered. 'Too big for his boots, that's the trouble with him.'

Steve edged away, only to end up within range of Annette.

'Do you know the time?' she snapped. 'Where've you been?'

'Sorry. Had a job.'

'What? On a Saturday night?'

'Well, you know what it's like. Ronnie rang up. Bit of linage for the nationals. Couldn't refuse.'

'Could have let me know, couldn't you?'

'How could I? You're not on the phone.'

'You could've called round. Pushed a note through the door.'

'No time, Annette. Didn't know myself till five o'clock. Bloody nuisance. Had to go all the way to – '

'I don't want to know. I don't believe you.'

'What?'

'You heard. I don't believe you. You're lying.'

'Lying! Me!'

'Yes you, little Lord Fauntleroy. Don't make out your Mr Perfect. I'll – '

Catapulted forward by a rush of human bodies, her head knocked Steve's cheek. Stumbling back, he fell over a chair, sprawling tipsily to the floor. Her shiny black shoes seemed ominously close as he wheeled around, trying to pull himself to his feet.

A blast of whistles signalled the arrival of two burly constables. Shouting commands, they forced their way through the melee. Only the record player continued to bawl until, suddenly, that too was silenced.

'Now would you kindly leave in an orderly manner,' commanded PC Thomas, famous for his Laurence Olivier-like presence in the witness box. 'And don't make any noise outside, or you'll get something you're not expecting.'

'Are you threatening me, officer?' a thin youth piped up.

'No sir, I'm not threatening anyone. I'm just doing my duty.'

'It's a private party, dammit.'

'We've had complaints about noise and a disturbance of the peace,' said the constable calmly. 'And if you have any questions, I suggest you ask your father.'

A mock cheer from Dennis, who knew the whippersnapper to be the son of a beak.

'And now, if you please, I'd like a word with whoever organised this shindig.' He glowered impressively.

'Don't worry,' Steve whispered to a white-faced Annette. 'I know him. He's all talk.'

'Dad'll kill me,' she murmured. 'Oh God.'

PC Thomas lumbered up, winked at Steve. 'Press here too, eh? Front page next week, is it?'

'Not quite.'

'Oh, thought it was for a minute. You the tenant, miss?' Annette nodded. 'Just a quiet word when they've all gone. God, it's hot in here. Can't you open them windows?'

The flat, emptying, was suddenly no more than a huge dustbin of dregs and dogends and party detritus.

The constables sat down heavily, their helmets perched on their knees.

'Just one or two things, if you don't mind, miss,' PC Thomas began.

Having said their piece, at great length and with infinite satisfaction, they took off into the night.

Annette silently wept. Shirley flopped down, exhausted.

'Get me a Scotch, Steve, for Godsake,' she said. 'Kitchen cabinet. By the sink.'

Tired to the bone, he swilled a glass under the kitchen tap and sloshed some whisky into it. He didn't pour any for Annette. She'd had enough to drink already. So had Shirley, come to that, but he didn't care too much about Shirley. He was sure she was a bad influence on Annette; the whole evening had been a mistake. All those freeloaders and poseurs, the very worst that Glanaber youth could offer! He wouldn't give tuppence for the lot of them.

He debated giving Shirley the Scotch straight, but relented and topped it up with a little tap water. If she got more drunk, she'd only puke over him probably. Not that he'd be staying long; he'd had enough. He should never have gone there from Sara's; Annette was in a vile mood anyway. Was she at all suspicious? In his heart he knew that nothing remained secret for ever in Glanaber, but for the moment it suited him to ignore this. Yet there was a fear in his stomach that had not been there before; the taunts of the peroxide blonde made it clear he'd been rumbled.

He took the Scotch into the living-room. 'Here you – ' he began, then stopped. Both the girls had dropped precipitately into sleep. Shirley was snoring, her mouth open.

Steve allowed himself a momentary sense of superiority. Then he tipped the Scotch ceremonially into the aspidistra pot by the window, and left.

Part Four

BLACK COTTON

15

'Can I come with you?' asked Lennie.

'No,' replied Ivor.

'Why not?'

'You know why. You might catch it.'

Lennie scuffed his shoe on the garden path, frowning. He knew TB was catching, because everyone said so. But Sally was his sister, and he wanted to see her. She'd been in the San for ages, and he missed her: terribly, sometimes. Mostly he'd got used to it, or pretended he had, but then a feeling washed over him and he wanted to cry.

And there was another thing. They'd lied to him. They'd told him she'd be home in six months. Now it was nine months, nearly. It wasn't fair. They were treating him like a kid.

'You're treating me like a kid,' he complained.

Ivor scuffed his hair, laughing. 'What d'you think you are then, old man?'

'Geroff,' cried Lennie, pretending to be annoyed but loving it. If anything happened to Ivor . . . Tears started in his eyes and he ran to the end of the garden to stare unseeingly at the chickens clucking and squawking in the fenced-off enclosure.

He heard Ivor come up behind him but stayed where he was, unmoving.

'Look,' said Ivor gently. 'I'd take you if it was up to me. But Mam says no. She doesn't want you to. She's afraid.'

'Of what?'

'You catching it, of course. It's a terrible thing, Lennie. You don't want to be ill, do you?'

The boy shrugged.

Ivor put a hand on his shoulder.

'I'll make you a promise,' he said. 'When she's up and about, I'll take you to see her. She'll be able to go for walks then – you can go with her.'

Lennie said nothing. A huge question formed in his brain but got stuck there.

'OK then, kid?' Ivor gave his shoulder a squeeze.

Suddenly, out it came. 'She isn't going to *die* in there, is she?'

Ivor took his hand away. The brothers stood side by side.

'No,' said Ivor at last. 'I don't think so.'

Lennie looked up. He would never forget the look on Ivor's face. Nor the feeling he had: that at last he was being treated like a grown-up.

He looked back at the chickens scrabbling at the earth, fussing and crooning and cluck-clucking like the daft things they were.

'OK then,' he said.

On Sunday mornings, the bus left at ten-thirty. Ivor was there early, waiting at the stop by the station. His old school was just down the road, Alexandra Road Boys', now *Ysgol Gymraeg*, one of the new-fangled schools where everyone was taught in Welsh instead of English. It would have made no difference to him, he reflected, without self-pity: he'd been a dunce, only good with his hands, hadn't even bothered to sit the scholarship at eleven. He knew he'd fail it, so what was the point?

He felt sorry for them, truth to say, those boys and girls going up to the County School, the place for bright kids. They had to wear silly caps on their heads, and green uniforms that looked as though somebody'd been sick on them. And they had piles of homework, like Lennie. He'd been much better off, leaving school at fourteen and making money. And he loved carpentry, shaping things and feeling them fit snugly into joints. That was something real, not like adding up rows of figures and writing daft things about what you did on holiday and getting your brain in a twist with stupid problems about if A had six apples and B four bananas, how many oranges would be left if . . . ? Anyway you hadn't been able to get bananas for love or money then, that's how barmy the whole thing had been.

Yes, he'd loved carpentry. Then. Now he wasn't so sure. He didn't like anything much. Least of all Sally being so ill.

The empty bus trundled up to the stop and they piled in.

'Late last night, weren't we?'

Edna Lewis, thin-lipped, gave her son a small, poisonous smile.

Steve crunched his toast.

His mother sat opposite, tried again.

'I heard you come in. Your father didn't. He was out for the count alright.'

Steve's head thumped, his mouth felt like the inside of a bran tub.

'At Annette's, were we?'

The 'we' scalded Steve. Who did she think she was, Queen Victoria? Two pressure points, one each side of his skull, throbbed with tension.

'Lost your tongue, Steve?' she asked icily.

'Mam,' he said thickly, 'I don't feel very well.'

'And whose fault is that?'

'Please, Mam. Not now.'

She looked at him, gathering her forces, deciding strategy.

'Not now. Not any time,' she murmured. 'That's it, isn't it?'

Steve sighed, put his hand to his head.

'How's she getting on these days? In her new flat?'

'Alright.'

'Must be funny for her. Living on the prom like that. After Penbryn.'

'They like it.'

'Ah yes. They. That girl Shirley.'

She dropped the name, disapprovingly, into the cold Sunday morning breakfast room.

'Strange thing to do, Steve, if you don't mind me saying. Leaving her parents like that. When her father's in such trouble.'

'Leave it, Mam.'

'I thought she'd be more – concerned. She's such a warm-hearted girl, isn't she?'

The bait plopped invitingly into the water.

'When's the case coming up?' she asked.

'I don't know.'

'Can't be long now, can it?'

'Probably not.'

'Will you be reporting it?'

'Good God, no!'

Edna frowned at the blasphemy.

'Someone else can do that,' added Steve.

'Pick and choose then, do you? Must be quite important on that paper, son.'

He drank his coffee, quickly.

'Was she in here?' asked Edna suddenly.

'What?'

'When we were away for the weekend. Did you bring her back here?'

'What if I did? No harm in it, is there?'

'That depends, son.'

'What do you mean?'

'You know very well.'

'If you're suggesting – '

'I'm not suggesting anything. I wouldn't dare. She's a nice girl, isn't she?'

Her eyes hooked into his. He saw something in them that held him.

'You've got your life ahead of you, Steve,' she said softly. 'Don't want to be stuck, do you? Like I was.'

Had he heard those last words, or imagined them?

Suddenly he was alone, staring at the empty space opposite.

He stood in the doorway a moment, as if afraid to step in. She was lying on her side dozing, but opened her eyes suddenly, then smiled, beatifically.

'Ivor!'

'Alright, Sal?'

'Oh, it's so good to see you!'

She sat up, raising her arms in welcome.

'Good to see you too, Sal.' He kissed her cheek awkwardly then stepped back, frowning down at the steeply tilted bed.

'What's all this in aid of then? You've got half a forest under your bed, mun.'

'Oh, don't worry about that. They're to help me get better.'

'Can't see how. Not very comfy is it, lying like that all the time?'

'It's alright, honestly. You get used to it after a while.'

'Don't think I could. Anyway, how are you feeling?'

'Much better now, thanks.'

He looked at her dubiously, pulled up a chair.

'Brought some things for you to read.'

He handed her the magazines: *Woman's Own*, *Picture Post* and *Illustrated*.

'Oh, Ivor, you shouldn't. Spending all your money.'

'Go on, enjoy them. Haven't read them, have you?'

'No,' she said, lying, for she had the *Picture Post* in her locker, thankfully out of sight.

'There you are then.'

He was shocked by the change in her. When he'd seen her last, in the ward with the three other women, she hadn't looked too bad. He'd wondered, then, why they were keeping her in here so long. Why not get her on her feet, send her home? Now there were bright crimson spots in her pinched cheeks, a look of sickness about her that had not been there before. This whole block she was on too, Powys Block so-called, had a smell and a feel to it that made him think of graveyards and wreaths. He felt uneasy and nervous; he wanted to get out and run miles.

'What's all your news then?' asked Sally brightly. 'How's the football?'

'OK. We're in the final. Playing Borth.'

'Great! When's that then?'

'Next Saturday.' He didn't tell her that he wouldn't be playing; that he was in disgrace.

She smiled at him. They'd always been close, she and Ivor. Ever since they'd been kids.

She remembered much the same things as he did, but in a different way. And some of the things he remembered best of all she had entirely forgotten.

'Lennie sends his love,' he said, as the time approached when he should be leaving. 'He wanted to come with me.'

'Bless him. And Megan?'

'Crazy about dancing. As usual.'

She looked away, seeing them all clearly. Mam, Ivor, Lennie, Megan, bustling about the house where she still lived in her imagination.

She kept her eyes turned to the window, for suddenly they were filled with tears.

'Sorry I haven't been to see you much,' Ivor said awkwardly. 'I mean, not as often as I should have, like.'

'Oh, Ivor,' she said, turning, not caring about the tears. 'You've got your own life to lead. You mustn't bother with me.'

'Bother with you?' His voice cracked. 'Don't be daft, mun.'

She reached out a hand. He gripped it tightly.

'You're going to get better, Sal,' he whispered. 'I know it. You're *going* to get *better*.'

She pursed her lips, unable to speak. Her eyes said everything.

'When you get home . . . yes?' He paused, not knowing quite what he was saying.

She gazed into his eyes, holding on to his hand as if to life itself.

'We'll . . .,' he said, and could not go any further. Tears ran down his cheeks, but no sound escaped him.

At last their grip slackened. She turned away, looking up at the ceiling.

'Anything you want, Sal? I mean, can I send you anything?'

She shook her head. 'Just bring yourself,' she said. 'When you can.'

He nodded, not trusting himself to say any more.

'I'm tired now,' she said softly. 'See you again soon, OK?'

He nodded, choked. Quickly he pecked her cheek, left the cubicle, and was gone.

16

'What's wrong, 'Nette?' asked Rita.

'Nothing. Why?'

'You look like death.'

'Do I? Fancy that.'

Annette whipped the cover off her typewriter, screwed a piece of stationery into position, glared at her notepad and began typing.

Rita sighed. She didn't know what had come over her. Ever since she'd moved in with that mad-hatter Shirley . . .

Big Bertha emerged from her morning consultation with old Richards the senior partner. She paused, hand still on the doorknob, scrutinising Annette with a lethal half-smile.

'So,' she said. 'You've made it after all, then.'

Annette ignored her. Rita coughed anxiously.

'I'm talking to you, Annette.'

'Yes?'

'I said you've made it. To the office.'

'Why shouldn't I? It's Monday morning, isn't it?'

'I'm perfectly well aware of that.' Magisterially she took her place at the desk placed right outside Mr Richards's door, as befitted the rank she assumed for herself. 'But we weren't sure if you'd be in a fit state to come in or not.'

'Oh? Who's 'we' exactly?'

Big Bertha flushed. 'Mr Richards and myself, of

course. And don't take on that tone of voice with *me*, my girl.'

Annette looked at her coolly, the original ice maiden. Rita glanced from one to the other, transfixed.

'May I ask what you're talking about?' said Annette.

'You know very well. That – that – *outrage* on Saturday night.'

'Do you mean our flat-warming?'

'Flat-warming! That's what you call it, is it? More like a riot, from what I've been hearing. They say you could hear the noise half a mile away.'

'I wasn't aware that you lived down there, Mrs Bevan?'

'I don't, thank goodness. Or I'd soon have put a stop to it, don't you worry. I'd have called the police a lot sooner.'

'The police?' said Rita, goggle-eyed.

'Oh, don't listen to her,' said Annette impatiently. 'You know what they're like round here.'

'Yes, indeed we do,' spat out Big Bertha. 'Thieves and robbers!'

'What?' Annette, rigid, stared at her. 'What did you say?'

Big Bertha, realising she had gone too far, breathed heavily, not replying.

'Are you calling me a thief?' persisted Annette.

'Not you, no.'

'Who then?'

The door to the inner sanctum was flung open and Mr Richards stood there, glowering. Tall, dark-suited, pulpit-mannered, his presence filled the room.

'What's the matter with you all? It's like a bear garden out here.'

'I'm sorry, Mr Richards,' fawned Big Bertha. Rita thrust her face into a file.

Annette met his eyes steadily. He hesitated, then slowly closed the door.

A few seconds of utter silence followed. Then Big Bertha came to life, picked up the phone, dialled a number.

'Richards and James Solicitors here,' she intoned. 'May I talk to Mr Peregrine please?'

Annette began typing a letter. Rita stared at her wonderingly.

Bill Merrick strode into the reporters' room, hung up his mac, put his fly-fisherman's hat on a peg.

'There's someone downstairs to see you, Stephen,' he said.

'Who is it?' asked Steve, fearing that Sara Baker had come round the office.

'Search me,' said Bill indifferently, flopping his notebook down on the table. 'Bit of a wide boy, by the look of him.'

'Why didn't you ask him up?'

'I didn't know if you wanted to see him, did I? He's down in the Small Ads, if you're interested.'

The stranger had his back turned, flicking through the file of back numbers.

'Can I help you?' Steve asked politely.

'I don't know about that,' the man drawled, turning. 'Depends who the hell you are, doesn't it?'

'Brian!' They pumped each other's arms, delighted. 'Good God, great to see you again!'

'Same to you, pal.' Brian Tate, tall, dark-haired, lugubrious, seemed to fill the small space where the customers came to place their ads.

'What on earth are you doing here?'

'What are *you* doing, more's the point. Fancy a coffee?'

'Yes, hang on a minute, I'll just go and tell them upstairs.'

Behind the counter Arnold Lucas, advertisement manager, distastefully eyed the two friends. He had little time for journalists, who seemed to come and go as they pleased. He worked strict office hours, nine to five-thirty, and believed people bought the paper for the adverts, not the so-called news. If he'd had his way, the entire paper would be filled with honest, decent ads, not flim-flam about football and silly news items and court reports of goings-on not fit to print, in his opinion.

He managed to ignore the stranger in the short interval before Steve's return.

'I've got 20 minutes,' said Steve.

'Wow. Can they spare it?'

'There's a coffee bar just down the road,' said Steve, as they stepped into the street. 'Nothing great, but it'll do.'

'Surprised there's one here at all. Thought you'd all be drinking woad or something.'

'You don't drink woad. You slap it on your body.'

'I'll take your word for it, son.'

Steve could forgive Brian the clichéd English humour because he knew it was not meant unkindly. They had been friends since their schooldays, when they had found themselves in the sixth form of Cowbridge Grammar School together. Brian had fitted in well with the snottier element in a school which liked to think it stood for eternal verities in a rapidly changing world. He had played the insolent Englishman to perfection, enjoying the hatred he aroused in those who did not see it was simply a game, the self-protective shield of a boy who did not know quite where he stood in a Welsh context. Steve had sussed it out quickly and made friends with the aloof stranger, not caring what anyone thought. Brian had been there only a year before his engineer father moved back to England, leaving a gap in Steve's life.

The Chelsea Cafe was neither as large nor as popular as The Pelican. It stood between the Bon-Bon sweet shop and Daniel's Gents' Outfitters, cultivating a quasi-metropolitan ambience with blown-up photographs of London Bridge and Nelson's Column and the Houses of Parliament. It courted a young clientele of the more ambitious souls in Glanaber, those who might cast envious eyes at the passers-by in the photographs and harbour hopes, however faint, of emulating them.

Brian was predictably amused by it all.

'Where'd they think this is, Oxford Circus?'

'I thought you'd approve, English git that you are.'

'I think it's pathetic.'

The coffee was less frothy than The Pelican's but cost a penny more, sixpence instead of fivepence. It was brought to the table by a busty waitress whom Brian eyed appreciatively.

'Got some talent here, I see,' he said, licking his spoon. 'Even if there's none on the local rag.'

'You keep your eyes off her. She's married to a local bruiser.'

'Of which there are many, I'm sure. All neolithic with an IQ of twelve.'

'Six, actually. Well, tell me what's happening. You on a job here or something?'

'Spare me. What could possibly be of interest round here?'

'That wench for a start. So what are you doing?'

'Actually I'm on holiday.'

'You've come on holiday – here?'

'Only passing through, old chap. Don't get excited. We're touring this wretched country of yours, if you really want to know.'

'We?'

'Margaret and I.'

'Who's Margaret?'

'My wife, you moron.'

'You're *married*?'

'Don't be so surprised. I'm entitled to, you know.'

'Why didn't you tell me?'

'Why should I? You'd only have turned up with your putrid Welsh ways and ruined everything.'

'Well, where is she now?' Steve was hurt, that he hadn't been told, but tried not to show it.

'Doing some shopping. If she can find anything worth buying in this godforsaken hole, which I doubt.'

Brian seemed uncomfortable, so Steve changed the subject.

'Anyway, how's life on the *Sketch*? Crappy paper, isn't it?'

'Not in the same league as the *County Dispatch*, I grant you. The only difference is, we sell a million more copies. At a rough guess.'

'Why don't you join a decent paper?'

'Meaning?'

'Well – the *Manchester Guardian*.'

Brian gave a good impression of a hollow laugh. 'I'd rather not work for a kept woman, thank you. It would've gone under years ago if it wasn't for the M.E.N.'

'M.E.N.?'

'*Manchester Evening News*, ignoramus.'

'Well, it's a better paper than the *Sketch*, you have to admit.'

'Depends how you look at it. I'm quite happy, thank you. Anyway, you're a fine one to talk. Working for a crap weekly in a dead-end dump.'

Steve flinched. 'I won't be here for ever.'

'Won't you? You will if you're not careful.'

'What d'you mean by that?'

'Well, how old are you now?'

'Twenty-three.'

'Better wake up then. If you're not in The Street by twenty-five you've had it.'

Steve fell silent, all too sure Brian was right.

'Don't look like that,' Brian said, relenting. 'I can put some feelers out for you if you like.'

'Could you?' asked Steve eagerly.

'Might not come to anything. But I don't mind trying.'

'Where've you got in mind?'

'Not the *Manchester Guardian*, that's for sure.' A smile flickered. 'Just another provincial, isn't it?'

'*The News Chronicle*?'

'*News Chronicle*,' groaned Brian. 'What would you want to go there for?'

'It's a good paper.'

'Good for wrapping chocolate bars in, that's about all. If the Cadburys pulled their money out it'd go under. Join a decent paper, son, if you're going to move at all.'

'Where then?'

'Fancy the *Daily Mail*?'

Steve frowned. 'It's a Tory rag.'

'Well, so what? Most of them are, Christ! Anyone'd think you were doing them a favour. Chances are you'll still be knocking out lists of mourners when you're forty.'

Steve thought so too, in his more depressed moments.

'Do what you can then, will you? I've *got* to leave here soon.'

'You're not kidding.'

He met Brian's wife before he returned to the office. She was dark, good-looking in a sullen way, and very pregnant.

'Thanks for looking me up then,' said Steve. 'It's great to see you both.'

Margaret offered a small, tense smile. Steve caught, for a moment, Brian's unguarded expression.

'Do your best then,' he said heartily. 'Keep in touch.'

Lost for words for a moment, Brian raised a hand. Steve ducked his head and hurried away, the sight of the doomed couple impressed forever on his mind.

But Brian had got there, that was the thing. He'd made it to Fleet Street before getting her up the bung!

If he didn't do the same . . .

He couldn't bear to think of it.

17

There were times, in the early hours of the morning, when Ted Morris thought he could hear Annette move around in her bedroom. It was still Annette's room to them both, though she had been gone now for several weeks. There was not a moment when he did not blame himself for losing her: oh, the stupidity of his thieving, and all to pay his debts to that vulture Don Tremlett the bookie!

He knew he wouldn't get away with it, but what else could he do? Don was at him every day, cornering him on his postman's round, the sly word in his ear, the threats that had seemed empty at first, then the blackmail. 'Lorna wouldn't like to know about that little tart of yours, would she, Ted? Break her little heart it would, thinks you're the cat's whiskers, don't she? Never mind Ted, give me ten bob next Friday and we won't say a word, oh no, no-one can say Don Tremlett's a hard man...' All uttered in that soft Cornish accent of his, devil that he was. Why hadn't he stayed where he belonged instead of coming to plague them all here?

Of course, he could have gone to the police. Don was running an illegal business. But how could he have done that without revealing his sneaky visits to the woman in Back Row? Word would have got back to Lorna, and that would have been the ruin of everything. Now she suspected nothing, and was standing by him. She'd known about his gambling, and made allowances for it, but allowances for a bit on the side? He'd rather go to jail than let that out; he simply couldn't do it.

And now the time had come to face the music.

'Well?' said Lorna bravely. 'Ready?'

She stood before him in Sunday best, feet firmly planted, holding her brown handbag in front of her with both hands, as if for protection.

'Suppose so,' said Ted.

He attempted to smile but his mouth got stuck in a grimace.

'Oh Ted,' she said, her voice breaking. 'What they gonna do to you, love?'

'I dunno. Fine me, maybe.'

But he feared the worst. Postmen who stole went over the wall; he knew it.

'They're not gonna send you to Swansea, are they? I couldn't stand that.'

'Nah. Won't do that. Don't worry.'

It had seemed so easy at first, nicking a few letters. It was amazing what people put in them; uncrossed postal orders, ten shilling notes. Even pound notes. They sent them to pay bills, or slipped them in with birthday cards. Crazy.

He thought he'd been clever, but had done it once too often. He remembered, with shame, the interview with his supervisor, John Bowen: a nice man.

'Why'd you do it, Ted? Bad debts or something?'

Ted shook his head. But the young solicitor had got it out of him.

'Gambling,' he said thoughtfully. 'Got a chance there. An outside one, but a chance. Won't get your job back, of course, but it may save you from prison. Don't bank on it, though.'

He'd asked him about Tremlett. 'How long's he been running this business?'

'I don't want to say nothing,' said Ted. 'He'd have my guts for garters.'

'You've got to, man. It's your duty – to yourself, if no-one else.'

Ted shook his head miserably. But it had come out all the same. Don was for the high jump; as if the cops hadn't known about it for years, and turned a blind eye.

What mustn't come out was his visits to the woman.

Lorna entered the courtroom stiffly, looking straight ahead. She had no idea what to expect nor what was expected of her. For all she knew, Ted would be put in handcuffs and led away any minute.

Instead he sat beside her, eyelids flickering, mouth twitching. The young solicitor, Roberts, came across to them, beaming encouragement. He had a few words with Ted and tried to engage Lorna in conversation. Distrusting him, she made little response and he rejoined the other solicitors at the front of the court. Amicably they all chatted together, as if in a private club where only they were the members.

'Silence in court! Stand please!' barked a burly police sergeant. Ted scrambled to his feet like all the rest, feeling weak and helpless. The magistrates filed in, two men and a woman. Mrs Doctor Rees, smartly-dressed in dove-grey suit, a county councillor and public figure to her fingertips, took the chairman's seat with a male colleague on either side.

They looked dauntingly severe and respectable. Ted knew he was for it before the case even began.

'We'll have to plead guilty,' Roberts had said, as if he himself had opened the mail as well as Ted. 'No point in doing otherwise. But I'll plead extenuation.'

The long words had wearied Ted; it all seemed little to do with him.

He stood in the dock. The top of his thighs would not stop trembling.

'Do you plead guilty or not guilty?'

'Guilty.'

The clerk of the court sat down with a bored expression. Ted felt Mrs Doctor Rees's eyes on him but he could not meet hers.

'You may sit down,' she said clearly. Ted sat, a policeman at his side.

The words droned on; strangely, he began to feel sleepy. His head ached slightly, his mouth was dry. And out of nowhere came a picture of his old headmaster, Mr Jenkins, swinging a cane in his hand. They had all been terrified of his tall, lean figure, and of the way the cane whipped down on the outstretched hand of his victim. It left the hand cut and bruised, incapable of anything for hours. Ted almost swooned; he gripped his chair tightly.

Dimly he was aware of young Roberts's voice, straining higher and ever higher. What was he saying? He caught only disconnected words which hardly made any sense. Suddenly the policeman was prodding him. 'Get to your feet, man,' he hissed. Ted stumbled up, holding the rail of the dock to stop himself falling.

'Mr Morris,' Mrs Doctor Rees was saying. 'We've listened carefully to what Mr Roberts has to say on your behalf. Is there anything you'd like to add?'

He shook his head.

'Very well then. We shall adjourn to make our decision.'

'All stand please!' bawled the sergeant, and the trio of justices went through the door behind the bench.

'You can sit down now,' said the policeman, tugging at Ted's jacket. He did so and sat immobile, shielding his eyes with his hand. 'Like a mint?' asked the policeman gently. For the first time Ted looked at him properly and saw it was Hugh Price, son of Dai Price the butcher. 'Thanks,' smiled Ted, taking one. But he could not look around as the professionals' chatter resumed. He slumped again, closing his eyes. Until the door opened again and he knew his moment had come.

He barely heard the words 'six months' imprisonment' because already he had fainted.

Bill Merrick strode into the reporters' room, slung his notebook on the table, avoided Steve's enquiring gaze, slipped into Ronnie's office.

'Well?' said Steve when he emerged after a minute or two. 'What happened?'

'Six months,' replied Bill, unconcerned.

'Christ.'

'Didn't expect anything less, did you?'

'I didn't know what to expect,' said Steve hotly. His temper raged up, his fists longed to punch Bill on his thin, grudging nose.

Ronnie padded across. 'Take it easy, boys. I feel sorry for him, mind. Poor bugger. Lot more to it than came out in court, I'd say.'

Bill coolly lit a cigarette, twitched out the match. 'There've been rumours,' he said levelly.

Ronnie suddenly found an interesting story on the front page of that morning's *Western Mail*, spread out on the table.

'What rumours?' asked Steve tightly.

Bill gave him a glance. 'You don't know?'

'No, I don't.'

'I'm surprised.'

'Why? What are these rumours, then?'

Bill took a long drag, blew out a long jet-trail of smoke.

'They concern a Mrs Sara Baker,' he said.

Steve felt a flush coming to his cheeks and forced it back, with all his strength.

'You know her, don't you?' said Bill, looking at him directly.

'Not really. I just did a story about her, that's all.'

'Of course!' Bill snapped his fingers theatrically. 'Good story it was too, wasn't it, Ronnie? Wanted a council house, from what I can remember.'

Ronnie, engrossed in the *Western Mail*, said nothing.

'What's she got to do with Ted Morris?' Steve managed to ask.

'Ah. Well may you ask.'

Bill flicked his notebook open, grooved a page of paper into his typewriter.

'I'm going out for ten minutes,' said Ronnie. 'Got some shopping to do.' He prowled back to his cubbyhole.

Bill, eyes on his notebook, began touch-typing.

'I've asked you a question,' said Steve.

Bill stopped. 'There are ladies present.'

Brenda, white-faced, said in a low voice, 'Don't mind me.'

'You really want to know, do you?' asked Bill.

'Yes, I do,' said Steve.

'He's been seeing her. Professionally, you might say.'

The blush, breaking free, flooded Steve's face. 'You bloody liar,' he said.

'Don't you call me that, you little worm.'

'I'll call you what I like. Ted would never do a thing like that.'

'Oh, wouldn't he? Wouldn't he? You wouldn't either, I don't suppose. Would you?'

'What? You –,' Steve flung himself at Bill, pressing his hands deep into his shoulders, squeezing him.

'Get *off* you swine!'

Bill tried to shove Steve away but his chair toppled back so that the two men sprawled on the floor. Brenda screamed.

'Jesus Christ.' Ronnie scampered about ineffectually. 'Break it up, boys, no sense in this.'

'What's up mister?' cried Scoop Matthews innocently from his corner, newly aware of the rumpus.

'Little bastard,' said Bill shakily, scrambling to his feet. 'Sorry, Brenda. His fault, filthy swine that he is.'

The door of the reporters' room opened. Gwyn Meredith, editor, éminence grise, rarely seen, stood there towering like a prophet.

'What on earth is happening?' he gloomed slowly. 'Merrick? Lewis?'

Bill's hands fluttered. 'I'm sorry, sir,' he fawned. 'I was attacked.'

'Attacked?' Meredith frowned. 'By whom?'

'Me,' said Steve. 'He made some insulting remarks.'

'Did he indeed?' Meredith breathed heavily. 'Then you'd better explain yourself, boy. Come inside.'

He returned to his office. Steve, bracing himself, followed.

Lorna sat at home dry-eyed, drinking her tea, surprising her daughter, not for the first time, with her self-control and fierce determination. Annette had feared she might disintegrate with the sheer distress and shame of it, but from the moment Ted had been taken away she had braced herself, the steel in her almost visible. Annette, sitting beside her then, having arrived at the court just in time for the case, had been ready to console her, but it was she who had been the emotional one, tears streaming silently. Her mother had been rigid, every feature harder, more pronounced, her brown eyes lacking any softness now. She had brushed aside the solicitor who had failed her, the sympathetic attention of the bubble-haired policewoman, like some high priestess impatient with the weakness of the rabble. They had gone home on the bus, sitting in silence, Lorna blind to the glances of the shoppers and seemingly deaf to their murmurs. In the house she allowed Annette to make the tea, sitting not in her favourite chair but at the table, and as they drank it from china cups with a rose-entwined pattern, mother and daughter sat opposite one another, saying little.

'I never thought they would,' Annette ventured at last.

Lorna exhaled breath sharply, glanced fleetingly at her then away.

'His first offence,' said Annette. 'They had no right.'

'Can do what they like, them buggers.'

'You can appeal, I suppose.'

'Don't be soft, girl.'

The silence returned, tightening itself around them, so that Annette felt incapable of movement, speech, anything.

'This is terrible,' she cried at last, tearing herself from the table.

'No use getting in a state,' said her mother tautly. 'What's done's done.'

Standing by the cold Rayburn, her back to Lorna, Annette said quietly, 'I'll come back home.'

'No you won't.'

'Why not? It'll be company for you.'

'I don't want you here, that's why.'

Annette turned, unable to believe the hurt so wantonly inflicted.

'Do you mean that, Mam? You don't want me?'

'Not like that, I don't. Don't want your pity.'

'It's not pity, Mam!' She looked in dismay at her mother, remembering how once before she had wanted to embrace her but could not, as she could not now for a different reason. Then the resistance had been inside her but now it came from her mother, oozing out of her like something physical. 'Oh Mam,' said Annette wearily.

Lorna seemed to have forgotten she was there. She sat staring through the window at nothing.

18

Sally coughed gently into her handkerchief: a damp, slimy cough, like something reptilian. Eileen feared to look at the hankie, afraid it would be flecked with blood. She flinched, then deliberately drew nearer, lest her daughter might think she had been repelled by her coughing.

'You want some water, darling?'

Sally shook her head, dabbed her lips, put her hankie back in the pocket of her bedjacket. She was sitting up in bed; the blocks under it had been removed, so that it no longer tilted up at the foot. Eileen, seeing this, had at first harboured a wild hope that it was because Sally's condition was improving. But the merest glance at her daughter had brought disillusion. She looked feverish, more ill than she had ever seen her, and the smell of illness hung heavy in the cubicle. She sat by the bedside, hiding her despair.

Sally smiled. 'Sorry about that, Mam. Comes over me now and then.'

'That's alright, love. Can't help it.'

'How's – ' The beginnings of a cough, bravely checked. 'How's Megan's dancing?'

'Oh, so-so. Doesn't work at it hard enough. You know what she's like.'

'I thought she was – keen.'

'She is but Miss Wyatt says she won't do as she's told. Goes her own way.'

Sally smiled, concealing the pain she felt at never seeing her little sister. She would not have had it otherwise; the danger of infection was too high.

'Ivor OK? Nice seeing him last time.'

Eileen looked set to say something, changed her mind. Sally closed her eyes, exhausted. Eileen sat in silence, afraid to move for fear of disturbing her.

Sally's eyes opened. 'Sorry Mam,' she whispered. 'Not much of a welcome, is it?'

'Don't worry, darling.'

A shadow passed over Eileen's face that Sally could not miss.

'I'll be alright, Mam,' she managed. 'You'll see.'

'Of course,' said Eileen tightly.

The editor's inner sanctum, like the editor himself, seemed out of place in a newspaper office. It had a cloistered air, as if far removed from the hustle of the newsroom. Unlike Ronnie's office, it was impeccably tidy. The latest copy of the *County Dispatch* was spread out on something resembling a large dais in a corner, with recent copies of the paper neatly stacked beside it. The walls, soberly but not forbiddingly papered, were hung with paintings of Glanaber and its environs, interspersed with framed photographs of the harbour as it had been during its Victorian heyday.

Gwyn Meredith lowered himself into the old armchair behind a large desk singularly uncluttered. Steve often wondered what he did in here; some answer seemed to be provided by the book of Welsh poetry reposing by his left elbow. Steve relaxed, the initial fear he had felt at following his titular boss into his lair after the newsroom rumpus dissipating in the face of the man's ecclesiastical mien. His short, bristly hair, lean face, dark eyes behind thick horn-rimmed glasses all spoke of restraint and civilised response to crisis.

Majestically, Meredith looked up. 'Well?' he said, with an attempt at severity. 'And why did you attack Merrick?'

'He made some remarks – sir,' replied Steve, the deferential final word being an obvious addition, uttered with difficulty.

'In respect of what?'

'I'd rather not say.'

'I think you should.'

Steve paused. 'They were about someone I know – Ted Morris,' he said quietly. 'He was up in court today.'

'So I believe. And sentenced to six months' imprisonment, I believe. An unfortunate affair. Very unfortunate.'

It did not strike Steve until later that, since Bill Merrick had come straight into the reporters' room from the court, the editor must have obtained this news from a more direct source.

As Steve stood in silence, unsure if any further response were called for, Meredith said quietly: 'You are a friend of his daughter's, I believe?'

'Yes,' replied Steve, colouring.

'A smart young lady. She is a credit to her parents.' Meredith played thoughtfully with a paperweight shaped like a frog. 'Sit down, Stephen,' he said at last.

The chair was more modern than the one in which the editor sat but exuded the same air of comfort and detachment.

'I'm going to ask you a very personal question,' Meredith said, after a pause. 'What is your ambition in life? Assuming you have one, that is.'

'To write good poetry,' Steve surprised himself by replying.

A thin smile played around Meredith's lips. 'Indeed. And what have you done towards achieving that objective?'

'Not much. But I will.'

Meredith tapped the frog's nose on his desk. 'You surprise me, Stephen. I thought you had more worldly ambitions.'

Steve, flummoxed both by the editor's line of questioning and his own response, said nothing.

'You intend staying here then, do you? To pursue the Muse in your spare time?'

'No. I want to get to Fleet Street.'

The tapping ceased. 'Fleet Street – and poetry! How do they mix?'

Steve shrugged. 'I don't know.'

Meredith sighed. 'You put me in a very difficult position. I can't have my senior reporter attacked by the office junior.' He gave Steve a direct look. 'You *are* still officially a junior reporter – you realise that, don't you?'

'Yes, sir,' replied Steve, more easily. 'Until my next birthday.'

'Twenty-four,' mused Meredith. 'You will then be twenty-four. A coming of age, according to the National Union of Journalists.'

He pushed his chair back, stood looking out through the big bay window with his hands clenched behind his back.

'I'll make no bones about it, Lewis,' he said, turning. 'You're a very good reporter. I'd like you to stay here.'

'Thank you,' Steve felt obliged to say.

'Wouldn't that be better for you? You wouldn't find much time for writing poetry in London.'

'I could try.'

'You don't understand. Those papers would suck you dry. You'd have nothing left after a day's work.'

Steve flinched inwardly, at hearing his own secret fears voiced so clearly.

'Think about it, I implore you. Before it's too late.'

Steve looked curiously at the older man, surprised by the urgency in his voice. Why did he care what happened to him?

'I can't stay here anyway,' he heard himself saying.

'Why not? Is it so uncomfortable? Oh, I know Merrick can be difficult but – ' He lowered his voice. 'It's the result of an unhappy marriage, boy,' he confided.

As if disturbed by this revelation, Meredith sat down again, frowning.

'I don't know your poetry,' he said. 'But you can write. You have a feeling for words rare in a journalist. At any level. Most of them are just – ' He brushed the air with his hand.

'Do you write poetry yourself, Mr Meredith?'

Again the faint smile, not of amusement. 'I try. Not very successfully.'

'In Welsh or English?'

'Welsh, of course. The language of heaven,' he added dryly.

Steve felt a rush of warmth for a man who kept so much hidden. Sensing it, Meredith withdrew slightly.

'I can't stop you leaving, if you wish. But if you stay, I can offer you prospects.'

Steve waited.

'I am considering opening an office in Carmarthen.

We are already making inroads there. I would like to put you in charge of it – at a considerably enhanced salary, of course. And after two or three years, assuming you've been successful, you would come back here – as assistant editor.'

Steve did not move.

'I shall then be approaching retirement. Need I say more?'

Their eyes met. Steve's heart was thumping.

'Think it over, Lewis. And don't you dare breathe a word of this to anyone.'

'Of course not,' Steve managed.

'That is all.' Meredith stood imposingly, stretched a hand out.

Steve grasped it, gave the editor a steady look, and left.

'You sure?' asked Shirley.

'Positive.'

'God help. What you gonna do now?'

'Have it of course,' said Annette simply.

The girls had drawn their easy chairs into the bay window of their flat in South Marine Terrace. The evening had turned sour after an oppressive Sunday which had clamped skullcaps of heat upon the people of the town. Around tea-time, leaden clouds had slowly thickened until now the entire sky was a pall. Far out at sea, lightning flickered and dark thunder rumbled war-like.

'When you gonna tell him?'

'I'm not.'

Shirley glanced fearfully at her friend, unsure that she had heard properly.

'You can't mean that.'

'No?'

'But you got to tell him, mun!'

'Why?'

Shirley frowned angrily. 'Because he's the bloody father, that's why. He is I suppose, is he?'

'Course.'

'Well then. He's got to marry you, hasn't he?'

'Not necessarily.'

Shirley's dusky blonde hair caught the thin light, a brief illumination in the darkening room. 'Christ Annette, you're talking rubbish. What sort of girl are you?'

'I don't know. That's the point.'

Her face crumpled suddenly into tears. She turned away.

'I'm sorry, 'Nette. I didn't mean it. Please.'

'That's OK.' She found her hankie, dabbed her eyes.

'Just thinking of you I am,' said Shirley. 'What's your Mam gonna say?'

'How do I know?'

The rain swept in suddenly from the bay, hissing and spattering on the window, conjuring miniature waterspouts from the hard paving slabs on the prom, drenching the few holidaymakers running cheerlessly for shelter. Lightning slanted viciously, followed closely by a broadside of thunder.

'Jesus,' cried Shirley, pushing her chair back. 'I can't stand this.'

She did not know quite if she meant the storm or the situation.

'Don't sit there. You'll be struck by lightning. Come back a bit, Annette, for Godsake.'

Annette obliged indifferently. She sat by the table. Shirley stood by the fireplace, gazing at her helplessly.

'I don't know what I'm gonna do with you,' she confessed.

'Don't bother. It's up to me, isn't it?'

'Aye, it is. Worse luck.'

Annette smiled faintly, blew her nose. 'Funny thing to say.'

'No funnier than you. I've never known anyone like you.' Shirley tried again. 'You *got* to tell him, girl!'

Annette shook her head slowly.

'Not yet. I'll see how it goes.'

Shirley stared at her as if at a stranger. Then, as if struggling to move against the weight of the air, she went to put the kettle on.

'I want to bring her home,' said Eileen abruptly. 'She's dying.'

She plopped her gloves down on the sideboard, a statement of intent. The word 'dying' took Ivor by surprise, like a blow in the stomach.

'Do the doctors say that?' he asked feebly, hearing the falseness in his voice. He became suddenly aware of how tired his mother sounded, how much older; it was something to hold on to, as he felt the ground begin to slither away under his feet.

'Of course they don't,' she said sharply. 'They don't tell you anything, do they? Give me a cup of tea, there's a good boy.'

Filling the kettle in the scullery, Ivor felt he was enacting a part which had been written for him long ago. He knew it would come to this, some day. His mind could not grapple with the idea of Sally dying so it latched on to narrower matters: what her homecoming would mean to him, and his younger brother and sister. He felt, too, a fear he did not wish to acknowledge. He forced himself to think of Sally, her alone, and of her imprisonment in that gloomy place high up in the hills.

'Want something to eat?' he called out.

'No thanks. The tea'll be fine.'

Crouched in the chair by the cold summer grate, his mother seemed shrivelled. The children were in bed asleep; he was glad about that. Her bus had been late getting back from Highland after a mechanical breakdown; it was a wonder it didn't happen more often, in his opinion, the state those buses were in.

'Thanks.' She gulped the tea thirstily. 'Lovely. Just what I needed. I'm parched.'

'Didn't they stop to let you have a cup of tea anywhere?' he grumbled. 'Miserable things.'

Eileen seemed not to hear him. 'I need to talk to you, Ivor. You're the man of the house now.'

Ivor grunted, feeling a sense of unreality. Even after all this time, he could not get used to being the man of the house. He had never been able to rid himself of the strange feeling that somehow his father was still around, to take all such burdens on his shoulders. He could not be responsible for everyone; coping with his own life was enough.

'You saw what she's like when you were there,' said Eileen. 'She's going downhill fast.' She paused. 'She should never have gone there in the first place.'

'You can't say that. Dr Cullen said it was the right thing to do.'

'Dr Cullen! What does he know about it? A tea planter, that's all he is.'

'What d'you mean?'

'Didn't you know? He was a tea planter one time. Out in India or somewhere.'

Ivor shuffled uneasily in his chair. 'I don't know about bringing her home, Mam.'

'Why not?'

'Well, what do the doctors say? Do they think it's right?'

Eileen made a dismissive sound, her face taut. 'They want to bury her up there in that horrible place.'

'Don't talk like that, Mam!' He felt suddenly cold, as if the clamminess of the grave were enclosing him. 'What makes you so sure she's dying anyway? She could still get better.'

'Don't be so stupid,' said his mother contemptuously. A silence fell upon the pair, like a shroud.

'What about the kids?' asked Ivor at last.

'What about them?'

'They might catch it.'

'Not if they don't go near her. We'll put her in the back bedroom. Megan can come in with me. You can move in with Lennie.'

'You're going to give her *my* room?'

'Well? Do you object?'

He got to his feet, stared out at the darkening garden. 'They told me what to do,' said Eileen. Her voice sounded oddly detached, like one of those that came out of the wireless. 'We must keep all her things separate. Cups and saucers and plates. Cutlery too. We'll put black cotton round her knives and forks, make sure we know which they are.'

Ivor felt, for the first time in his life, the sensation of his flesh crawling.

'I'll nurse her,' said Eileen. 'I'll give up my job. We can claim from the Assistance.'

'It's not *right*, Mam,' he said heavily.

He thought he saw, across the void outside, his father looking at him.

'Scared, are you?' she taunted him.

'Not for myself, no.'

'No? You sure about that?'

He turned to face her. 'It's not right for *them*,' he said quietly. 'Megan and Lennie.'

'They'll survive,' said Eileen coolly. 'Anyway it's done now. I've told them. She'll be coming home in a couple of weeks' time.'

Part Five

BLOOD

19

Steve awoke from a troubled night with dreams still clustered in the forefront of his skull. They were ugly and impenetrable and filled his mind like jagged spears. He went to his bedroom window, the ticking of his bedside clock loud in the silence. The first light of Monday morning was bringing a pencil-line of illumination to the hills to his left, along the valley of the river that rushed down from the boggy heights of Plynlimon.

He knew what had caused the dreams: his own corruption. He felt consumed by hatred of the person he had become through soiling himself with the woman of Back Row. She had thrown a spike of alienation between him and Annette just as they had fulfilled their love in the most intimate way. They should be in Paradise, after all that had happened, but instead they had grown sulky and remote from each other, and she was the reason!

He knew now what he had to do. He would go to the woman and tell her all was over between them. Then he would go to Annette and say he was sorry. He would propose to her – yes! – and they would go to London together. They had to get away from this horrible little town, which dragged everyone down to its level. He would find a job up there – Brian would help him – and they would be in the swim of things! He saw them going to the West End theatre together, sitting up in the gods maybe but *there*, holding hands. Then seeing all the sights, going for trips along the Thames, standing below Big Ben as it boomed out the hours and quarter-hours – *that's* where their future lay! Meredith could stuff his job in Carmarthen – who on earth wanted to go *there* – and the *County Dispatch* could go to hell!

He shivered, with excitement not cold. The slough of his dreams was swept away by the exultation that surged through him. He felt a sense of purpose that made his toes tingle. As a red, fevered sky spilt its blood on the hills he slipped back into a deep, dreamless sleep from which he awoke cleansed and renewed.

There was a letter in the post for him. It told him the poem he had sent to *John o'London's Weekly* had been accepted.

It was a rancid, bitter day at the *County Dispatch* office. First the typewriter carriage kept sticking and he ended up writing out the copy by hand, then someone rang to complain that he had made a mistake in a story about sheep farming. The error was trivial, but a bad-tempered Ronnie made the most of it. He was glad, finally, to get out of the office to cover an inquest. It was a sordid case involving child neglect but Steve shut his emotions off and simply concentrated on the facts. From time to time he glanced at the parents, who didn't seem to know who they were or what was happening. Shabbily dressed, defeated, they gave off an odour of failure that was almost physical. When they gave evidence they answered questions monosyllabically, the woman's voice barely audible. They had left their six-year-old daughter asleep and alone to go out drinking and in their absence the house had caught fire. Their eyes were vacant, as if they knew nothing about any of these matters. The verdict was misadventure, with heavy hints of a prosecution pending in another court. Steve thrust his notebook into his pocket and hurried up Darkgate Street; the town clock struck five as he went past it on the way to Back Row.

It was not an ideal time for a visit as people were coming home from work and he could not expect to go there unobserved. He did not care any longer. His feelings for her had changed since finding out that Ted had been one of her regulars. To follow Annette's father into her stinking bed! He felt ashamed and disgraced. Now rumour had been given a tongue, it would be all over town. Annette would hear of it, and his parents! He would *have* to leave now, whether he wanted to or not. But first he must see her, to confront her with what he'd found out about Ted and to tell her his decision.

He plunged down the steps from Shipwrights Road two at a time, knocked the door of No. 4. He was about to knock again when it opened, and a man stood there. He was tall, with jet-black hair, beetle brows and a corrugation of wrinkles etched deeply into his forehead. His eyes shaded with dislike and knowing as they looked at one another.

'Is Mrs Baker in?' asked Steve.

'Who's asking?'

'My name's Lewis. Steve Lewis. I'm with the *Dispatch* – there's something I'd like to check up on.'

'Oh, is there now?'

'Yes. If I could come in for a minute.'

'Piss off.'

'What?'

'You heard me –'

'Let him in, Jack.' Sara Baker, brown eyes flecked with fear, edged into the door frame.

'Why should I?'

'Please.'

With a jerk of the head, the man complied. He slammed the door shut. Steve felt trapped, scared, the situation out of control. There was no sign of young Vi. He stood in the small, dark room he had come to know so well, facing the older man and woman.

'You shouldn't have come, Gerry,' murmured Sara. 'I told you.'

'What you calling him Gerry for?' the man demanded roughly. 'Thought his name was Steve.'

'It is,' said Steve. 'I –'

'Who's asking you? I'm talking to the organ grinder, not the monkey.'

'Leave him be, Jack,' she said wearily. 'He's only a boy. Just let him go.'

'A boy, is he? We'll see about that.' He stepped forward truculently. 'Been hearing a thing or two about you, I have. Little skunk that you are. Put her name in the paper, didn't you? Don't say you didn't.'

'She wanted me to!'

'Liar! What'd she want that for? Full of villains, that rag of yours. All papers are, I know – I've had my fill of 'em!'

He shot out an arm, grabbed Steve by the lapel.

'And that's not all you've been doing here, is it? I've heard, don't you worry! Think you can get away with anything, don't you? Little rat.'

'Please take your hands off me,' said Steve deliberately. His heart was pounding; his voice seemed to come from someone else.

'Ho! Listen to him. "Please take your hands off,"' the man mimicked in a high, effeminate voice. His eyes, almost black in the perpetual gloom, glistened viciously. 'Fucking nancy boy. Bet you toss yourself off every night. I've a good mind to –' He raised his free fist menacingly.

'Don't, Jack, don't – you'll go to jail!' cried Sara.

'Who fucking cares.'

For a few seconds they remained poised, Steve on tip-toe staring straight into his tormentor's eyes, Jack's big fist ready to strike. Then, suddenly, the tableau collapsed.

'Nah. Not worth it,' Jack said contemptuously. 'Don't mind doing time, but not for a piece of shit like him.'

Steve, unexpectedly released, smoothed his jacket down, his hands trembling.

'Now hop it,' said Jack. 'Go on. Get lost.'

Sara nodded slightly, confirming the command. She looked ill and weak and, moved by pity for her, Steve resolved not to be rushed.

'I just came to give you my news,' he said, despising the tremor in his voice. 'I'm leaving Glanaber.'

A look he could not interpret briefly crossed her face. 'Where you going, lad?'

'London. I've got a job up there,' he lied.

'Good riddance,' the man said.

Steve stood his ground. 'Aren't you going to introduce me?' he asked Sara boldly.

Renewed fury flared in the man's eyes. 'You –!'

'Easy, Jack.' Emboldened by Steve's manner, she said simply: 'My husband, Gerry. Jack Baker.'

'*Mr* Baker to him,' Jack snarled. He turned away suddenly, as if embarrassed.

Sara and Steve exchanged glances.

'Go on now,' she said quietly.

'Right.' He brushed past her, their last touch.

He let himself out into the empty street.

'It's true,' insisted Shirley. 'I tell you, it's true.'

She felt scared at the way Annette was looking at her, from across the room. But she had to know, didn't she? There was no holding it back from her any longer!

'Who is she, this person?' Annette breathed. 'I've never heard of her.'

'I told you, she lives down Back Row. You know, those little houses butting on to the harbour.'

'He's never mentioned her.'

'Course not. Not likely to, is he?'

They had just finished the meal they often took together before going out for the evening. The remains of it were still on the table.

'I don't believe you. He's not like that.'

It was on the tip of Shirley's tongue to say 'All men are like that,' but she bit the cynical words back.

'I just thought you ought to know,' blustered Shirley. 'You're living in a dream world, mun.'

'Dream world? Why?'

'You know . . . not telling him about the baby and all.'

'That's my business, isn't it?'

Shirley gave her a close, anxious look. Why was she talking like this? She didn't seem angry in the least. Just puzzled; crushed, even.

'You seeing him tonight?'

'No.'

'Not seeing much of him these days, are you?'

Annette, pale and withdrawn, made no reply.

Anger flared up in Shirley. If it was her, by God! She'd be giving him what for. She'd have his guts for garters, no messing.

'You've got to tell him, 'Nette,' she said brutally.

'Tell him what?'

'About the baby, of course. And this! You can't let him get away with it, girl!'

'Who says I am?'

'It certainly looks like it.'

Annette looked down at her hands.

'How old is she, this woman?'

'God knows. Got a little brat anyway – probably more, if the truth be known.'

'Is she married?'

'No-one knows. She's from away. There's something else you should know. She's a part-timer – you know.'

Annette frowned. 'Part-timer?'

Shirley felt she could scream. 'For God's sake. Don't have to spell it out, do I? She takes men in – on the side.'

'Oh.'

Annette sat perfectly still for a moment.

'Well,' she said, 'thanks for telling me.'

She rose to her feet and walked to the door.

Shirley, with a strange sense of having disgraced herself, cried: 'Where are you going now? I had to tell you, didn't I?'

Annette went to the bedroom without replying, and turned the key in the lock.

He had intended going straight on to Annette's flat, but at the top of the steps from Back Row he was shaking

217

so much that he had to lean against the wall outside the small gospel hall that stood there. He grasped the spiky iron railings, feeling deathly cold. Suddenly he spewed, coughing and retching. Someone passed quickly, he knew not who. Slower footsteps ascended the steps. He wiped his mouth.

'Got your come-uppance at last, have you?' a sneering voice said.

He turned to face a short, thick-set man in paint-streaked blue overalls.

'We've been waiting for it. Stupid bugger.'

Steve knew him by sight, in the way that most people in Glanaber were familiar with one another.

'Don't know what you mean,' he said boldly. 'Just got an upset stomach, that's all.'

'Don't give me that! I saw you go in there. Lucky your head's not broke in two.'

The man stepped close. He was fortyish, prematurely bald, beer-bellied, blue eyes glinting with malice.

'If you've stopped spewing your ring up, bugger off now quick. We don't want your sort round here. Get back where you belong.'

Steve glared back at him, fists clenching spontaneously. Then, overcome with a fresh wave of sickness, he leaned back weakly against the wall.

The man lunged, catching him a blow on the shoulder. Steve slumped, his knees buckling, as if he were suddenly drained of all substance. His assailant struck out again. Steve fell heavily, his head thudding on to the pavement. The man looked around wildly, swung a boot into his ribs, then ran back down the steps.

She put only a few things into the small overnight suitcase her parents had given her for her twenty-first, and left a note for Shirley, who had gone off in a huff.

> Dear Shirley,
> I'm sorry but I can't live here any longer and am going back to my mother's. It's nothing you said, just everything. Thanks for telling me about Steve, I'd suspected something was going on. I'll be back for the rest of my things tomorrow. I'll go on paying my share of the rent till you find someone else or whatever. Please try to understand though it must be difficult.
> Your friend
> Annette

After a few moments' thought, she added xxx to her name.

As she walked along Shipwrights Road on her way to the station, she noticed that someone had been sick on the pavement at the top of the steps by the little gospel hall. She remembered where the steps led, and shuddered. She tried to blank Steve out of her mind but somehow his voice entered her head and she could not get rid of it. She could not make out any words, just the sound of his voice droning on. Then Shirley's voice took over, repeating 'You're living in a dream world, mun.' First Shirley's voice, then his, going on and on in her head. The evening was warm and the further she walked, the heavier the case felt. When she reached the bus stop she felt dizzy, and sat heavily on the green bench outside the greystone primary school where she used to go as a child. She wanted to hold her head in her hands but shrank from making an exhibition of herself. Her stomach was queasy and she forced her mind away from thoughts of the small pool of brown vomit at the top of the steps. Dad's in prison, Dad's in prison, she told herself over and over. It was a diversion from thoughts of the vomit and of Steve. She touched the handle of her small cream case, its coolness and firm surface a consolation. At last the bus arrived, three or four people stepped off and she went on it. She sat heavily and shielded her eyes with her hand.

'Not feeling too good, Annette?' said a sympathetic voice. It was George the bus conductor, whom she had walked straight past without a word, unaware of him.

'I'll be OK, thanks,' she replied, her wan face belying her words.

'Shall I open the window? Bit stuffy in here.'

'Thanks.'

She closed her eyes, trying to think about nothing. The bus fired into life, and the sound of its engine roared like a furnace in her head. She dare not open her eyes, for fear the movement outside the window would make her sick. She could guess where they were by the way the bus slowed down or accelerated and turned bends in the road. Half-way up Penbryn Hill she forced her eyes open. The bus had nearly reached her stop. She opened her handbag to pay the fare but George touched her wrist gently and whispered, 'I've bought your ticket, pay me back again.' She mouthed her thanks, the bus slowed down and stopped. She stepped off with her case and waved to George as the bus trundled away. Slowly she walked down the slope. It was cooler here and her feeling of nausea had gone. She nodded and smiled at a neighbour working in his garden, then opened the gate and walked down the path. The side door was open and she stepped in. 'Mam,' she called out, then suddenly her legs slipped from under her and she fell full-length in the kitchen.

20

His side hurt like hell and his head was throbbing. He lay in the semi-darkness, not sure where he was. Adrift in the grey country between sleeping and waking, he kept remembrance at bay. Instinctively he knew it was safer like this, that remembering would bring pain of a different kind altogether. He courted sleep, wanting to slip back and forget . . .

Someone coughed. Awake now, he caught his breath with the pain. He turned on his back, realising why he felt this strange constriction in the chest: there was some kind of binding around it, obviously linked with the pain in his side.

He moaned softly, remembering. A car stopping, a stranger helping him in. Sickening pain as he lay slumped in the back seat, reassuring words from the stranger. A sense of shame and disgust, of being polluted beyond redemption. The face of Jack Baker, ugly, threatening. His huge fist poised to strike. And then that other face, mean, repulsive. The boot crunching into his ribs. And then darkness.

The hospital; disconnected faces. His mother's among them? He seemed to see her, then she was gone. Being trundled to the X-ray room in a wheelchair, feeling stupid. Getting into bed, comforting voices. Then the dreams. All gone now. Only the knowledge of who he was, what had happened. The hurt in his side and his head. The shame of it. Oh, Annette. How could he face her?

The swish of a stiff, starchy dress. Someone peering down at him, torchlight glaring at first, then deflected. 'Awake then, are you?' Soft Irish brogue. A face dimly seen. Smiling. 'How are you feeling then?'

'Lousy.'

'Well now, that's a surprise. Is your head hurting much?'

'Quite a bit.'

'Let's take a look at you.'

She peered into his eyes. 'Are you feeling sick at all?'

'No.'

'Good.'

He could not see her face now, the torchlight shutting it out. She moved back, satisfied. 'How's the pain in your side?'

'Pretty bad.'

'I'll get you something for it. Would you fancy a cup of tea?'

'I'd love one. Nurse?' As she was moving away.

'Yes?'

'What time is it?'

'Three o'clock, just about. You be quiet now, or you'll wake all the ward up. I'll be back in a mo'.'

She swished away. Another cough, from somewhere to his left. He raised his head slightly. Long rows of beds on either side, dimly visible in the eerie blue light from a central lamp in the ceiling. A constant susurration of breaths from the sleeping patients, overlaid by creaking and shuffling as bodies turned in their beds. A rasping cough, much harsher than the others. Christ! He was in the men's ward of the infirmary on the hill, a slab of late Victorian do-goodery overlooking the town and the bay. That bastard had put him there, with his ugly great boot. But it was not the face of his attacker he saw clearest but that of Jack Baker, leering, threatening. A wave of revulsion engulfed him. The shabby net curtains, the reek of cheap perfume, the hot smell of her. How could he have done it? Who had he become?

The nurse bustled back, helped him sit up in bed. He gasped, pain clawing through his chest and then subsiding.

'Easy now . . . that's it.'

She gave him the tablet, a glass of water.

'Thanks.'

'How's the head?'

'Hurting.'

'It will do for a while. You've had quite a bang from somewhere. You sure you're not feeling sick at all?'

'Positive.'

'Good. I'll get you your tea now. Would you like sugar in it?'

'Yes please. One.'

Again the swish-swish in the semi-darkness. Someone cried out in his sleep. He hadn't been in hospital since he was eight, when he'd had his tonsils out. He remembered coughing blood into an enamel bowl, the raw feeling in his throat. What was wrong with him now? There was a dressing on the back of his head, binding round his chest.

When she came back, he could see her a little better. A small face, friendly eyes. He sipped his tea.

'What's wrong with me then, nurse? Nothing much, is it?'

'Nothing a bit of rest won't put right. You've bruised a rib, don't ask me how.'

'What's this thing they've put round me?'

'Only a bandage. Something to hold you together, in case you fall apart.' Her smile, a tonic.

'I want to go home now. I'm OK.'

'In the middle of the night? You'll be lucky.'

'I mean in – '

A jab of pain in his side.

'Be still with you now! And stop talking or I'll get cross, you see if I don't.'

Annette had imagined she might sleep late, that first morning back in her old bed, but she was awake at her usual time, soon after seven. She indulged herself by simply lying there, slipping back to the borderland of sleep as she luxuriated in the sensation of being where she belonged, with all the sounds she had so briefly discarded falling on her ears with the reassurance of the familiar. Gates creaking open, doors closing, men coughing as they set out for another day's work. Then the whistle of the train from Shrewsbury, the sputter of a car starting-up down the hill. She had told her mother not to disturb her; she would not be going to work that day. She found herself listening for something else, pulling the bedclothes over her head to shut out the day a little longer. Then she realised what she was missing: her father's early morning cough on the days when, like herself at that moment, he manufactured a reason for not going to work.

Dad in a prison cell! She moaned softly, thinking of it. She imagined it as dark, bare, with a tiny barred window, scarcely anywhere to sit down. The kind of torture chamber she had visualised at school, in history lessons about the terrible things people had suffered. Her mother, who had visited him in Swansea, assured her he was in pretty good spirits. She had been allowed to take him some 'books' (the word her mother applied equally to magazines), though he wasn't a big reader; cigarettes too, but only so many. 'He'll be home by the new year, with remission,' Lorna assured Annette, more bravely than she felt. 'Soon go, you'll see.' She was determined to make light of it all, almost to deny that her husband's prison sentence had any relevance at all. But for Annette it was still something horrible, an ugliness that would remain to the end of their lives, and she doubted that her father would be able to shrug it off like a snail sloughing away its old shell.

She tried not to think about Steve. Had he really been seeing another woman? She wouldn't put it past him. It would explain a lot. But . . . a *prostitute*! No! She couldn't imagine Steve doing that. He wasn't the type. Ugh!

It was Shirley, making things up. Gossipy Shirley, who thought she knew everything. She probably fancied Steve herself, if truth be known. She'd caught them exchanging looks once or twice. It was all horrible, horrible. Except for the baby. Ah, the baby! She wanted that, whatever happened between her and Steve. And she couldn't make her mind up about him. He was still a mystery to her. He was the father of the baby inside her: but did she want him? In many ways yes; he excited her, and there was so much about him she loved. But loved in total, enough to marry him? Enough to spend a lifetime with him, forsaking all others? She was awed by those words in the wedding service: how could you promise to forsake all others, for ever? Unless you were truly, deeply in love? Oh Steve, Steve! Suddenly she felt sorry for herself. Who was she, this Annette Morris? Sniffling with self-pity, she opened her eyes under the bedclothes, as she had done when a kid. A pinkish glow, as the morning light permeated the bedsheet. All so safe, calm, comforting. Then a figure appeared at the edge of her consciousness: Ivor! She breathed the forbidden name, pushed the image away. It remained at the edge of her awareness, tall, serious, solid.

Her mother slip-slopped downstairs and, not long afterwards, Annette followed. She was not sure what mood her mother would be in; she had been all concern the night before, but who knew what morning might bring? They had not yet spoken about her reasons for coming back, setting everything aside in the interest of an initial peace and (to some extent) reconciliation, but there would have to be some explaining today. Annette had vowed to be as open and honest as she knew how but still feared her mother's reaction; there was no knowing which way she would jump, once the truth was out.

Lorna was sitting reading yesterday's *Daily Mirror*, smoking her first fag of the day, ash-tray poised on the arm of the chair.

'Up early?' she said, slewing an ambiguous look Annette's way. 'Thought you might have had a lie-in, seeing as you're not working today.'

'No, I'm alright. No point in lying in bed all day.'

Lorna made a noise in her throat it was hard to interpret. 'Fancy making me a cup of tea then? Kettle's on.'

'OK, if you like,' said Annette, surprised. She had not bargained for the immediate demand, the assumption that since she was back the old relationship still applied.

In the kitchen, she looked around with distaste. Last night's dishes were still unwashed, a grubby tea-towel had been thrown down anywhere. Worse, an ash-tray full of dog-ends lay by the sink. Everything smelt of neglect and disarray. She recalled, with a pang, how neat and clean their own kitchen had been in their flat; Shirley may be careless in her behaviour but she was scrupulously clean in her habits. Resisting the urge to wash the dirty dishes, she took two cups and saucers from the cupboard and the jug of milk from the larder. Suspiciously she sniffed it but it seemed fresh enough. She made the tea, took the cups in.

'Oh – like a biscuit?' she asked.

'No thank you. Ta.'

Lorna took the cup without glancing up, sipped the tea. 'Not enough sugar, girl,' she said, handing it back.

Annette stared; Lorna avoided her eyes. For a moment a decision hung poised. Then, with an angry flicker of the eyes and a gesture of impatience, Annette went back to the kitchen and heaped a spoonful of sugar into her mother's cup. She handed it back to her defiantly and sat waiting for a reaction. There was none. Calmly Lorna sipped her tea, read the paper, appeared completely absorbed in its contents.

Annette's tea went cold as realisation of her situation sank in. Why on earth had she imagined anything different? The echo of words thrown at her a few weeks ago drummed dully in her head. 'Slut-slut-slut.'

So she was. The fault had been only in saying them prematurely.

'I'm sorry about last night,' Annette said clearly, the cut-glass brilliance of her voice sounding unnatural.

'Not your fault. Comes to us all sometimes. Feeling better now?'

'Yes thank you.'

Lorna turned a page, crossed her legs, a faded blue slipper hanging half off her gently moving foot.

Annette was dazed by her indifference. Had she imagined her reception the evening before, her mother's calm acceptance that something had gone terribly wrong between her and Shirley?

'I shan't be staying,' Annette said suddenly, 'if that's what's worrying you.'

'Who says I'm worried? You can come here when you like, you know that.' She did not add, 'It's your home,' and the absence of the words increased Annette's sense of finality.

'I've got something to tell you, that's all.'

'Oh?' Lorna looked at her calmly. 'What's that then?'

'You won't like it, Mam,' said Annette, her voice suddenly shaky. 'I'm having a baby.'

Lorna's eyes changed, taking on a blankness that was full of meaning.

'I'm sorry, Mam. I'm dead sorry.' Tears long withheld spilled from Annette's eyes. She wept quietly, blind to everything.

Lorna knelt before her, wrapped her arms round her.

'God help you,' she said. 'Why din't you tell me before?'

She hugged her daughter, stroking her head and crooning softly.

21

Jim Lewis stared gloomily through his office window overlooking the prom. He'd known Annette was big trouble as soon as he'd set eyes on her. That red hair, those wicked eyes! If only he'd been thirty years younger...

'She's behind this, I'm sure,' Edna had complained over breakfast.

'What are you talking about, Ed? She wouldn't beat him up, would she?'

'No, but it could be that rough-house from Brynpadarn she was going with! I wouldn't trust him an inch.'

'Don't be silly, Edna. How can you possibly say that? Anyway, we don't know he *was* beaten up. The fellow just found him lying there, by all accounts.'

'Yes, with a cracked rib and concussion! You don't get that from just falling down, do you? You must get it out of him, Jim. Whoever did that mustn't get away with it.'

'Well, let's just get him out of hospital first. That's the important thing.'

The gulls screeched and whirled in the high wind that roughed up the sea, but Jim saw nothing of this. The crisis he'd feared all along had arrived. Once Edna got her teeth into something she wouldn't let go. What had that boy of his been up to?

'Coffee, Mr Lewis?' asked his secretary, Linda, sympathetically.

'What? No, no thanks . . . yes please,' he corrected. 'I think I will. I can do with something.' He clicked his knuckles, a sure sign he was worried.

He went back to his desk, opened a file with a sense of futility. He wasn't in the mood for work, wasn't in the mood for anything. His thoughts veered suddenly along a well-worn track, taking him to someone he preferred not to remember, who with dangerous calm looked at him with deep brown eyes and asked unspoken questions to which he did not have the answers.

He shut the file, tossed it back in its tray.

'You should have taken the morning off,' said Linda reprovingly. 'You're bound to be worried about him.'

'I'd have been just as worried at home. I'm better off here, working. Or trying to.'

He gave Linda a small, appreciative smile. She knew things about him his wife didn't. He noticed touches of grey in her hair that hadn't been there before. Comes from working for me, he thought ironically, while not really believing it.

Alone, as she went to make the coffee in the small room set aside for that purpose, he allowed himself a brief, unappetising look at the years ahead. He couldn't see Steve staying home much longer, whether or not he made a go of it with Annette. Best for him if he *did* leave; there was no future for him in this tin-pot town. Especially now, with whatever muck this business would throw up. He wasn't too worried about his state of health; from what the doctors had told them last night, his injuries didn't seem serious. 'We'll keep him in overnight for observation and see how he is in the morning,' was their line.

To be truthful – and he was more candid with himself than with anyone – he was more worried about himself than about Steve; he had to admit he'd grown tired of Edna. She'd become so petty-minded, as if small-town life had narrowed her down to nothing. It had been a mistake coming up here; he knew it now in his bones. Perhaps, when Steve had gone, he could get a transfer back to Cardiff. They'd both be happier there, he was sure.

'Thanks, Linda.' He smiled up at her as she put his cup down. What did he know about her? Not much; she was a very private person. Just as well. He flicked the file open again, frowned down at it.

When the hospital rang he listened, then told her: 'They're letting him out right away. I'll go and collect him.'

'Oh, I *am* glad,' said Linda. And she meant it. She was a jewel.

'Shan't be long then. If Brookes rings tell him I'll be back within the hour.'

'Alright, but don't rush back. Everything will be fine.'

Her trace of pure, Scottish-highlands accent had never seemed more attractive. He clattered down two flights of stairs and out into a sudden shaft of sunlight.

'A nice to-do,' tutted Edna Lewis. 'A nice to-do, I must say.'

She fussed over her son as he stretched out on the settee in the room they called the 'lounge', as opposed to the best room at the front of the house where, not long before, he had made love to Annette on the carpet. If only she knew this, he found himself thinking, if only she knew!

'Now,' she said, 'what can I get you? A nice cup of coffee, yes?'

'OK then, Mam. Thanks.'

Everything was to hand: the *Western Mail* and *Daily Telegraph*, the library book he was reading, even the *Radio Times* in case he wanted to know what was on the wireless. It stood on a small occasional table, next to the new record player that had replaced the bulky radiogram they had brought up from South Wales. The record player was smart, fawn-coloured, with shiny silver clips holding the top down when closed. It took the best fibre needles: you sharpened them with a special contraption, feeling infinitely superior to anyone daft enough to persist in using those scratchy old steel needles.

Steve relaxed; it was good to be home. He'd been discharged that morning, after the night's 'observation' of his condition. There was nothing seriously wrong, but he'd have to go easy for the next few days. That suited him; he could do with a few days off work. He'd work on his poetry a bit, see Annette in the evening (nothing to stop him going out for an hour or two), spend some time reading and listening to the radio. He'd keep away from trouble now; avoid Back Row and all it stood for. As soon as he felt better, he'd make a real effort to get a job up in London. But he'd have to take Annette with him; he couldn't bear to part with her.

He'd have to ring her soon, to tell her what had happened. He didn't want her to find out from anyone else: God knows what garbled story would be getting around town already!

He sat up; every movement made his head thump. Steeling himself, he got to his feet and walked shakily to the hall. He felt dizzy and sat suddenly on the chair by the phone. He closed his eyes, waiting for his head to clear. Then, slowly, he dialled the number of Annette's office.

'Hullo? Richards and James Solicitors?'

The haughty voice of Big Bertha, giving information as if it were a question.

'Can I speak to Annette please.' Crisply self-confident; Steve's best telephone manner.

A moment's pause. 'Who is that speaking?'

'It's Steve, Mrs Bevan – Steve Lewis. I'd like a word with Annette – I won't keep her long, I promise.'

'That's not possible, I'm afraid. Annette isn't in the office today.'

'Oh, isn't she? Has she got the day off then?'

'We are led to believe she's indisposed,' replied Bertha distantly.

'Indisposed? You mean she's ill?'

'So we are told.'

'What's wrong with her, do you know?'

'I can't tell you that, I'm afraid.'

'But haven't you any idea? I'd like to know. I – '

'Mr Lewis, I've told you all I know. There's no point in prolonging this conversation.'

'But – hello? Hello?'

The bitch! She'd put the phone down. Who the hell did she think she was?

'What on earth do you think you're doing?' His mother, hastening in from the kitchen.

'Phoning Annette, Mam, that's all.'

'But you're ill, boy! You should have asked me to do it.'

'Don't worry, Mam, please.'

'Don't worry! That's a fine thing to say. When you get yourself beaten up by goodness knows who – who was it, anyway? You've got to tell us, Steve.'

'Please, Mam. Give me a break.' He put his hand to his head, pistons banging inside, a distant roaring.

Her tone changed. 'You look like death, boy. Come on – back where you were. Or would you like to go to bed? That's where you ought to be, from the look of you.'

'I'm alright, Mam. Really.' But he did not object as she helped him back to the settee. He lay back, his head cradled on a purple cushion, eyes closed.

'I'll draw the curtains. You'll be able to rest better then,' she said softly.

She was all tenderness now, the whys and wherefores set aside till a more appropriate moment. A fear, long suppressed, suddenly surfaced; the fear of losing him, of a lifetime just with Jim, her only boy gone away, perhaps for ever. A physical pain gripped her; she put a hand to her chest, her breath quickening. Instinctively she grasped the lifeline she had disdained before.

'What did she say then? About all this?'

'Who?'

'Annette, of course. You've just been speaking to her, haven't you?'

'She wasn't in work. She isn't well.'

'Why, what's wrong with her?'

'I don't know. They didn't say.'

'That's funny. It's not like her to be ill,' Edna found herself saying.

Steve looked at her curiously. She was not usually so solicitous towards Annette.

The curtains drawn, Edna seemed reluctant to move.

'She'll need to know. When are you supposed to be seeing her next?'

'Not till tomorrow. Why, Mam? What're you so worried about?'

'I'm not worried – I'm just trying to help you, boy. Do you want me to try and get a message to her?'

'How can you do that? She's not on the phone.'

'Your father can call round to that flat where she lives. After he's finished work.'

'Good Lord, no. There's no need for that. I'll drop her a line, if you'll post it for me. She'll get it tomorrow.'

'You sure now?'

'Of course. She'll only panic, if Dad goes round there. She'll think it's something drastic.'

'It's drastic enough, son. I hate to see you like this.'

She was close to tears. He looked away, embarrassed.

'Don't worry, Mam. I'll be alright soon.'

'Well, keep out of trouble in future. I can't stand . . .'

She blew her nose, shook her head fiercely. 'It wasn't that boy from Brynpadarn, was it? Did this to you?'

'What're you saying, Mam?'

'The one Annette was going with? That Ivor?'

'Good God, no. Don't *say* things like that, Mam!'

'Well, somebody did it! It wasn't the man in the moon, was it?'

'Please, Mam!'

'We've got to know, son! We've –.'

Her voice broke. With tortured face, she hurried out.

Nurse Sandy Dewhurst, auburn-haired, broad-shouldered, butch, plumped up Sally's pillows in Highland Sanatorium. 'Better put on a clean nightie,' she said censoriously. 'The old man's coming to see you.'

'Old man?'

'Dr Campbell. The boss.'

'Coming here? Why?'

'Don't know. Have to wait and see, won't we?' She rummaged in Sally's locker. 'This one'll do. Come on, take that off. It's wringing wet.' She put the clean blue nightie on the bed, waited impassively.

Sally coughed, reached for her sputum cup, spat into it. Shakily she wiped her mouth.

'Sweating a lot, aren't you?' said the nurse. The look she gave Sally was her nearest approach to sympathy.

'Tell me something I don't know, Sandy.'

'Hey. No need for that.'

The laconic conversation, edging on banter, was the common currency between patients and staff. Both, to differing degrees, felt a sense of exclusion from the workaday world; the patients more severely, because of their enforced isolation, but the nurses and orderlies too, by reason of the location of the sanatorium and its connotations of a leper colony.

Sitting up in bed, Sally took off her nightie. Sandy helped her put on the clean one.

'When will he be here, d'you know?' Sally asked.

'Any time now. Mind you're on your best behaviour.' She gave Sally a lugubrious wink, and left the cubicle.

Dr Campbell was broad, leathery-faced, a stubble of grey hair coating his scalp. He gave an impression of physical power not long past its peak, like an ageing pugilist. He tended to exert his authority as medical superintendent of the sanatorium from afar, controlling everything through his minions. His appearance at the bedside of a patient was a rarity, and Sally feared the worst. They must be sending her away for a thora, the dreaded operation by means of which a diseased lung was permanently disabled. The operation was performed not at Highland but in a chest hospital by the sea, a chaste white heap created in the 1930s as a temple of modern medicine.

Sally knew that if she went there she would never come back. She would die under the knife; she knew it.

She looked at Campbell steadily. She would not flinch, nor go under easily.

He was accompanied by the virago known to the patients as Sister Bronwen, the most senior nurse at Highland apart from the matron. She had the air of a high priestess, her prim, starched uniform exuding the very essence of discipline and good order. Her dress, her iron-grey hair, her remote unsmiling eyes and cold efficiency, all expressed the underlying assumption of Highland, that only by such rigorous self-control could the ravages of the tubercle bacillus be held in check.

She stood stiffly by the medical superintendent's side, her presence silently underlying the wisdom of his words, the completeness of his authority.

'I'm told your mother wants to take you away from here,' said Campbell accusingly. His voice was higher-pitched than one might have expected from his build, rasping and hectoring, as if he were confronted always by a recalcitrant band of trouble-makers.

'I'm not going. I've told her,' replied Sally calmly.

'Oh, ye have, have ye? That's news to me. Sister Wyatt told me your mother had been demanding your release. There's nothing to stop you going, you know. There's no barbed wire around Highland.'

'I know that, doctor. But I want to get better.'

'I'm glad to hear it.' Campbell grimaced suddenly, an unexpected flash of white dentures more like a snarl than a smile. 'So you've told her you're staying, have you?'

'Yes. Right away. It was her idea, not mine.'

'Well, it's a pity she didn't believe you. It causes us no end of trouble, this sort of thing. There's plenty waiting outside who'd be only too willing to take your bed, you know.'

'I know that. But I'm not leaving here till I'm cured.'

'Good. Good. You hear that, sister?' Campbell wagged his head approvingly. She nodded impassively.

'Well now. Let's get down to business. Pass me the file please.' He took it from Sister Bronwen and flapped it open on the bed. Broodingly he studied it, and Sally suddenly saw him for what he essentially was, a born actor playing the role of benevolent dictator.

'You've had a bit of a setback lately. You know that, don't ye?'

'Yes. That's why they moved me here, I suppose.'

'Exactly. But there's nothing to be alarmed about. We've got it under control. You've stabilised nicely, the last week or so. But still . . . we think something more is needed.'

He shot her a glance, inquisitive, good-humoured.

'You're wondering what I'm going to suggest, I suppose, aren't ye?'

Sally met his gaze levelly. 'A thora?'

'Thora? Who put that idea in your head?' He swivelled round. 'Has anyone mentioned the word thoracaplasty to this young woman, Sister Miles?'

'Not to my knowledge,' she replied, with thin-lipped austerity.

'Sister Wyatt wouldn't have done that, would she?'

'I'm quite sure she wouldn't.'

'Well now. Where'd you get that idea from, Sally?'

'Because I'm on Powys Block, I suppose.'

'It's not a place apart, Sally. Just part of the sanatorium.' Suddenly he softened. 'Look, Sally. I'll be honest with you. We were thinking of giving you a pneumothorax but it's not appropriate any longer. We're going to try something else. Something new.' His eyes glistened theatrically. 'Streptomycin. Have you heard of it?'

'Yes. You gave it to that woman on Knighton Block, didn't you? The one with TB meningitis.'

'Indeed we did, Sally. And remarkable results we had, too. She is now on her way to a full recovery.'

It had happened three months ago. Word had spread around of a new wonder drug from America, something suitable only as a last desperate throw of the dice. Sally's face clouded.

'I'm not as ill as that, am I?'

'Of course not. Did I say you were? It's coming into wider use now. We think it's the right thing for you. We've got every confidence in it. But there are some side effects you ought to know about.'

He explained that the drug left patients prone to varying degress of deafness and attacks of giddiness. 'We're learning to counteract this. I'm sure we'll be using it in combination with other drugs before long. But it's the way forward, Sally.'

Sally felt a veil lifting, a shaft of hope long suppressed. 'I'll take anything you want me to, doctor. You know best.'

Campbell smiled. 'Good girl. Didn't I tell ye, sister? This one's a sensible patient.' He touched Sally's arm, as it lay on the counterpane. 'I was very concerned when I heard you might be discharging yourself, Sally. That's why I wanted to see you myself.' He stepped back, added brusquely: 'We'll start the treatment right away. Sister Wyatt will be along here in a moment.' He turned, paused in the cubicle doorway. 'Just remember one thing though, Sally. Mental attitude is still important. Keep your spirits up.'

Sally, suddenly overwhelmed, could only nod.

22

She felt terrible, going back to see Shirley, but it had to be done. There was no getting away from it.

She went down on the six o'clock bus, nearly empty as usual after disgorging the homeward-bound office workers on its outward journey. The driver was the one they called Stirling Moss, who went round corners on two wheels. Or so it felt like. The conductor, not George this time, stood at the front whistling softly, swaying in a practised manner with the bus's violent motions.

Annette looked through the window, contented. She had made it up with her mother. They had spent a lovely day, doing things together they had not done for ages: baking cakes in the kitchen, going shopping, drinking afternoon tea in the little cafe by the station. Steve was hardly mentioned. By unspoken assent they shelved the question of what was to be done about things, simply building bridges between each other, putting their relationship on a new footing.

She walked along Shipwrights Road, her high heels clacking on the pavement. A chill was in the air, a foretaste of autumn. Through gaps between houses to her left, she caught glimpses of the harbour. She felt warm, comforted by these sights of the familiar. Reaching the prom, she was surprised to see huge dark clouds out to sea. The sheer bulk of them dismayed her. She did not know why, but they struck her as terrible. Quickening her step, she reached Shirley's place and rang the bell.

She almost rang a second time, but then Shirley opened the door. 'Well well,' she said coldly. 'The wanderer returns.'

'Don't be like that, Shirl. Can I come in?'

Shirley opened the door wider, avoiding Annette's eyes as she stepped past her. 'Better come on up, I suppose,' she said. 'I've just put the kettle on.'

Following her upstairs, Annette noticed a scag in one of Shirley's stockings. The stairway smelt musty. Had it been this way before? Their footsteps echoed strangely, as if nobody had inhabited the place for ages. The remains of a skimpy meal were on the table in the front room, where they'd so often sat together. Already it seemed light years away.

'Didn't expect to see you here today, I must say,' said Shirley shortly.

'I'm sorry about last night. I know I shouldn't have left like that, but I couldn't help it. I – '

'I don't mean that. How's Steve?'

'Steve?' repeated Annette, puzzled.

'Well, is he home from hospital, or what?'

'Hospital? What do you mean, hospital?'

Shirley looked at Annette strangely. 'You mean you haven't heard?'

'Heard what?'

'Jesus.'

'What're you talking about, Shirley?'

'You're going to have a shock, kid. You'd better sit down.'

'*What's happened?*'

'He had a going-over last night. I thought everyone knew.'

Annette stared at her, as if she had trouble understanding. 'Going-over?'

'I'm sorry, 'Nette. Look – '

'Is he hurt bad?'

'I don't know. I don't think so. I – '

'You say he's in hospital.'

'Yes, that's what we heard but – '

'I must go and see him.'

'I'm sure he's OK, 'Nette.'

'Who did it?'

'What?'

'Who beat him up?'

'I don't know.'

'Where'd it happen?'

'Look, let me just get you something – '

'Tell me, Shirley!'

'By those steps. Going down to Back Row.'

'I see,' said Annette, white-faced. She felt, for a moment, the sensation of her legs giving way, then straightened up.

'Where you going now?' cried Shirley, distracted.

'To see him of course.'

'But why? After all he's done to you!'

'I've got to.'

'Don't be such a fool!' Shirley called down the stairwell. 'He's not worth it!'

The kettle shuddered to the boil, steaming and spitting.

The first specks of rain hardly wetted the pavements. They fell unheeded on Annette, hurrying along with her head down, thinking of Steve. How badly had he been beaten? She saw his face, a mask of blood, felt the ache of his body. She beat back a sense of panic, the sense that something was lost irretrievably. They had made love and then . . . the past few weeks seemed unreal, she could not believe they had happened. Had he really been to a prostitute? How could he, why would he want to? It was all a nightmare, along with the sending of her father to prison. What was wrong with the world, that such things could happen?

In an obscure way she felt she was to blame. If she hadn't been so damn proud, wanting things on her own terms instead of taking what she could like other women . . . But even as she entertained this thought, she rejected it. It was far more mixed-up than that, beyond any reasoning.

She wrenched open the red door of a telephone kiosk, flicked through the tattered pages of the directory. Glanaber General Hospital, there it was . . . she put two pennies in, dialled the number.

When the operator answered, she pressed button A.

'Hullo? Can you tell me if Mr Steve Lewis is still in there, please?'

'What ward is he on?'

'I don't know . . . he had an accident yesterday.'

'Just a moment, please.'

A long silence. Rain spattered the windows. Suddenly a grotesque picture formed itself in her brain – of a pool of brown vomit at the top of the steps leading up from Back Row, the day she'd walked out on Shirley. Was that when it had happened? Could that have been . . . ?

'Mr Lewis was discharged today . . . Hullo? Are you there?'

'Yes . . . Thank you.'

She rattled the phone back into its cradle. She could not move for a moment. Now she could see Steve's face in the vomit, looking up at her. She felt faint; her hands were shaking.

A shadow was outside; she cringed from it fearfully. It took shape, became a man looking in at her; not unpleasantly. She gathered herself together, put her purse back in her handbag, pushed the door open.

'Sorry,' she murmured.

'No hurry, love,' the man said, smiling.

She stood uncertainly for a moment, then decided to go to Steve's house. She had to see him, find out for herself what had happened!

The rain beat down faster; she was getting very wet. She had left the house without a raincoat, wearing only a light jacket over the cotton dress she'd had on all day. It was too late to go for a bus now, she was already in the long road out of town leading to Dewi Avenue. She began to run, the skirt sticking to her thighs. She'd look a right mess when she got there; what on earth was she up to? But there was no turning back, even though it meant facing Steve's mother looking like something the tide had washed up.

Gasping, a stitch in her side, she stopped at the gate. His father's car was in the drive; remembering the last time she had been there, she hesitated. How could she think of going inside? She was about to go away when the door was flung open. Jim Lewis, head down against the buffeting rain, hurried to the car. He looked up, saw her.

'Annette!'

It was too late now. She cursed herself for coming.

'What you doing here, girl? You're like a drowned rat.'

'How's Steve?'

'Not too bad. Come on in.'

'No, really. I – '

'Don't be soft. He'd like to see you. I've just posted you a letter. I'd have come round to tell you myself, but –' He hustled her up the drive.

'What happened?'

'I'll tell you inside, look,' said Jim, his native dialect coming through.

They were in the hall now, and she dripping over the nice carpet.

'Edna!' he called. 'Annette's here. She's soaking wet. Come on, girl, let's get you dry.' He tries to usher her towards the living-room.

'Goodness gracious!' exclaimed Edna, coming out of the front room. 'I couldn't believe it when – How'd you get in that state? You look like a drowned rat, girl!'

Feeling profoundly rat-like Annette held her ground, miserably.

'Don't just stand there, come on in and see Steve. He's had a nasty turn. I'll get you some dry clothes in a minute. Good heavens above, fancy coming through the wet like that! I don't know what the world's coming to.'

She allowed herself to be led to the lounge where Steve, woken up by the noise, gave her a dazed look. The babble of voices, his parents both talking the same time, Annette assuring them she was alright, made his head thump. He thought, for a moment, that his father had fetched her in the car and wondered why she was so wet.

'How'd you know?' he said eventually, when they were alone.

'Shirley told me. What happened then?'

'Oh, nothing much.'

'Nothing much! You've only had a pasting, that's all. Who did it, Steve?'

'I don't know. Honest,' he said, seeing her face. 'I don't know him from Adam.'

'But why? Were you in a fight?'

'Not really. I – '

Edna fussed in, talking twenty to the dozen. 'I've got some dry clothes for you upstairs, now come along they ought to fit you. Would you like a bath now, you'll feel better after – she'll be back in a minute Steve, just you lie down nice and quiet.'

Annette, protesting that she was fine, was jostled upstairs into a spare bedroom and handed a towel.

On her own, in the sudden quiet, she felt very lonely.

She was in Steve's house. He had been beaten up by God knows who. She was having his baby. Her father was in prison.

She began to cry.

She sat by the settee, in borrowed nightie and dressing-gown. She felt weird, wondering why the old cow hadn't simply sent her packing; she'd never had much time for her before. Drying her clothes out, letting her sit by her precious son like this, and she scarcely decent. It made her head whirl, thinking of it.

But she was so relieved to find Steve OK. There didn't seem much wrong with him really. A bang on the head; bruised ribs or whatever; nothing broken, at any rate.

Talking to him as he lay on the settee, she'd let him hold her hand at first, but she'd found an excuse to let go and now her hands were folded quietly in her lap. He hadn't come clean with her; hadn't really explained what he'd been doing down that filthy Back Row. He was looking at her soulfully, wanting a snog in spite of his condition, and she was having none of it. She knew she had to have it out with him but the words stuck in her throat.

'What's wrong, love?'

'Nothing.'

'You seem a million miles away.' He stretched out a hand, gazed at her meltingly. 'Aren't you going to give me a kiss?'

'I've given you one.'

'That's not enough.'

'It wouldn't be good for you,' she said, listening to her mincing tone in horror. 'You've just come out of hospital, remember?'

'It'd make me better.' He put his hand on her leg, just above the knee; she wanted to brush it away but instead burst out, 'Who's this woman you've been seeing then, Steve?'

'What woman?' he replied, recoiling.

'You know. The one in Back Row.'

'I haven't been seeing anyone. I don't know anyone in Back Row.'

'Don't lie to me, Steve. You were there yesterday, weren't you?'

She crossed her legs suddenly, ridding herself of his touch.

'What makes you think that?'

'It's obvious, isn't it? That's what you were doing down there.'

His face was flushed, guilt-ridden.

'It was her boyfriend, was it? Did this to you? Or her *pimp*.'

She dragged the word from her subconscious, unaware that she had even known it.

'What are you saying? That's a horrible word to use.'

'Well, she's one of them, isn't she?'

'No! She's not!'

'So you *have* been seeing her!'

'Not like that though!'

'How then?'

'She's a friend,' he answered, after a pause.

'*Friend*?'

'Yes. Nothing wrong with that, is there?'

'It depends. What's her name, this person?'

'Mrs Baker – Sara Baker,' he answered reluctantly.

'Oh! So she's married. How old is she?'

'I don't know. I haven't asked.'

Annette stared at him, confused. She hadn't expected him to admit seeing anyone.

'Why haven't you told me about her then?'

'I didn't like to. In case . . .'

In case I got the wrong idea, she answered for him silently.

'I'm sorry, 'Nette. I should've told you.'

'Yes. You should.'

The house was wrapped in an uncanny silence. No sound came from the front room where, presumably, his parents were sitting. She had a sudden suspicion that they were spying on them. Was his mother listening at the door? She felt the beginnings of a scream inside her, a scream of desperation.

But what was Steve saying now? He was giving an explanation of how he had got to know this woman, something about going to her house to do a story for the paper and, looking at and listening to him, she knew he was lying. Knew, too, what sort of a woman this Mrs Baker was, even though she'd never met her.

Knew what Steve had been doing with her, even while his baby was growing inside her.

'So who did this to you then?' she asked abruptly, cutting him short.

'I don't know. I've never seen him before in my life.'

'You must have!'

'I tell you I haven't! I don't know everyone in this town, you know.'

'You surprise me. Was it her husband?'

'What?'

'This Baker woman. Was he the one who hit you?'

'No! What makes you think that?'

'Well, that's where it happened, isn't it? By those steps.'

'Who told you that?'

'Shirley. Everyone seems to know except me!'

'I'm sorry,' he said wretchedly.

'Sorry! You should be sorry for yourself.'

Her hands were shaking. She thrust them deep in the pockets of her dressing-gown. A door opened somewhere, a murmur of voices. The door closed, someone padded upstairs.

'I've stopped seeing her,' said Steve. 'That's what I went to tell her. I came up the steps, and this guy hit me.' He looked pleadingly at the silent Annette. 'That's all that happened, 'Nette – I swear to God.'

This was the moment to tell him. She felt empty.

'I hate myself,' he said miserably. 'I really do. I want to get away from here – both of us.'

The baby, she thought. I must tell him about the baby.

'Look,' he said eagerly. 'I'm going to apply for a job in London. I met an old mate of mine not long ago

– he'll help me get a job in Fleet Street. Just think of that, love. I'll be in the big time!'

He put his hand back on her thigh. She let it stay there.

'And there's something else – I haven't had a chance to tell you yet. I've had a poem accepted by *John o' London's*. Isn't that marvellous?'

She nodded, unable to speak.

His voice changed, became huskier.

'I want you to come with me. To London. You will, love, won't you?'

He squeezed her thigh. 'Please.'

'I don't know,' she said slowly.

'I mean – when we're married.'

He was looking at her strangely. She felt the word pressing down on her.

'You will though – won't you?'

He tried to take her hand. His eyes were shining.

'I can't, Steve.'

'Why not?'

'I just can't.'

'Because of her!' he cried out in anguish. 'I told you – there's nothing in it!'

'No – not that!'

'What then?'

'I don't know.'

'Christ.'

They sat in silence. She thought of his baby, growing inside her.

23

Ivor came home exhausted. His boss had sent him up to a hill farm ten miles away, to lay down floorboards for a loft conversion. The wrong measurements had been given and he'd had to go all the way back to the timber yard in town for replacements. Not only that, but the crappy old Morris van had broken down on the return journey. Ivor had tinkered with the engine and got it going, but the spluttering and misfiring afterwards stretched his nerves to breaking point. What's more the farmer was a surly old bastard who pretended he only spoke Welsh, and got in the way a lot just to be awkward.

Only one thing soothed Ivor. He'd have a skinful at the Black Lion later and forget everything.

He knew something was wrong as soon as he set foot in the house. There was a tension in the air like a physical presence. His little sister Megan was upstairs doing her homework, while Lennie was scuffling his feet moodily on the black rug by the fireplace.

'What sort of time do you call this?' his mother asked. 'Your dinner's gone cold so don't expect anything special.'

'Don't worry. I'll make something myself. I'm perfectly capable.'

'I'll warm it up for you, so keep a civil tongue in your head. You've got too big for your boots, that's the trouble with you since your father's gone.'

She banged some dirty crocks down in the kitchen, scattering the cutlery from the plates.

Ivor scowled. He hated it when Eileen brought his father into this. It seemed to be exploiting the dead, as if they were capable of taking sides. Without a word, he brushed past her and went upstairs.

'And where d'you think you're going now? You lost the use of your tongue?' she shouted after him.

'I'm going to wash and change. I'll have something out, don't worry about me.'

'Oh, the devil with you!'

Stripped to the waist in the tiny bathroom, swilling himself with his soapy hands – he disdained the use of a flannel, something cissyish in his opinion – Ivor calmed down, wondering what had bitten his mother. He tried to make allowances, but it was hard. He wondered, not for the first time, if he should move out and get his own place. He'd have a lot more freedom, and he was sure they'd all be better off for it; all he and his mother seemed to do these days was quarrel. But how would she manage without his money, and how would he manage on his own? Flats weren't all that easy to come by; most of them went to students sharing, or young couples without children. None of his mates had them, they all lived at home or in lodgings. He didn't want to go into lodgings, and what was the point of that anyway? He'd be going from the frying pan into the fire, from a quarrelsome mother to a bossy landlady. No thank you; he was better off where he was, for all the drawbacks. Anyway he'd miss Lennie and Megan, and miss Mam too, that was the trouble.

He didn't allow himself to think, for more than a second, of what might have been: he and Annette getting married, setting up a home of their own and having children.

He briskly towelled himself dry, his skin turning pink with the rubbing.

He put on the nice green tweedy jacket he'd bought at a summer sale, and did his tie up with a flourish. Whistling, he went downstairs, looking like a man without a care in the world.

His mother was sitting in the kitchen, and his heart went cold when he saw her.

'What's wrong, Mam?' he asked anxiously, 'got a headache or something?'

She did not answer for a moment, then said: 'She's not coming.'

She was resting her head on her hand, the fingertips pressed close to her scalp.

He saw the letter on the table. She gestured to it, aware of his gaze although not looking at him.

'From Sally?'

She nodded.

He opened it out and read it, then put it back on the table.

'I know what you're thinking,' she said. 'You're glad, aren't you?'

He did not answer.

She took a hankie from her apron pocket and blew her nose quietly.

'God help me,' she said. 'I wanted her here, to look after. Even though she might have – '

She choked on the word.

'Don't,' said Ivor. 'You mustn't say that. Never.'

The house was silent. Lennie had gone out to play.

'It wouldn't have been right, Mam. For the other two.'

'Doesn't matter now – does it?' she said bitterly.

She pushed her chair back, scraping it along the red-and-blue flagstones.

She began heating his dinner up.

'You didn't tell him?' said Lorna disbelievingly. 'Why not?'

'I didn't feel like.'

Annette sat in her pink dressing-gown, after the bath she had scorned to take in Dewi Avenue. She could still feel the touch of those strange clothes on her skin, the humiliation of it.

'You gotta tell him some time,' declared Lorna.

'Have I?'

'Course you have.' Lorna looked at her daughter as if she were a rare zoological specimen. 'What're you thinking of?'

Shrieks of laughter from the wireless greeted Frankie Howerd's catchphrase, 'Ladies and gentle-*men*.' With a swift, impatient movement Lorna switched it off.

'So what you gonna do then?'

'About what?'

'The baby, of course.'

'I don't know . . . Have it I suppose.'

'Just like that.'

Annette shrugged.

Lorna sat down heavily on her favourite chair, facing the Rayburn.

'You planning to marry him?'

'He hasn't asked me yet,' she lied. 'Anyway, I don't know if I want to.'

'Should've thought of that sooner, shouldn't you?'

Lorna, remembering her own past, felt a twinge of conscience at this harsh judgement.

'How're you gonna manage if you don't? Babies cost money, you know.'

'I'll go on the Assistance.'

'Assistance!' scorned Lorna. 'You'll be lucky if you get enough to keep you in nappies.'

Annette's silence goaded her.

'You ought to have come home anyway,' she grumbled, ''stead of going to his house like that, shaming us.'

'Oh! So you think I should be ashamed then, do you?'

'Not of having the baby. Going round there I mean, in the pouring rain and that. She must think we're queer.'

'Who?'

'His mother, of course. Mrs Thingummy.'

'Their name's Lewis.'

'Don't be cheeky!' snapped Lorna. 'I don't know what your father will say about this, an' all.'

Annette pulled her dressing-gown tighter around her, as she'd pulled the one she'd been wearing a few hours earlier in Steve's house. She'd asked for her clothes, still damp, had been given a lift home by Steve's father. She could still see Steve's face as she left, the hurt and confusion it registered.

'Who had a go at him then, anyway?'

'He doesn't know.'

Lorna gave her a sharp look. 'Sounds a bit fishy to me. Was he in a fight or what?'

'No. Someone just hit him, that's all.'

'People don't just go round hitting, unless they've got a reason . . . He must've seen who it was, in broad daylight.'

'He says he doesn't know him.'

Lorna sniffed. Annette suddenly felt tearful. Sensing this, Lorna softened.

'Don't get me wrong,' she said gently. 'I feel sorry for the boy.'

I don't, Annette wanted to say. He's been seeing a prostitute.

'Cup of tea?'

Annette shook her head.

'You must be worn out, girl.'

'I'm OK.'

The two women sat in silence, steeped in thoughts they could not share.

There had been a terrible row and then silence. He knew Betty would not be bothering him again.

He set his mind on little things, trying not to look too far ahead. Another football season had begun and he was back in the team, under a new captain. He had started to build a new shed, where he could do his carpentry after work and at weekends. Some day he might be his own boss.

What bothered him most was his feeling of being at odds with everything. He was irritable, moody, not really enjoying anything, even his football. People looked askance at him, taking care not to cross him for fear of having their heads bitten off, or worse.

He forced himself to go out and socialise, even though he liked nothing better these days than being alone. At the Black Lion in Brynpadarn he put on an act, capturing something of the old devil-may-care Ivor everyone knew.

That evening, however, things took a strange turn. Sitting quietly at the bar, smoking a Woodbine and supping a pint of Roberts Dark, he clocked on to the fact that the talk around him was oddly muted and that people were giving him peculiar looks.

It was Will Dubbin who finally detached himself from the rest and shuffled over. He was slackmouthed, smelly, a little simple.

'Give it to him then boy, eh?' he grinned. His fists opened and closed emptily, his head slanted lop-sided towards his left shoulder.

Ivor ignored him, dragging on his Woodie.

'Time too. Had it coming to him.' Ivor caught a whiff of his breath and said irritably, 'Bugger off Will, leave me in peace.'

'Should've killed him. Had it coming,' he parroted, the words coming blindly from his skeewiff mouth.

'For Chrissake. What're you talking about, mun?'

Will rolled up his fist, thrust it under Ivor's nose. 'Thass what you did, yeh? Hit him cross the chops, yah yah yah!' He jabbed the air futilely, his movements releasing a reek from his fetid clothing.

'Piss off, you stupid bugger!' Ivor thrust him away disgustedly. 'What the 'ell's he on about, anyone know?'

The staring faces in the silent bar gave him the uncanny sense of acting out a dream.

Will stood there confused, opening and closing his hands.

'We thought it was you,' said a sober voice quietly at his side. Job Monk, black-haired, tanned face, serious-minded.

'Thought what was me?'

'Duffed up that reporter feller. If it wasn't, OK. Don't blame him.' He nodded at Will. 'You know what he's like.'

'What reporter?'

Job gave him a look. 'Pull the other one, Ivor.'

'I tell you I don't know!'

'Jesus. Where you been all day, boy?'

'Don't mean that bastard Lewis, do you?'

'The same.' Job pushed his empty glass along the counter. 'Pint again Joan, please.'

'Alright, pet. Just a minute.'

She shot a glance at Ivor, who looked stunned.

'No need for that,' grumbled Will. 'Pushin' and shovin'. No need at all.' He loped back to his cronies, the murmur of renewed conversation dispelling the tension.

Ivor stood in silence a moment, then edged over to Job. 'What happened then?

'You really don't know?' said Job incredulously. 'Not taking the piss?'

'Shit, no.'

'Well, I'll be buggered. You're the only one that doesn't.' He swigged his ale. 'Someone give him what for, that's all. Not before time too, big-headed sod that he is.'

'You mean someone had a go at Lewis? When?'

'Last night.'

'Was he hurt?'

'Not much, worse luck. Few bruises, by all accounts.'

'Bloody hell. Where was this then?'

'Down by the harbour.' He gave Ivor a close look. 'You sure it wasn't you?'

'No! First I've heard of it. Why should it be me, anyway?'

'Now you *are* taking the piss. Bugger off, Ivor.'

'I'm not! I want to know! Tell me!'

'Well, he's going out with your old girlfriend, isn't he?'

'Yes, but – '

'And having his end away with that tart in Back Row.'

'He's what?'

'Don't say you didn't know! For God's sake man – '

'You telling me that Lewis . . . oh no . . . '

Job stared at him, alarmed. 'You must have known *that*. Every bugger knows that, Ivor.'

'Christ,' murmured Ivor. 'Holy Christ.' He leaned heavily on the bar.

'Hey – sit down a minute. Come on now.' He put a hand on his elbow.

'No!' cried Ivor passionately. 'Leave me alone!' He pushed Job away, elbowed some drinkers aside and lurched out of the bar.

Part Six

DEPARTURES

24

In his prison cell in Swansea, Ted Morris looked at the last of the day through the barred window. His cellmate snored on his bunk. He had a great capacity for sleep.

To Ted's eye, the patch of sky he saw was like the pale blue of a box of paints someone had given him as a kid. He'd forgotten it till now, the pale blue of the box's cover.

Everything kept reminding him of something else in this place. The screws were like the army sergeants he'd known in the Pioneer Corps; the prisoners like kids he'd known at school; the food like army grub, only worse. The man snoring in the bunk was like his Uncle Ben, only fatter.

It was worse than he'd expected at first, but he'd got used to it all now; the hot, stifling smell of male bodies, the slopping out, the pathetic bullying. He'd seen worse things in the army, much worse. And he'd be home after Christmas.

He stretched out on his bunk, trying not to think of home too much. He thought instead about the first girlfriend he'd had. Joyce was from away, and came to Glanaber on holiday with her parents. He used to meet her in the amusement arcade under the King's Hall, and if he had enough money he treated her to a ride on the dodgems. He showed off something awful, banging into other cars like fun. He was never sure if she liked it or not but it made her shriek and she clung tight to him, and that was nice.

She couldn't stay out late; she was only fourteen. But sometimes they found somewhere quiet, where he kissed her. She pursed her lips up and closed her eyes, as if afraid to see what she was doing. He had never done anything he shouldn't.

There were times when he thought of the woman in Back Row. He couldn't see her half so clearly as his childhood sweetheart. Nor (and this was strange) could he remember what her lips felt like on his. But Joyce's tight, innocent kisses, and the smell of her skin, were as real to him as the rattle of keys in the lock.

In a few days' time, he'd be seeing Lorna. He wasn't sure if he wanted to or not. She reminded him of things he'd put aside for the duration (his private word for his incarceration); the comforts of home, all that went by the name of normality. He preferred to serve his time in a kind of vacuum, as if nothing existed outside the prison. And her visits dragged anyway, with the screws watching over them. They found little to talk about, and with those bastards listening you couldn't say much anyway.

He lit a fag; he rolled his own now. It was something to do and saved money.

The man in the top bunk started to snore. Ted looked at the blue, drifting smoke, and tried not to hate him.

Annette took another day off before returning to work. The office was curiously hushed, as if it were waiting for her. Rita gave her a strange, almost scared look, while Big Bertha's air was one of undisguised triumph.

'Better today, Annette?' she asked, with a poisonous smile. 'We've missed you, haven't we, Rita?'

Rita nodded dumbly.

'Nice of you to say so,' Annette said politely.

'We were very busy as it happens,' Big Bertha steamrollered on. 'But I'm sure you wouldn't have stayed away unless you had to.'

Annette pursed up her lips, and her temper.

'Oh – by the way. Your boyfriend rang up the other day. We told him you were off sick. You've seen him since, I suppose?'

'Yes.'

'Alright then, is he?' Big Bertha asked sweetly.

'Yes, fine.'

'Ah, good. Funny how rumours start. We were told he'd had a nasty accident, weren't we, Rita?'

'He did, but he's better now,' said Annette.

'Oh, that's nice. I don't like to see anyone in trouble.'

At home, Steve fretted. He wanted to go back to work, but for two whole days he had an aching side and thumping headaches. The doctor, summoned by Edna, examined him gravely and prescribed pain killers. If the headaches persisted, he would recommend another X-ray.

He was filled with remorse, and cursed the day he had met Sara. Yet Annette's attitude puzzled him. He could understand her being angry, but why so cold and remote? He'd rung her at work, and it was like talking to a stranger. She'd made excuses for not coming to see him for a day or two.

Not only his heart was hurt, but his pride. He'd convinced himself that the mere mention of marriage would make things right between them, but she'd thrust him away as if he were a leper. If only she knew! That woman had thrown herself at him! How many other blokes would have acted so decently by her?

Outside the summer months, Annette and Rita had a lunchtime snack at a cafe opposite the railway station. There were old GWR holiday posters on the walls and photographs of giant steam engines. It had a mixed clientele of office workers, rail travellers and country people in town for a bit of shopping before going home again on the bus.

Rita wanted to know everything.

'What happened to him then? They say someone half murdered him.'

'Rubbish. There's hardly a scratch on him.'

'But who'd want to do a thing like that, Annette? In broad daylight too.'

'Leave it be, Rita. I don't want to talk about it.'

'Well, alright, but I was only thinking of you.'

'What d'you mean?'

'Well, not very nice for you, is it? The things people are saying.'

Annette looked at her sharply. 'Like what?'

'I don't like to say, Annette. It's not decent.'

Annette gave her a straight look. 'You don't want to listen to rumours. This town's full of them. There may be some about you, for all you know.'

Rita blushed. 'I don't think so, Annette. Not like this, anyway.'

'You never know. Be like the three monkeys.'

'Oh?' asked Rita, mystified. 'Who are they then?'

'Hear no evil, see no evil, speak no evil.'

Back at the office, a strange idea possessed her. It

frightened her at first, so that she tried to forget it. But it refused to go away, and became irresistible.

Jack had gone away again; he never stayed long. He was up in Scotland on a job, she didn't know exactly what; she never asked too many questions. He sent her something every week, money orders she cashed in the post office. He kept a lot more for himself, she knew that for a fact, but she didn't grumble. There were some who got bugger-all from their husbands, and she was glad of something regular coming in.

Sara got Vi off to school, and sat down with a cup of tea and a fag. The day stretched before her; she had nothing to do, except a bit of shopping. Normally she'd be at work now, but her cleaning job had come to an end; not that it had paid much. She got more for an hour or two a week upstairs with her regulars, but that had stopped as well. She didn't feel up to it, and the bobbies were turning nasty. One had been sniffing round the other week, standing outside for ages just staring. She'd had a good mind to go and tell him to buzz off, but didn't. He hadn't had the cheek to knock the door, or she'd have told him a thing or two. She wasn't breaking any law, and they knew it. She didn't go out displaying herself, and no-one could just knock the door and expect to get it. She just entertained a few friends, and if they wanted to leave a little something that was up to them.

She couldn't say she missed them though, apart from Ted the postman. He was nice, a real pal. He'd only come a few times, late at night when he thought no-one was watching. He'd felt dead guilty about it too, she could tell that. When it was over they used to talk, about all sorts of things. He was very proud of his daughter, but felt he wasn't good enough for her. He never mentioned his wife, but the nice ones didn't. She'd given up wondering what it was drove men to the likes of her; it wasn't just the sex, she was sure of that. Men were funny creatures.

But now Ted was in the jug, poor sod. All over money. She'd have given it him for nothing, if he'd asked.

She was better than she'd been, but still felt like a washed-out rag. And she'd be moving house soon, from what the council said. They still hadn't told her where she'd be going, but the way she felt now she didn't care. All she wished was that someone could wave a magic wand and set her up there, without all the bother of moving.

She tried to keep cheerful for Vi's sake, but it was hard. Everything was such an effort. If she didn't get another job soon she'd have to go on the Assistance, but she couldn't face all their questions. And the cops would start nosing round again, prying into her business. Oh God! If it wasn't for Vi she'd top herself, she was sure.

But that afternoon, something happened. She'd been having a bit of a rest when she'd looked out and seen someone tapping Nancy Pugh's door. A slim girl with reddish hair, hadn't seen her before. Not that she'd stood staring at the girl, wasn't one for things like that. She'd got on with tidying the place up, before Vi came home; she was a terror these days, like a little old woman. But then there came a tap at the door, and she'd opened it to find the girl there.

'Excuse me calling, but is Mrs Baker in?'
'Who's asking?'
'I am.' A quick smile.

'And who might you be?'

'My name's Annette. Annette Morris.'

'I'm Mrs Baker. What do you want?'

The girl looked surprised. 'Can I come in please? I won't keep you long.'

She let the girl in, if only to get away from Nancy Pugh staring at them from her doorway, nosy bitch. Annette . . . the name rang a bell, but not very strongly.

In the dim afternoon light, half her face was in darkness.

'Well?' said Sara. 'What can I do for you?'

'I just wanted to meet you, that's all,' Annette said levelly.

'From the council, are you? Where you gonna put me then, eh? Cos if the rent's too high I'm not going, I can't afford it – '

'I'm not from the council, what makes you think that?'

'Well, where you from then? Don't know you, do I?'

'No. But I think you know my boyfriend. Steve Lewis.'

'Steve? I don't know no Steve.'

'Yes you do. He works on the paper.'

Sara's expression changed. 'Oh. You mean Gerry.'

'*Gerry*?'

'Oh Christ. Sit down, girl.'

To her own surprise, Annette sat. She hadn't known what to expect, but certainly not this. She'd expected to see a brazen young tart gashed with lipstick and rouge, not this ill-looking woman nearly old enough to be her mother. Could this be the wrong Mrs Baker? She had a terrible sense of making a fool of herself.

'What about a cup of tea then, eh? I'll put the kettle on.'

The dark, tiny house, the tatty furniture, the air of poverty, seemed all wrong for the trade the mysterious Mrs Baker was said to live by. Annette sat on the edge of her seat, wishing she hadn't come.

But she had to know; how else could she explain her presence? And what was this about 'Gerry'?

Emboldened, she said: 'You are Sara Baker, aren't you? Or -?'

'Oh yes,' acknowledged Sara, with a queer, twisted smile. 'I'm Sara alright.'

She struck a match, lit the gas. 'I know why you've come here. I've been expecting you.'

'You have?'

'He often talks about you, you know. He thinks the world of you.'

'Oh!'

'Look,' said Sara firmly. 'I won't beat about the bush. He shouldn't have come here. I told him, stick with your girlfriend. Not that he did anything wrong, mind. He's a good lad.'

Annette flushed angrily. Did this woman think her a fool?

'He come here first for the paper, that's all. I was after a council house like. For Vi's sake, not mine. Well, she deserves better'n this, don't she? Every kid does.'

'I'm not talking about that!' cut in Annette shrilly. 'It's the other things.'

'What other things?'

'You know.'

'Oh,' said Sara flatly. 'So you think that.'

'What do you expect?'

Sara made a hopeless gesture, let her hands drop. 'Look at me, love. What'd he be wanting with me?'

'That's what I'd like to know.'

Sara knew, from her manner, that she'd guessed right. Gerry hadn't split on her.

'I don't blame you for thinking that, mind,' she said in a low voice. 'It's only natural.'

Annette looked down at her hands.

'He's been a good friend, your boy has. If it hadn't been for him – well.'

'How'd you mean?'

'Well, he's got us that house, hasn't he? That bit he put in the paper. We'll be moving soon, Vi and me. Don't know where yet, mind.'

'So I gather,' said Annette primly, determined not to be easily won over.

The kettle began singing.

'How is he now anyway?' asked Sara. 'After his – accident.'

'So you know about that then, do you?'

'Everyone does, pet. Stands to reason.'

'Who did it then, do you know?'

'No, wish I did. I'd tell you straight love, don't worry. I'd have his guts for garters, see if I wouldn't . . . Better now, is he?'

'Getting better.'

'That's good.' She set the cups out, put an opened bag of sugar on the table.

'He'd been here to see you, hadn't he?'

'Aye, he had. Said he's off to London. Going with him, are you?'

'I don't know. I don't expect so.'

'Oh . . . thought you would be, like.'

She turned to make the tea. Annette looked at her broad back, the strands of grey in her hair. It seemed impossible, and yet . . .

'What I can't understand,' she said slowly, 'is why he kept coming back here. If it was only about this council house.'

She did not know what it was; a stiffening in the woman's posture, a psychic emanation . . . but Annette knew she'd struck home.

'Oh, he just liked talking to me,' said Sara amply, putting the cups on the table. 'And Vi. You should see 'em together, they're like . . .' Her voice trailed away, in the face of Annette's steady look.

'You call him Gerry,' said Annette, in an odd voice.

'Aye, I do,' acknowledged Sara, laughing it off. 'I –'

'Why?'

'Just a little joke, that's all. Can't stand the name Steve, see. Help yourself to sugar, love.'

Annette looked at her directly. 'You've done it with him, haven't you?'

'Done what, love?'

'Don't pretend, you . . .'

The unspoken word touched Sara on the raw. Her mouth twisted. 'What if I have? What's one more slice off a cut cake?'

Annette pushed the cup away, and stood up.

'Go on then!' cried Sara furiously. 'You young madam. Think you're so precious, don't you? You'll learn.'

Annette looked at her coldly. 'I'm having his baby,' she said.

'Oh!'

'I just wanted to see what you were like, that's all. Now I know.'

'Well, take a good look girl. You may end up like me some time. I've got a man too, you know.'

'Only one?'

For a moment, Sara looked as though she might strike Annette.

The younger woman stood her ground, glaring.

'Out,' hissed Sara.

'Don't worry, I'm going.'

The door slammed behind her.

Ted looked at her incredulously, hardly taking in what she was saying. She had found it hard to speak, with that vicious-looking screw standing just a few yards away, staring at them. Her first hesitant words had been accompanied by a vague gesture which he interpreted now as a sign that Annette's midriff would soon be expanding.

'You mean? No!' he said, in a low voice.

Lorna nodded mutely.

'I don't believe it. Not Annette.'

Lorna gave him a strange look, the look women give when confronted by the obtuseness or naivete of the male.

Ted glanced at the screw, who looked away, a faint smile on his pale gangster face. He knew the screw, a hard Northerner called Skinner, could hear every word they were saying.

'Are you sure?' Ted hissed.

Lorna nodded again.

'Christ. When?'

Lorna held up all five digits on one hand and two fingers on the other.

'She OK?'

'So far.'

Ted considered this. Skinner glanced back at him, then away again.

'Who was it?'

'What?' asked Lorna, startled.

Ted leaned forward across the table. 'Who did it to her?' he whispered.

'Who d'you think?' responded Lorna, in her normal voice.

'Keep your voice down, woman!' hissed Ted, anguished.

The gleeful look that had crossed the screw's face was a torment to him. He knew Skinner would make the most of this, make sarky comments, spread the gossip. Annette's name would be mud! And here of all places.

That reporter feller, Steve. He didn't dislike him, but he was a bit too clever for his taste. But then, he might suit Annette. She'd changed so much, these past few years.

Lorna was still giving him a funny look. He'd no idea what she was thinking. But he'd never known that, all the time they'd been married. And that reminded him how they'd jumped the gun too, and got away with it.

'You had a word with him?' he asked. 'Steve?'

Lorna shook her head.

'Why not?'

'No point.'

'No point? What you mean, girl?'

Lorna glanced over her shoulder, looked back at Ted. Cautiously, her finger hidden by her body, she pointed warningly at the screw.

'Never mind,' said Ted quietly. 'I want to know.' He leaned forward again. '*Is he going to do the right thing?*' he whispered intensely.

Lorna swayed back in her chair, distancing herself from the wild look in his eye.

'Well?

'She doesn't want him to,' replied Lorna distinctly.

'*What*?'

The screw looked as though he might intervene, then stared again into the far distance. Ted remained as he was for the moment, a caged animal reaching out in its distress, then he leaned back and moaned softly.

'Don't worry, Ted,' said Lorna calmly. 'She'll be OK.'

'Oh aye,' said Ted bitterly. 'You bet.'

Abruptly he stood up, his chair toppling over. Skinner and another screw sprang into action, grabbing his arms.

'Orright orright,' he cried. 'I'm not doing nothing, don't worry.'

He fixed Lorna with an accusing eye. 'Best be going,' he said. 'You've said enough.'

She stayed where she was, all eyes in the room veering between her sitting there quietly and Ted being marched away.

Suddenly she had a clear picture of Ted as he used to be, before they were married. He'd been a smart young chap then, keen on bettering himself. All that had slipped away slowly . . . like so many things.

As she saw him being hustled away now, between two brutes who weren't fit to lick his boots, a black despair engulfed her. How had he ended up like this? What would become of them now?

25

'Oh!' exclaimed Lorna. 'It's you. Come in, *bach*.'

He had knocked the side door, as always, and entered the kitchen. He felt strange, as if he had stepped over a threshold in other ways too.

'How are you? Annette's out. Are you feeling better?'

'Yes thanks. Where is she?'

'Only up Sutton's. She's gone shopping. I'm sorry 'bout what happened.'

He flinched. 'Forget it. It was nothing.'

He felt suddenly dizzy, and clutched the draining board for support.

'You look awful, boy. You shouldn't be out. Here, come and sit down.'

'I'm OK.' But he stayed still till his head cleared.

She tried to take his arm but he shook it off. 'I'm alright, honest.'

He shuffled into the living-room, with Lorna following. He slumped in the chair by the window, the chair he always thought of as Annette's. He held his head in his hands.

'How'd you get here?' asked Lorna. 'Your dad bring you?'

'No. Bus.' Eyes closed, he fought back a wave of nausea.

'You should be in bed. I'll get you a cuppa tea.'

He did not argue. Slowly his stomach settled.

The side door opened and closed. He heard low voices in the kitchen.

Someone came into the room. He knew it was Annette.

She looked at him, then sank into her mother's chair. He felt that if he opened his eyes, he'd feel sick again. His head was split by the axe of pain. His ribs were on fire.

Lorna came into the room, exchanged glances with Annette. He knew they were looking at each other, even though his eyes were still closed.

Lorna put his cup on the table near him. She sat on the low chair by the Rayburn.

Annette stared down at her hands. She had not wanted a tea.

Steve opened his eyes. 'Thanks,' he managed.

'You like a rest upstairs, love?' Lorna asked quietly.

He shook his head, smiled wanly at Annette. 'Hullo. Sorry about all this.'

She fluttered a smile back at him.

'Done your shopping?' he asked.

'Mm-hm,' she nodded.

He closed his eyes again, beginning to feel a little steadier.

'Get me a new head if you like,' he said.

'I would if I could,' said Annette.

Lorna looked from one to the other. It was as if she were seeing them anew.

She stirred her tea, sipped it. The rattle of her cup back in its saucer seemed to rouse him.

'Thanks for the tea,' he said. 'I'll drink it in a minute.'

'Take your time, *bach*,' said Lorna.

Annette hardly moved. One leg was crossed over the other. She looked neither at Steve nor her mother. But when he spoke again her eyes darted at him, full of unexpected light.

'I'm sorry to cause you all this trouble, Annette. Could we talk somewhere?'

'Talk here,' said Lorna eagerly. 'I've got some things to do upstairs anyway.'

'No!' he cried. 'We'll go next door. Really.'

They both knew he meant the next room where he had snogged so often with Annette.

Surprised by his authoritative tone, Lorna didn't argue. 'I'll put the fire on in there,' she said. 'Wait here a minute.'

When she left the room, Steve and Annette looked steadily at each other.

'You shouldn't have come here, Steve,' Annette murmured.

'Why not? Don't you want to see me?'

'Of course I do. But you're ill. You shouldn't have risked it.'

'No,' he said mischievously. 'I shouldn't have, should I?'

She turned pink. He felt another threshold had been crossed.

Lorna came back in, closing the door behind her. 'There,' she said. 'It'll soon warm up.'

Steve began drinking his tea. His fingers were icy-cold. Lorna went straight into the kitchen.

After a silence he said, 'Coming then?'

'If you like.'

In the parlour they sat side by side on the small settee, not touching.

'Don't you want a cup of tea?' he asked, noticing the absence of one for the first time.

'No thanks. I'm not thirsty.'

'It's nice seeing you.'

'And you.'

'I've missed you.'

She said nothing. She looked pale now, even drawn.

'Look,' he began abruptly. 'I want to say I'm sorry. About all that – you know – '

She made a motion with her hands. 'Don't bother. I've been to see her.'

'Sara?' he asked, dumbfounded.

She nodded.

'Good God. Why d'you do that?'

'Because I wanted to.

His heart began to thump wildly, as though he had been running.

'What she tell you?'

'Everything,' she lied.

'Oh hell.'

She let him suffer.

'I feel sorry for her,' she said at last.

'Sorry!'

'Don't you?'

'I don't know,' he confessed. 'I don't know what I feel.'

'She says you got her a house.'

He shrugged it off. 'She'd have got it anyway.'

'That's not what she told me.'

'What else did she say?'

The ghost of a smile played around Annette's lips.

'That you're a good boy.'

'Oh yes,' he said sarcastically.

'She thinks a lot of you.'

He gestured impatiently. 'Stop playing with me, Annette.'

'Playing?'

'I said I'm sorry. What else do you want?'

'Oh,' she said queerly. 'Listen to Mr Hoity-Toity.'

He looked at her, then relaxed. 'I'm sorry.'

'I should think so.' She touched his arm. 'You feeling better now, Steve?'

'Yes thanks.'

'It was good of you to come.'

'Had to, didn't I? Since you wouldn't come to me.'

'I couldn't.'

He didn't ask why.

'I'm pregnant, Steve,' she said.

A thrill ran through him like wildfire. He put his hand over hers.

'You're not cross?' she asked wonderingly.

He squeezed her hand.

'Sorry I couldn't – tell you – '

He stopped her words with a kiss, the clumsiest he had ever given her. They looked at each other, their eyes so close that they gazed at each other's reflections.

They kissed again.

The next day, a Sunday, Ivor took the bus to Highland alone. His mother, still downcast by Sally's decision to stay in the sanatorium, went to early Mass while he stayed home with Lennie and Megan. He left as soon as he could afterwards, to avoid another day of taut nerves and needless quarrels. He had enough troubles of his own, without having to cope with his mother's moods. The encounter in the pub with Will Dubbin and the others had resurrected all his old feelings for Annette. To be thrown over for that crappy bastard from South Wales, who was now playing fast and loose with a prostitute! He knew that woman in Back Row, everyone did, she was just a cheap shag for anyone who had no respect for himself. Did Annette know what he was up to? She couldn't! He felt he ought to warn her, but how could he? Best not to get involved. But he longed to hammer hell out of that shithead, just as he'd been suspected of doing. His fists clenched and unclenched as he thought of it.

As the bus made its slow, grinding way through the hillside villages of Goginan and Cwmbrwyno, he began to feel oddly soothed. There was something in these ancient hills to which his soul responded. He came from long generations of mountain dwellers on his father's side, dark, unyielding men and women as tough as the terrain they inhabited. They had slogged hard on the farms and in the lead mines of north Cardiganshire, often going to early deaths but never surrendering their dignity. In the softer life of the coastal town he would sometimes forget this but today, as his fraught nerves settled, he had a sense of belonging.

There were few people on the bus, which suited his mood perfectly. He gazed out at the dark tarns and cold streams of this high moorland that stretched between the wild western sea and the lowlands of the English border. Lean sheep cropped the thin grass, the hawk hovered over fastnesses little changed since the days when Owain Glyndŵr's warriors ambushed the king's men, and the boggy heights of Plynlimon still squeezed out the chilly headwaters of a dozen rivers. Through Eisteddfa Gurig they went, the last outpost before the slow descent to the gentler hills of Radnorshire, where the bus at last ended its journey outside the white gates of Highland Sanatorium.

He went straight to Powys Block, up the stairs then stopped, disbelieving. Her bed was empty. What's more, it had never been slept in. The startling white sheet, doubled back neatly over the dark grey blanket, seemed to glare back at him. What had happened? For a manic moment he wondered if she had died, without them knowing. He looked into the next cubicle. A girl, even younger than Sally, lay on her back reading. A ribbon was in her fair hair, haemorrhage-red. She looked wasted, exhausted. 'Where's Sally?' Ivor asked awkwardly. The girl looked at him indifferently. 'Gone,' she said.

'Gone? Gone where?'

'Don't know. Better ask sister.' She turned on her side, away from Ivor. Her thin shoulder blades pointed up the rebuff. He felt angry, wanting to shake her. Footsteps to his right. A nurse in white uniform. 'Excuse me, but are you the sister?'

'No, I'm Nurse Shaw.' Sweetly. 'Can I help you?'

'I want to know where my sister is – Sally Morgan.'

'Oh, she's been transferred to Knighton Block. Didn't you know?'

'No. Nobody told us. Why's that then?'

'She's on different treatment now. Sister will tell you all about it.'

In the small office where Sister Barnes sat, prim and censorious, he listened to her explanations. Sally was being given injections of a new drug, only now coming into wider use. She was already making progress and her prospects were good. Knighton Block was the best place for her, for reasons he couldn't quite fathom.

'But why weren't we told? Why keep us in the dark?' asked Ivor.

'It's Sally's place to tell you. Doesn't she write home regularly?'

'Yes but – she hasn't mentioned this.'

'Then I'd ask her why not, if I were you. Come along, I'll take you to her.'

Ivor followed her down the stairs, and along the covered way to Knighton Block. Everything in this place conspired to make him feel small. He was unwanted, a fit stranger in the halls of the diseased. Sally was propped up on pillows, listening to the radio on headphones. Her face brightened when she saw him.

'Why didn't you tell us?' he asked, when they were alone.

'I did. I sent a letter off yesterday. I've only been here a few days.' She coughed. Still the sickly wet rasp, but those hot crimson spots had gone from her cheeks and her whole demeanour had altered. 'I'm going to get better now, I know.'

'Good. That's the spirit, Sal.'

She told him about the new treatment. He only half took it in. What was important was that her whole outlook had changed. She had lost that terrible fatalism, little short of a death wish. She had faith in the wonder drug.

'Great, Sal. Great.'

'And how about you?' she asked suddenly.

His face darkened. 'Oh, I'm OK.'

'What's wrong, Ivor? Tell me.'

He pretended it was to do with their mother, but she knew there was something more.

'How's Annette these days? Do you see anything of her?'

'No. Nothing.'

She knew she had hit on it. She was afraid to mention Steve, but how could she avoid it?

'Don't talk about him, Sal,' he said irritably.

'Why, what's he done to you then?'

'Not to me – her!'

Sally put a hand on his arm. It seared him to the bone.

'He's been seeing a prostitute, Sal,' he said, snatching his arm away. 'What do you think of that?'

Sally felt a twin shock, that of her sisterly touch being rejected as if it were dirty, and of the accusation against Steve. The one acted on the other, turning her sympathy away from her brother.

'How do you know that?' she asked coldly.

'Everyone knows. He was beaten up because of it.'

'Beaten up? When?'

He told her what he knew. Seeing her face, he felt confused yet defiant.

'He's a load of rubbish, Sal – he must be.'

She was silent. He knew he had damaged her, but did not know how.

'Tell you what,' he said impulsively. 'When you get out of here – let's get away, shall we?'

'What do you mean?'

'Leave Glanaber. Both of us. I'm sick of the place. I want to live somewhere else.'

'But where? What would you do?'

'Go to Birmingham. Work in a car factory or something.'

'I can't see you doing that. Anyway, you wouldn't want me there with you, would you?'

'Why not? We've always got on alright, haven't we?'

'It wouldn't work, Ivor – you know it wouldn't. Anyway, I've been in this place long enough. I just want to get home.'

'OK then,' he said sullenly. 'Forget it.'

She felt resentful and unhappy. Why had he come here, destroying her dreams? The image she'd cherished of Steve, that entirely innocent image, now lay in ruins. She knew it had been foolish, yet it had helped to sustain her.

'I'm sorry, Sal,' he said, relenting. 'I didn't want to upset you.'

'You haven't,' she said wearily.

She coughed, pressing her handkerchief to her lips. She kept it there when the coughing ceased, squeezing saliva into it against all the sanatorium rules, instead of spitting into the metal pot by the bed.

'Sorry about that,' she said eventually.

'Don't worry. Soon be right as rain, won't you?'

She gave him a tired smile, put the hankie under her pillow.

The tension eased. She closed her eyes, resting.

'Ivor,' she said suddenly.

'Aye?'

'Don't mind me asking but – how is he now? That reporter?'

'Oh . . . alright I think.'

'He wasn't badly hurt then?'

'No.' He nearly added 'More's the pity' but checked himself.

He was sorry now he had brushed her arm away. It had been something instinctive, rooted in a past he should have outgrown.

'You'll have to forget her, you know,' she said gently.

'Who?'

'Annette.'

He shook his head. 'No,' he said. 'Never.'

26

October roared in with high winds and huge seas. The waves, cresting and foaming, smashed against the promenade before spouting high and soaking the red-and-green-scarved students who hopelessly tried to dodge them. Their laughter and shouts reached Shirley as she stood in the window of her flat in South Marine Terrace. 'Silly buggers', she said out loud.

She was feeling restless these days. Annette's engagement to Steve, for all its practicality, had come as a mild shock. Although far from being obsessed by dreams of marriage, Shirley had always assumed, deep-down, that one day she would have a husband. Had she been forced to analyse her feelings she might have admitted that she thought her own chances in the marriage stakes greater than Annette's. Her urging of marriage on her friend, once she knew she was pregnant, had been purely altruistic. Now it was becoming reality she felt uncomfortable, even – though she would never have confessed this – resentful. You've been left behind, a small voice inside her insisted. Better get your skates on, kiddo.

One evening, after a lonely supper – she still missed Annette more than she cared to admit – she saw a man walking towards the wooden jetty at the end of the prom. There was something familiar about him – the set of the shoulders, the way he walked – but it took a few moments for her to place him as Annette's ex, Ivor Morgan. She was surprised by how downcast he appeared: was he still pining for Annette? Acting on impulse, she put on a jumper and top coat and, hurrying downstairs, stepped into the stiff breeze.

The last of the daylight was fast being consumed by the dusk which seemed to drift out to sea from the land. The waters, still greeny-blue an hour earlier, were now leaden, and the sole atmospheric survivor from the day was a line of pale, ghostly-yellow light just above the horizon.

He was standing at the far end of the jetty, staring down at the water. The nearer she approached, the more conspicuous did she feel. She was tempted to turn tail before he was aware of her, but that would have implied some dubious behaviour on her part. What harm was she doing, simply taking an evening stroll?

She rested her arms on the jetty rail, looking over the tidal river to the hill fort that rose above the town's outlying houses. She felt his eyes on her; she wondered if he'd speak. They were not friends, but still they knew one another. In Glanaber the townspeople – as opposed to the visitors and students – were hardly ever complete strangers. Only degrees of acquaintanceship existed.

Suddenly he found his voice. 'Still living up the road, are you?'

She half-turned to face him. 'Yes.'

'H'm . . . Like it there?'

'It's alright.'

She could not see his eyes. She felt a spasm, not of fear, but of unease, and was on the point of going when he said, 'Must find it funny there. Without Annette.'

'Yes,' she agreed, feeling a little twinge at the mention of her friend's name. 'I do.'

After a silence he said flatly, 'Back with her mother then.'

The statement seemed to call for no comment.

'Wouldn't mind living there myself. Where you are.'

She had no sense of being propositioned. The words hung there, small, harmless birds in the thickening dusk.

She remembered he had a sister, ill with some terrible disease. The girl's name suddenly came to her.

'How's Sally getting along?' she asked.

'Not too bad,' he answered, surprised. 'You know her then, do you?'

'A bit . . . In hospital, isn't she.'

'Not hospital. Sanatorium. She's got TB.'

'Oh. I'm sorry.'

He was looking at her closely, as if weighing her up.

'She's still very ill,' he said at last. 'But they're giving her some new treatment.'

He had drawn a little closer.

'So she's getting better?'

'I think so.'

'That's good.'

The ambiguity of their position made them suddenly feel awkward.

'Well . . . I'll be getting along then,' he said reluctantly.

'Right,' she said, with a small smile.

The wind, quickly rising, blew her hair about her face, and she pushed it back with a swift, glowing gesture. He stared at her, fascinated.

'Don't suppose you feel like a drink?' he asked abruptly.

'A drink?' she repeated, startled.

He could not believe he had asked the question, or that she would give a proper answer. But they both held their ground, looking at one another. She pushed her hair back again.

'OK then,' she said slowly.

They were almost shy with each other, as if they had never touched intimately. Steve had a delicacy that surprised her, contrasting as it did with his former boldness.

His return to the office, after a week away, had been less stressful than he'd imagined. The gossip soon died down, as there was nothing for it to feed on. He and Annette were seen around in the usual places, hand in hand. There were no obvious problems between them.

One day he was summoned to the editor's inner sanctum. Gwyn Meredith squinted up at him playfully. 'What's it like then? Being a published poet? You haven't seen it? Good heavens above.'

For the first time, Steve noticed what was on the desk in front of the editor. His heart leapt.

'A little strident, but then you're young. You have a poet's touch right enough.'

He handed the magazine to Steve. 'Sit down,' he said. 'Enjoy the moment.'

Steve looked wonderingly at his own words. They seemed familiar yet strange, as if the act of printing had given them more weight.

Meredith had wandered to the window. "In the December of my youth I sing," he murmured.

Steve tensed, afraid that the editor might be going to recite the whole poem.

'A good line,' Meredith acknowledged. 'How long ago did you write it?'

'Not long,' said Steve self-consciously.

'I wish I were you,' said Meredith unexpectedly. 'You know,' he went on, turning, 'you've got a great chance to do something with your life. But not if you go to London.'

Steve flushed. He did not want to be lectured by Gwyn Meredith again.

'You don't like me saying these things, do you? But it's for your own good, lad.'

His hands, clasped behind his back, flicked of their own volition, expressing the nervous emotion he subdued in his general manner.

'I've seen it happen before. There was a lad here twenty years ago – I wasn't much older than you are now – he'd have made a great writer. But he went off to Fleet Street and that was the end of him. He never wrote a thing after. Became a sub-editor on the *Daily Mirror*. A mere headline-monger! What a waste.'

Steve listened; he had no choice but to do so. And Meredith's words touched something inside him, a deep-buried doubt.

Meredith sat on a plain wooden chair in a dusty corner of the office, a chair even older than the one that stood behind his desk.

'Gifts like yours are rare,' he said soberly. 'Anyone can be a reporter. But a poet! You are of the gods, man.'

Steve felt a rush of pride and excitement. Meredith leaned forward. 'Look, Stephen,' he said urgently. 'It doesn't matter to me if you stay or go. I can bring out this paper without you – oh, not so well admittedly, but it would do. No-one would see any difference. But it matters to *you*, lad. I don't want you looking back in ten years' time, full of regrets. I beg you, think about it.'

He sat back, peered over the top of his horn-rimmed glasses. 'Don't forget what I told you last time,' he said weightily. 'My offer still stands.'

Something in his manner, a falseness and theatricality, grated on Steve. His suspicion of people slowly surfaced. He became conscious of the physical weirdness of the situation: the empty editorial chair, Meredith staring into space in a corner of the office.

Steve put the magazine back on the editor's desk. The slight movement broke the spell. 'Well,' said Meredith in a different tone. 'It's entirely up to you, boy.'

'Thank you,' said Steve awkwardly.

Meredith threw him an ironical glance, and moved heavily back to his desk. Already he seemed to be regretting his friendly advice, which in an odd way had put them on the same level for a few moments, nullifying their usual relationship.

'Have you finished that piece on the land dispute in Cardigan?' he asked brusquely.

'Not quite. I'm just finishing it off.'

'Bring it straight to me when you've done it. Don't give it to Banks.'

'Right.'

Meredith took two tablets from a small tin, washed them down with a swig from a glass of water on his desk. He nodded at Steve, who had reached the door, and lifted a hand in farewell.

Alone, he turned the magazine around so that he might read the poem again.

"Scorching my jungle veins," he murmured, and grimaced: perhaps with pain, perhaps regret.

Bill Merrick was off work, with some unexplained sickness. The atmosphere was easier without him. Without his side-kick Ronnie did not feel inclined to take the piss so often. Scoop Matthews cackled and crooned over his copy, Sam Evans typed endless rewrites of illiterate sports reports from part-time wannabes, and in her cherry-red office suit Brenda brewed tea with immense self-satisfaction and handed the cup to Steve, making sure their fingers touched.

Midway through the afternoon, the phone rang. 'It's for you,' said Brenda, smiling.

He snatched it from her, irritated by her Mata Hari seductiveness.

'Hullo? Steve Lewis here.'

'You don't say. Thought it might be Tarzan of the Apes.'

'Brian! Where you ringing from?'

'Where'd you think? Look, I've only got a minute. You still keen on coming up here?'

Steve's heart lurched. 'To work, you mean?'

'What d'you think, play the fiddle? . . . Well, are you or aren't you?' asked Brian impatiently.

'Yes. Of course.'

'You don't sound too convinced. Settling in nicely there, are you?'

'No need for that,' retorted Steve, bristling at the sarcasm. 'What've you got in mind?'

'A job. On the *Star*.'

'The *Star*?'

'Yes. You've heard of it, haven't you? Evening paper, if you know what that is.'

'I thought we were going for . . . something else.'

'Oh, getting picky are we? I know it's not good enough for you small-town hustlers, but all the same . . .'

'OK, what is it then exactly?'

'Reporter. Well-paid. Good stepping-stone. Might even make it to the *News Chronicle*, if you play your cards right.'

Sarky bastard. Steve took a deep breath, then plunged in. 'OK then. What do I have to do?'

'Good man!' returned Brian, all surprise and jubilation. 'Leave it to me. Give me your home number. I'll call you back.'

Steve put down the phone. He felt light-headed, and something more. Absolved. Free. A mixture of emotions that made it impossible to remain where he was, sitting opposite Brenda Marsden in this crummy office writing a stupid story about small-town hicks.

Brenda was looking at him narrowly, reproachfully, as if all his thoughts were written large in the space between them.

'I'm going out,' Steve announced to the room in general.

Sam took no notice. Neither did Scoop. Ronnie, hunched in his cubbyhole office, did not hear him.

'Where shall I say you've gone?' asked Brenda. 'If someone asks?'

He grinned across the table at her.

'For a date with destiny,' he announced grandly.

'Fancy that,' she said coolly.

27

'You know,' said Edna placidly, 'I think we should get a new three-piece suite.'

Jim looked cautiously across the top of his *Daily Telegraph*. 'Oh yes?' he said.

'It's ages since we had one.'

She bent over her knitting, counting the stitches on her needle before glancing again at the pattern.

'Where would we put it?'

Edna looked at him sharply. 'Where? In here of course.'

She knew what was coming next and braced herself for it.

'What's wrong with the one we've got?' he asked.

'Oh, Jim!' she cried, exasperated. 'You're impossible!'

She flung down her knitting and pressed a hand to her forehead, the picture of despair.

'Why, what's wrong now?' he asked, bewildered. 'What on earth's up with you?'

'It's no use talking to you, that's all.'

He put on his martyred look, which cross-faded easily into the resentful expression that inevitably followed. He shuffled his paper uneasily, the words blurring as his thoughts drifted away to more pleasant pastures.

She took up her knitting again, sighed, and with pursed lips let the silence extend to the point where she would not lose face by speaking again.

'There's some nice ones on offer in Astons,' she said. 'Blue and gold. They look very comfortable too.'

'Go and get one then,' he said, relieved that the tension had lifted so quickly.

'Wouldn't you like to see them first before deciding?' she asked sweetly. 'It's your choice as well. Or of course,' she went on, when he failed to respond to this, 'we could go up to Shrewsbury and see what they've got there.'

She ran her hand down the garment she was knitting, not looking at him but extending, unmistakably, the flag of peace.

'That's a good idea,' he said amiably. 'We haven't been there for ages.'

He felt decidedly more cheerful. He hated discord.

'Where's Steve?' he asked suddenly.

'He went out hours ago. Fat lot of notice you take!' she chaffed him, without acrimony.

'Gone to pictures, has he?'

'I doubt it.' She flattened the garment on her lap, gazing at it with narrowed eyes. 'I imagine he's with Annette.'

'Oh,' he said, uninterested. The words on the page sharpened; he resumed reading.

Edna gave him a coy, almost maidenly glance. 'You'd expect him to, wouldn't you? Seeing how things are.'

The words took a few seconds to sink in. 'How do you mean?' he asked cautiously.

'Oh, Jim,' she murmured, in a different tone from before. 'You don't notice anything, do you? The girl's pregnant.'

'Pregnant? You mean – good Lor'.'

Placidly she went on knitting.

'You mean – Steve's the father?' he asked, dismayed.

She looked at him reproachfully. 'I certainly hope so. You wouldn't like to think your future daughter-in-law's a slut, do you?'

'They're getting married? When? Nobody's told me!'

'Calm down, Jim, for heaven's sake. You'll give yourself a heart attack.'

'I think it's preposterous. The boy's throwing his life away!'

'Oh, is he now? Nobody said that when you married me, did they?'

'That was different. We'd been engaged.'

'Engaged *and* pregnant. You've got a short memory, Jim.'

He thought of the baby he'd never seen, its life snuffed out by miscarriage, buried without a name, its brief existence hushed up and never spoken of afterwards.

She had put her knitting down. She spoke to him quietly.

'Nobody's said anything, Jim. It's what I know for myself. I know it – here.' She put a clenched fist to her chest. 'That girl's pregnant as sure as my name's Edna Lewis.'

'But aren't you worried – for his sake?'

'Why should I be?'

'He's got a career to make – in London. This will put the kybosh on it.'

'That's all you want for him, is it? A career in London.'

'I thought you wanted it too. It's not so long since' – he forced the words out – 'you hated the girl.'

'I never hated her,' protested Edna, putting new fury into her knitting.

'You could have fooled me, Edna.'

In the long silence, Jim Lewis stared at his wife as if she were a stranger. She was detached from him now, living in a remote country of her own making.

He thought of the woman with the deep brown eyes, whom he preferred not to remember. He had let her go to remain with Edna, the wife of his body. God knows where she was now.

He took up the *Daily Telegraph* again. His eyes prickled with unmanly tears.

They spent more and more time in Lorna's 'best room' together, as if in training for domesticity. She sat reading, mainly light novels and thrillers, while he worked at his poetry. He enjoyed stealing glances at her, struck by her new, serious look, the way she became wholly absorbed in what he saw as trivial, empty tales. Sometimes they had necking sessions which, for all their excitement, never went beyond certain unspoken limits. They had reached mutual understanding which did not need expression in words. They would not go 'all the way' again before their marriage.

The call from Brian came soon after seven, just as he was getting ready to go round to Annette's place. 'Yes,' he murmured into the receiver in the hall, 'that's fine . . . great.' The ping as he put it back into its cradle sounded like a clarion call. He didn't want his parents to suspect anything yet.

His mother's complaisance amazed him. Her entire view of Annette seemed to have altered. And he could have sworn that she knew all about the baby, though no-one had said a word. It was weird.

He tried to dampen down his elation; he didn't want it to show just yet. He had to explain things properly to Annette, not be so excited that he'd fly off the handle if she opposed him. She must be won round, not bludgeoned into submission.

And part of him feared she would refuse him entirely. What would he do then, if he had to choose between her and his career?

She knew at once something was up. It was in the glint in his eye, the way he stepped into the house. She shrank back from it, but determined to show nothing. They chatted awhile with her mother until they went into the other room.

She did not pick up her latest library book. She simply sat and waited. He spoke of easy, inconsequential things, and she responded coolly, in control.

Then it came.

'I had a phone call from Brian today – you know, my mate in London.' His voice was strained, a semitone higher than usual.

'Oh yes. What did he have to say for himself?'

'Nothing much... There's a job come up on the *Star*. He thinks I've got a good chance of getting it.'

Nothing much indeed, she thought ironically.

'Do you want it?'

'I don't know... what do you think?'

'It's not what I think, is it? It's for you to decide.'

'No it's not. It's both of us. We're getting married, aren't we?'

'Are we?'

'Of course we are,' he said irritably. 'It's all decided, isn't it?'

She was silent, staring at nothing.

'It's a bloody good job,' he said, catching with

dismay the defiance in his voice. 'It's a stepping stone to a national.'

'You'd better take it then, hadn't you? If that's what you want.'

'I want *you*,' he cried, sitting beside her. 'I don't want to go if you don't.'

A smile flickered on the corner of her mouth, then was gone. He hated this detachment of hers. He wanted her to fling her arms around him, to say something that would take them to new heights of love and commitment.

She simply sat there, silent as a penny.

'Annette,' he said. 'I love you.'

'I love you too,' she responded mechanically.

Her eyes, looking down towards the floor but seeing nothing save her imaginings, were those of an older woman.

At last he ventured, 'So you'll come with me then – will you?'

'If you like,' she murmured.

He felt only the sadness of her surrender.

'I'll make it right for us,' he promised, taking her hand. 'For you . . . and the baby.'

She turned to him, and smiled. 'Will you, love?' she murmured.

The move went much better than Sara had feared. Vi was a little treasure, helping with an efficiency far beyond her years.

They'd given her a new two-bedroom flat right at the top of Penbryn, looking down the valley to the town and the sea beyond. It was so bright, so convenient, so full of good things she'd never had before, that she was bowled over.

'It's great in't it, Mam?' cried Vi, skipping round the kitchen with its reconditioned gas stove, courtesy of the Assistance Board.

'Aye, it is – now get out of the way you little minx, you're making the place look untidy!'

Vi laughed at the happiness in her mother's voice.

Now, thought Sara grimly, now to face the neighbours. She knew there'd be funny looks from some, but if they were only looks she'd manage.

No, she inwardly corrected. She'd manage anything. All that bad stuff was in the past. She'd make a new start.

The train to Shrewsbury and Birmingham, where it connected with the London-bound express, puffed out of the station and rattled along the track to her right. She could see it through the bathroom window if she wanted, but why should she bother? It was nothing to do with her.

Driving up to the hills in his employer's van, Ivor gave the train a glance and then forgot it.

Inside a compartment he had all to himself, Steve settled into his corner seat and watched the town slowly fall away before his eyes. He was filled with such conflicting emotions that, for a moment, he would have given anything just to be back there. Annette, Annette! His eyes filled with tears. Quickly he brushed them away and, looking up to the Penbryn estate across the valley, clearly made out the house where the Morrises lived. Because no-one was watching, he raised an arm in farewell.

In the office of Richards and James, Solicitors, Annette took a chocolate Penguin from her handbag and munched it with her morning coffee. The sound of the train did not reach her.

She had the provisional date of their register office wedding pencilled into her diary for two months' time. She flatly refused to rush it; she didn't care what people said.

When she went home that evening, she cried for Steve's absence. But as she looked through her diary the following week, the date she had scribbled down made her heart flip right over.

She frowned at it, as if seeking some special meaning. Two weeks later, she tore the page out altogether.

THE END

Also by Herbert Williams

Poetry
Too Wet for the Devil
The Dinosaurs
A Lethal Kind of Love
The Trophy
Ghost Country
Looking Through Time

Fiction
A Severe Case of Dandruff (novella)
The Stars in their Courses (short stories)
Stories of King Arthur (for children)

Biography
John Cowper Powys
Davies the Ocean: Railway King and Coal Tycoon

Other non-fiction
Voices of Wales
Come Out Wherever You Are: the great escape
from Island Farm POW Camp
Battles in Wales
Stage Coaches in Wales
Railways in Wales